W9-BUT-647

BLESS
ME,
ULTIMA

BLESS ME, ULTIMA

a novel

Rudolfo A. Anaya

TONATIUH–QUINTO SOL
INTERNATIONAL
Publishers
Post Office Box 9275
Berkeley, CA 94709
USA

Sixteenth Printing   September, 1984

Library of Congress Catalogue Card Number: 75-29996

ISBN: 0-89229-002-1

Tonatiuh International, *Publishers of Chicano Literature*, present this novel by Rudolfo A. Anaya. It is the winning entry in the Second Annual Premio Quinto Sol literary award for 1971.

Probably no other novel written by a Chicano has had such wide and varied acclaim as has Rudolfo A. Anaya's *BLESS ME, ULTIMA*, now in its FIFTH PRINTING. The admirers of Anaya's work span the public spectrum from junior high school students to universities throughout the nation, from university presidents to readers in England, France, Mexico, and Australia. From this standpoint alone, Rudolfo A. Anaya merits a preeminent place in the history of Chicano Literature.

Anaya's preeminence in Chicano Literature is merited from still another viewpoint, for *BLESS ME, ULTIMA* is even more popular today than it has ever been since its first printing in 1972 by Quinto Sol Publications. Clearly, from a literary and historical point of view, as well as from the general public's acclaim, *BLESS ME, ULTIMA* truly can be called a classic in Chicano Literature.

TONATIUH INTERNATIONAL, with RUDOLFO A. ANAYA, hereby presents this novel and thus participates in the evolution of Chicano Literature within the context of international literary currents.

Octavio I. Romano-V., PhD
Senior Editor, Literature
November *1975* Tonatiuh International, Inc.

Rudolfo A. Anaya

Con Honor

Para Mis Padres

Uno

Ultima came to stay with us the summer I was almost seven. When she came the beauty of the llano unfolded before my eyes, and the gurgling waters of the river sang to the hum of the turning earth. The magical time of childhood stood still, and the pulse of the living earth pressed its mystery into my living blood. She took my hand, and the silent, magic powers she possessed made beauty from the raw, sun-baked llano, the green river valley, and the blue bowl which was the white sun's home. My bare feet felt the throbbing earth and my body trembled with excitement. Time stood still, and it shared with me all that had been, and all that was to come. . . .

Let me begin at the beginning. I do not mean the beginning that was in my dreams and the stories they whispered to me about my birth, and the people of my father and mother, and my three brothers—but the beginning that came with Ultima.

The attic of our home was partitioned into two small rooms. My sisters, Deborah and Theresa, slept in one and I slept in the small cubicle by the door. The wooden steps creaked down into a small hallway that led into the kitchen. From the top of the stairs I had a vantage point into the heart of our home, my mother's kitchen. From there I was to see the terrified face of

1

Chávez when he brought the terrible news of the murder of the sheriff; I was to see the rebellion of my brothers against my father; and many times late at night I was to see Ultima returning from the llano where she gathered the herbs that can be harvested only in the light of the full moon by the careful hands of a curandera.

That night I lay very quietly in my bed, and I heard my father and mother speak of Ultima.

"Está sola," my father said, "ya no queda gente en el pueblito de Las Pasturas—"

He spoke in Spanish, and the village he mentioned was his home. My father had been a vaquero all his life, a calling as ancient as the coming of the Spaniard to Nuevo Méjico. Even after the big rancheros and the tejanos came and fenced the beautiful llano, he and those like him continued to work there, I guess because only in that wide expanse of land and sky could they feel the freedom their spirits needed.

" ¡Qué lástima," my mother answered, and I knew her nimble fingers worked the pattern on the doily she crocheted for the big chair in the sala.

I heard her sigh, and she must have shuddered too when she thought of Ultima living alone in the loneliness of the wide llano. My mother was not a woman of the llano, she was the daughter of a farmer. She could not see beauty in the llano and she could not understand the coarse men who lived half their lifetimes on horseback. After I was born in Las Pasturas she persuaded my father to leave the llano and bring her family to the town of Guadalupe where she said there would be opportunity and school for us. The move lowered my father in the esteem of his compadres, the other vaqueros of the llano who clung tenaciously to their way of life and freedom. There was no room to keep animals in town so my father had to sell his small herd, but he would not sell his horse so he gave it to a good friend, Benito Campos. But Campos could not keep the animal penned up because somehow the horse was very close to the spirit of the man, and so the horse was allowed to roam free and no vaquero on that llano would throw a lazo on that horse. It was as if someone had died, and they turned their gaze from the spirit that walked the earth.

It hurt my father's pride. He saw less and less of his old compadres. He went to work on the highway and on Saturdays after they collected their pay he drank with his crew at the

Longhorn, but he was never close to the men of the town. Some weekends the llaneros would come into town for supplies and old amigos like Bonney or Campos or the Gonzales brothers would come by to visit. Then my father's eyes lit up as they drank and talked of the old days and told the old stories. But when the western sun touched the clouds with orange and gold the vaqueros got in their trucks and headed home, and my father was left to drink alone in the long night. Sunday morning he would get up very crudo and complain about having to go to early mass.

"—She served the people all her life, and now the people are scattered, driven like tumbleweeds by the winds of war. The war sucks everything dry," my father said solemnly, "it takes the young boys overseas, and their families move to California where there is work—"

"Ave María Purísima," my mother made the sign of the cross for my three brothers who were away at war. "Gabriel," she said to my father, "it is not right that la Grande be alone in her old age—"

"No," my father agreed.

"When I married you and went to the llano to live with you and raise your family, I could not have survived without la Grande's help. Oh, those were hard years—"

"Those were good years," my father countered. But my mother would not argue.

"There isn't a family she did not help," she continued, "no road was too long for her to walk to its end to snatch somebody from the jaws of death, and not even the blizzards of the llano could keep her from the appointed place where a baby was to be delivered—"

"Es verdad," my father nodded.

"She tended me at the birth of my sons—" And then I knew her eyes glanced briefly at my father. "Gabriel, we cannot let her live her last days in loneliness—"

"No," my father agreed, "it is not the way of our people."

"It would be a great honor to provide a home for la Grande," my mother murmured. My mother called Ultima la Grande out of respect. It meant the woman was old and wise.

"I have already sent word with Campos that Ultima is to come and live with us," my father said with some satisfaction. He knew it would please my mother.

"I am grateful," my mother said tenderly, "perhaps we can repay a little of the kindness la Grande has given to so many."

"And the children?" my father asked. I knew why he expressed concern for me and my sisters. It was because Ultima was a curandera, a woman who knew the herbs and remedies of the ancients, a miracle-worker who could heal the sick. And I had heard that Ultima could lift the curses laid by brujas, that she could exorcise the evil the witches planted in people to make them sick. And because a curandera had this power she was misunderstood and often suspected of practicing witchcraft herself.

I shuddered and my heart turned cold at the thought. The cuentos of the people were full of the tales of evil done by brujas.

"She helped bring them into the world, she cannot be but good for the children," my mother answered.

"Está bien," my father yawned, "I will go for her in the morning."

So it was decided that Ultima should come and live with us. I knew that my father and mother did good by providing a home for Ultima. It was the custom to provide for the old and the sick. There was always room in the safety and warmth of la familia for one more person, be that person stranger or friend.

It was warm in the attic, and as I lay quietly listening to the sounds of the house falling asleep and repeating a Hail Mary over and over in my thoughts, I drifted into the time of dreams. Once I had told my mother about my dreams and she said they were visions from God and she was happy, because her own dream was that I should grow up and become a priest. After that I did not tell her about my dreams, and they remained in me forever and ever . . .

In my dream I flew over the rolling hills of the llano. My soul wandered over the dark plain until it came to a cluster of adobe huts. I recognized the village of Las Pasturas and my heart grew happy. One mud hut had a lighted window, and the vision of my dream swept me towards it to be witness at the birth of a baby.

I could not make out the face of the mother who rested from the pains of birth, but I could see the old woman in black who tended the just-arrived, steaming baby. She nimbly tied a knot on the cord that had connected the baby to its mother's blood, then quickly she bent and with her teeth she bit off the loose end. She wrapped the squirming baby and laid it at the mother's side, then she returned to cleaning the bed. All linen was swept aside to be washed, but she carefully wrapped the useless cord and the afterbirth and laid the package at the feet of the Virgin on the small altar. I sensed that these things were yet to be delivered to someone.

Now the people who had waited patiently in the dark were allowed to come in and speak to the mother and deliver their gifts to the baby. I recognized my mother's brothers, my uncles from El Puerto de los Lunas. They entered ceremoniously. A patient hope stirred in their dark, brooding eyes.

This one will be a Luna, the old man said, he will be a farmer and keep our customs and traditions. Perhaps God will bless our family and make the baby a priest.

And to show their hope they rubbed the dark earth of the river valley on the baby's forehead, and they surrounded the bed with the fruits of their harvest so the small room smelled of fresh green chile and corn, ripe apples and peaches, pumpkins and green beans.

Then the silence was shattered with the thunder of hoofbeats; vaqueros surrounded the small house with shouts and gunshots, and when they entered the room they were laughing and singing and drinking.

Gabriel, they shouted, you have a fine son! He will make a fine vaquero! And they smashed the fruits and vegetables that surrounded the bed and replaced them with a saddle, horse blankets, bottles of whiskey, a new rope, bridles, chapas, and an old guitar. And they rubbed the stain of earth from the baby's forehead because man was not to be tied to the earth but free upon it.

These were the people of my father, the vaqueros of the llano. They were an exuberant, restless people, wandering across the ocean of the plain.

We must return to our valley, the old man who led the farmers spoke. We must take with us the blood that comes after the birth. We will bury it in our fields to renew their fertility and to assure that the baby will follow our ways. He nodded for the old woman to deliver the package at the altar.

No! the llaneros protested, it will stay here! We will burn it and let the winds of the llano scatter the ashes.

It is blasphemy to scatter a man's blood on unholy ground, the farmers chanted. The new son must fulfill his mother's

*dream. He must come to El Puerto and rule over the Lunas of
the valley. The blood of the Lunas is strong in him.*

*He is a Márez, the vaqueros shouted. His forefathers were
conquistadores, men as restless as the seas they sailed and as
free as the land they conquered. He is his father's blood!*

*Curses and threats filled the air, pistols were drawn, and the
opposing sides made ready for battle. But the clash was stopped
by the old woman who delivered the baby.*

*Cease! she cried, and the men were quiet. I pulled this baby
into the light of life, so I will bury the afterbirth and the cord
that once linked him to eternity. Only I will know his destiny.*

-- The dream began to dissolve. When I opened my eyes I heard
my father cranking the truck outside. I wanted to go with him,
I wanted to see Las Pasturas, I wanted to see Ultima. I dressed
hurriedly, but I was too late. The truck was bouncing down the
goat path that led to the bridge and the highway.

I turned, as I always did, and looked down the slope of our
hill to the green of the river, and I raised my eyes and saw the
town of Guadalupe. Towering above the housetops and the
trees of the town was the church tower. I made the sign of the
cross on my lips. The only other building that rose above the
housetops to compete with the church tower was the yellow
top of the schoolhouse. This fall I would be going to school.

- My heart sank. When I thought of leaving my mother and
going to school a warm, sick feeling came to my stomach. To
get rid of it I ran to the pens we kept by the molino to feed the
animals. I had fed the rabbits that night and they will had alfalfa
and so I only changed their water. I scattered some grain for the
hungry chickens and watched their mad scramble as the rooster
called them to peck. I milked the cow and turned her loose.
During the day she would forage along the highway where the
grass was thick and green, then she would return at nightfall.
She was a good cow and there were very few times when I had
to run and bring her back in the evening. Then I dreaded it,
because she might wander into the hills where the bats flew at
dusk and there was only the sound of my heart beating as I ran
and it made me sad and frightened to be alone.

I collected three eggs in the chicken house and returned for
breakfast.

"Antonio," my mother smiled and took the eggs and milk,
"come and eat your breakfast."

I sat across the table from Deborah and Theresa and ate my
atole and the hot tortilla with butter. I said very little. I usually

spoke very little to my two sisters. They were older than I and they were very close. They usually spent the entire day in the attic, playing dolls and giggling. I did not concern myself with those things.

"Your father has gone to Las Pasturas," my mother chattered, "he has gone to bring la Grande." Her hands were white with the flour of the dough. I watched carefully. "—And when he returns, I want you children to show your manners. You must not shame your father or your mother—"

"Isn't her real name Ultima?" Deborah asked. She was like that, always asking grown-up questions.

"You will address her as la Grande," my mother said flatly. I looked at her and wondered if this woman with the black hair and laughing eyes was the woman who gave birth in my dream.

"Grande," Theresa repeated.

"Is it true she is a witch?" Deborah asked. Oh, she was in for it. I saw my mother whirl then pause and control herself.

"No!" she scolded. "You must not speak of such things! Oh, I don't know where you learn such ways—" Her eyes flooded with tears. She always cried when she thought we were learning the ways of my father, the ways of the Márez. "She is a woman of learning," she went on and I knew she didn't have time to stop and cry, "she has worked hard for all the people of the village. Oh, I would never have survived those hard years if it had not been for her— so show her respect. We are honored that she comes to live with us, understand?"

"Sí, mamá," Deborah said half willingly.

"Sí, mamá," Theresa repeated.

"Now run and sweep the room at the end of the hall. Eugene's room—" I heard her voice choke. She breathed a prayer and crossed her forehead. The flour left white stains on her, the four points of the cross. I knew it was because my three brothers were at war that she was sad, and Eugene was the youngest.

"Mamá." I wanted to speak to her. I wanted to know who the old woman was who cut the baby's cord.

"Sí." She turned and looked at me.

"Was Ultima at my birth?" I asked.

"¡Ay Dios mío!" my mother cried. She came to where I sat and ran her hand through my hair. She smelled warm, like bread. "Where do you get such questions, my son. Yes," she smiled, "la Grande was there to help me. She was there to help at the birth of all of my children—"

"And my uncles from El Puerto were there?"

"Of course," she answered, "my brothers have always been at my side when I needed them. They have always prayed that I would bless them with a—"

I did not hear what she said because I was hearing the sounds of the dream, and I was seeing the dream again. The warm cereal in my stomach made me feel sick.

"And my father's brother was there, the Márez' and their friends, the vaqueros—"

"Ay!" she cried out, "Don't speak to me of those worthless Márez and their friends!"

"There was a fight?" I asked.

"No," she said, "a silly argument. They wanted to start a fight with my brothers—that is all they are good for. Vaqueros, they call themselves, they are worthless drunks! Thieves! Always on the move, like gypsies, always dragging their families around the country like vagabonds—"

As long as I could remember she always raged about the Márez family and their friends. She called the village of Las Pasturas beautiful; she had gotten used to the loneliness, but she had never accepted its people. She was the daughter of farmers.

But the dream was true. It was as I had seen it. Ultima knew.

"But you will not be like them." She caught her breath and stopped. She kissed my forehead. "You will be like my brothers. You will be a Luna, Antonio. You will be a man of the people, and perhaps a priest." She smiled.

A priest, I thought, that was her dream. I was to hold mass on Sundays like father Byrnes did in the church in town. I was to hear the confessions of the silent people of the valley, and I was to administer the holy Sacrament to them.

"Perhaps," I said.

"Yes," my mother smiled. She held me tenderly. The fragrance of her body was sweet.

"But then," I whispered, "who will hear my confession?"

"What?"

"Nothing," I answered. I felt a cool sweat on my forehead and I knew I had to run, I had to clear my mind of the dream. "I am going to Jasón's house," I said hurriedly and slid past my mother. I ran out the kitchen door, past the animal pens, towards Jasón's house. The white sun and the fresh air cleansed me.

On this side of the river there were only three houses. The

slope of the hill rose gradually into the hills of juniper and mesquite and cedar clumps. Jasón's house was farther away from the river than our house. On the path that led to the bridge lived huge, fat Fío and his beautiful wife. Fío and my father worked together on the highway. They were good drinking friends.

"¡Jasón!" I called at the kitchen door. I had run hard and was panting. His mother appeared at the door.

"Jasón no está aquí," she said. All of the older people spoke only in Spanish, and I myself understood only Spanish. It was only after one went to school that one learned English.

"¿Dónde está?" I asked.

She pointed towards the river, northwest, past the railroad tracks to the dark hills. The river came through those hills and there were old Indian grounds there, holy burial grounds Jasón told me. There in an old cave lived his Indian. At least everybody called him Jasón's Indian. He was the only Indian of the town, and he talked only to Jasón. Jasón's father had forbidden Jasón to talk to the Indian, he had beaten him, he had tried in every way to keep Jasón from the Indian.

But Jasón persisted. Jasón was not a bad boy, he was just Jasón. He was quiet and moody, and sometimes for no reason at all wild, loud sounds came exploding from his throat and lungs. Sometimes I felt like Jasón, like I wanted to shout and cry, but I never did.

I looked at his mother's eyes and I saw they were sad. "Thank you," I said, and returned home. While I waited for my father to return with Ultima I worked in the garden. Every day I had to work in the garden. Every day I reclaimed from the rocky soil of the hill a few more feet of earth to cultivate. The land of the llano was not good for farming, the good land was along the river. But my mother wanted a garden and I worked to make her happy. Already we had a few chile and tomato plants growing. It was hard work. My fingers bled from scraping out the rocks and it seemed that a square yard of ground produced a wheelbarrow full of rocks which I had to push down to the retaining wall.

The sun was white in the bright blue sky. The shade of the clouds would not come until the afternoon. The sweat was sticky on my brown body. I heard the truck and turned to see it chugging up the dusty goat path. My father was returning with Ultima.

"¡Mamá!" I called. My mother came running out, Deborah and Theresa trailed after her.

"I'm afraid," I heard Theresa whimper.

"There's nothing to be afraid of," Deborah said confidently. My mother said there was too much Márez blood in Deborah. Her eyes and hair were very dark, and she was always running. She had been to school two years and she spoke only English. She was teaching Theresa and half the time I didn't understand what they were saying.

"Madre de Dios, but mind your manners!" my mother scolded. The truck stopped and she ran to greet Ultima. "Buenos días le de Dios, Grande," my mother cried. She smiled and hugged and kissed the old woman.

"Ay, María Luna," Ultima smiled, "Buenos días te de Dios, a ti y a tu familia." She wrapped the black shawl around her hair and shoulders. Her face was brown and very wrinkled. When she smiled her teeth were brown. I remembered the dream.

"Come, come!" my mother urged us forward. It was the custom to greet the old. "Deborah!" my mother urged. Deborah stepped forward and took Ultima's withered hand.

"Buenos días, Grande," she smiled. She even bowed slightly. Then she pulled Theresa forward and told her to greet la Grande. My mother beamed. Deborah's good manners surprised her, but they made her happy, because a family was judged by its manners.

"What beautiful daughters you have raised," Ultima nodded to my mother. Nothing could have pleased my mother more. She looked proudly at my father who stood leaning against the truck, watching and judging the introductions.

"Antonio," he said simply. I stepped forward and took Ultima's hand. I looked up into her clear brown eyes and shivered. Her face was old and wrinkled, but her eyes were clear and sparkling, like the eyes of a young child.

"Antonio," she smiled. She took my hand and I felt the power of a whirlwind sweep around me. Her eyes swept the surrounding hills and through them I saw for the first time the wild beauty of our hills and the magic of the green river. My nostrils quivered as I felt the song of the mockingbirds and the drone of the grasshoppers mingle with the pulse of the earth. The four directions of the llano met in me, and the white sun shone on my soul. The granules of sand at my feet and the sun and sky above me seemed to dissolve into one strange, complete being.

A cry came to my throat, and I wanted to shout it and run in the beauty I had found.

"Antonio." I felt my mother prod me. Deborah giggled because she had made the right greeting, and I who was to be my mother's hope and joy stood voiceless.

"Buenos días le de Dios, Ultima," I muttered. I saw in her eyes my dream. I saw the old woman who had delivered me from my mother's womb. I knew she held the secret of my destiny.

"¡Antonio!" My mother was shocked I had used her name instead of calling her Grande. But Ultima held up her hand.

"Let it be," she smiled. "This was the last child I pulled from your womb, María. I knew there would be something between us."

My mother who had started to mumble apologies was quiet. "As you wish, Grande," she nodded.

"I have come to spend the last days of my life here, Antonio," Ultima said to me.

"You will never die, Ultima," I answered. "I will take care of you—" She let go of my hand and laughed. Then my father said, "pase, Grande, pase. Nuestra casa es su casa. It is too hot to stand and visit in the sun—"

"Sí, sí," my mother urged. I watched them go in. My father carried on his shoulders the large blue-tin trunk which later I learned contained all of Ultima's earthly possessions, the black dresses and shawls she wore, and the magic of her sweet smelling herbs.

As Ultima walked past me I smelled for the first time a trace of the sweet fragrance of herbs that always lingered in her wake. Many years later, long after Ultima was gone and I had grown to be a man, I would awaken sometimes at night and think I caught a scent of her fragrance in the cool-night breeze.

And with Ultima came the owl. I heard it that night for the first time in the juniper tree outside of Ultima's window. I knew it was her owl because the other owls of the llano did not come that near the house. At first it disturbed me, and Deborah and Theresa too. I heard them whispering through the partition. I heard Deborah reassuring Theresa that she would take care of her, and then she took Theresa in her arms and rocked her until they were both asleep.

I waited. I was sure my father would get up and shoot the owl with the old rifle he kept on the kitchen wall. But he didn't, and I accepted his understanding. In many cuentos I had heard the owl was one of the disguises a bruja took, and so it struck a chord of fear in the heart to hear them hooting at night. But not Ultima's owl. Its soft hooting was like a song, and as it grew rhythmic it calmed the moonlit hills and lulled us to sleep. Its song seemed to say that it had come to watch over us.

I dreamed about the owl that night, and my dream was good. La Virgen de Guadalupe was the patron saint of our town. The town was named after her. In my dream I saw Ultima's owl lift la Virgen on her wide wings and fly her to heaven. Then the owl returned and gathered up all the babes of Limbo and flew them up to the clouds of heaven.

The Virgin smiled at the goodness of the owl.

Dos

Ultima slipped easily into the routine of our daily life. The first day she put on her apron and helped my mother with breakfast, later she swept the house and then helped my mother wash our clothes in the old washing machine they pulled outside where it was cooler under the shade of the young elm trees. It was as if she had always been here. My mother was very happy because now she had someone to talk to and she didn't have to wait until Sunday when her women friends from the town came up the dusty path to sit in the sala and visit.

Deborah and Theresa were happy because Ultima did many of the household chores they normally did, and they had more time to spend in the attic and cut out an interminable train of paper dolls which they dressed, gave names to, and most miraculously, made talk.

My father was also pleased. Now he had one more person to tell his dream to. My father's dream was to gather his sons around him and move westward to the land of the setting sun, to the vineyards of California. But the war had taken his three sons and it had made him bitter. He often got drunk on Saturday afternoons and then he would rave against old age, he would rage against the town on the opposite side of the river which drained a man of his freedom, and he would cry because the war had ruined his dream. It was very sad to see my father cry, but I understood it, because sometimes a man has to cry. Even if he is a man.

And I was happy with Ultima. We walked together in the llano and along the river banks to gather herbs and roots for her medicines. She taught me the names of plants and flowers, of trees and bushes, of birds and animals; but most important, I learned from her that there was a beauty in the time of day and in the time of night, and that there was peace in the river and in the hills. She taught me to listen to the mystery of the groaning earth and to feel complete in the fulfillment of its time. My soul grew under her careful guidance.

I had been afraid of the awful *presence* of the river, which was the soul of the river, but through her I learned that my spirit shared in the spirit of all things. But the innocence which our isolation sheltered could not last forever, and the affairs of the town began to reach across our bridge and enter my life. Ultima's owl gave the warning that the time of peace on our hill was drawing to an end.

It was Saturday night. My mother had laid out our clean clothes for Sunday mass, and we had gone to bed early because we always went to early mass. The house was quiet, and I was in the mist of some dream when I heard the owl cry its warning. I was up instantly, looking through the small window at the dark figure that ran madly towards the house. He hurled himself at the door and began pounding.

"¡Márez!" he shouted, "¡Márez! ¡Andale, hombre!"

I was frightened, but I recognized the voice. It was Jasón's father.

"¡Un momento!" I heard my father call. He fumbled with the farol.

"¡Andale, hombre, andale!" Chávez cried pitifully, "mataron a mi hermano—"

"Ya vengo—" My father opened the door and the frightened man burst in. In the kitchen I heard my mother moan, "Ave María Purísima, mis hijos—" She had not heard Chávez' last words, and so she assumed the aviso was one that brought bad news about her sons.

"Chávez, ¿qué pasa?" My father held the trembling man.

"¡Mi hermano, mi hermano!" Chávez sobbed, "He has killed my brother!"

"¿Pero qué dices, hombre?" my father exclaimed. He pulled Chávez into the hall and held up the farol. The light cast by the farol revealed the wild, frightened eyes of Chávez.

"¡Gabriel!" my mother cried and came forward, but my father pushed her back. He did not want her to see the monstrous mask of fear on the man's face.

"It is not our sons, it is something in town—get him some water."

"Lo mató, lo mató—" Chávez repeated.

"Get hold of yourself, hombre, tell me what has happened!" My father shook Chávez and the man's sobbing subsided. He took the glass of water and drank, then he could talk.

"Reynaldo has just brought the news, my brother is dead," he sighed and slumped against the wall. Chávez' brother was the sheriff of the town. The man would have fallen if my father had not held him up.

"¡Madre de Dios! Who? How?"

"¡Lupito!" Chávez cried out. His face corded with thick veins. For the first time his left arm came up and I saw the rifle he held.

"Jesús, María y José," my mother prayed.

My father groaned and slumped against the wall. "Ay que Lupito," he shook his head, "the war made him crazy—"

Chávez regained part of his composure. "Get your rifle, we must go to the bridge—"

"The bridge?"

"Reynaldo said to meet him there—The crazy bastard has taken to the river—"

My father nodded silently. He went to the bedroom and returned with his coat. While he loaded his rifle in the kitchen Chávez related what he knew.

"My brother had just finished his rounds," he gasped, "he was at the bus depot cafe, having coffee, sitting without a care in the world—and the bastard came up to where he sat and without warning shot him in the head—" His body shook as he retold the story.

"Perhaps it is better if you wait here, hombre," my father said with consolation.

"No!" Chávez shouted. "I must go. He was my brother!"

My father nodded. I saw him stand beside Chávez and put his arm around his shoulders. Now he too was armed. I had only seen him shoot the rifle when we slaughtered pigs in the fall. Now they were going armed for a man.

"Gabriel, be careful," my mother called as my father and Chávez slipped out into the dark.

"Sí," I heard him answer, then the screen door banged.

"Keep the doors locked—" My mother went to the door and shut the latch. We never locked our doors, but tonight there was something strange and fearful in the air.

Perhaps this is what drew me out into the night to follow my father and Chávez down to the bridge, or perhaps it was some concern I had for my father. I do not know. I waited until my mother was in the sala then dressed and slipped downstairs. I glanced down the hall and saw candlelight flickering from the sala. That room was never entered unless there were Sunday visitors, or unless my mother took us in to pray novenas and rosaries for my brothers at war. I knew she was kneeling at her altar now, praying. I knew she would pray until my father returned.

I slipped out the kitchen door and into the night. It was cool. I sniffed the air, there was a tinge of autumn in it. I ran up the goat path until I caught sight of two dark shadows ahead of me. Chávez and my father.

We passed Fío's dark house and then the tall juniper tree that stood where the hill sloped down to the bridge. Even from this distance I could hear the commotion on the bridge. As we neared the bridge I was afraid of being discovered as I had no reason for being there. My father would be very angry. To escape detection I cut to the right and was swallowed up by the dark brush of the river. I pushed through the dense bosque until I came to the bank of the river. From where I stood I could look up into the flooding beams of light that were pointed down by the excited men. I could hear them giving frenzied, shouted instructions. I looked to my left where the bridge started and saw my father and Chávez running towards the excitement at the center of the bridge.

My eyes were now accustomed to the dark, but it was a glint of light that made me turn and look at a clump of bullrushes in the sweeping water of the river just a few yards away. What I saw made my blood run cold. Crouched in the reeds and half submerged in the muddy waters lay the figure of Lupito, the man who had killed the sheriff. The glint of light was from the pistol he held in his hand.

It was frightening enough to come upon him so suddenly, but as I dropped to my knees in fright I must have uttered a cry because he turned and looked directly at me. At that same moment a beam of light found him and illuminated a face twisted with madness. I do not know if he saw me, or if the light cut off his vision, but I saw his bitter, contorted grin. As long as I live I will never forget those wild eyes, like the eyes of a trapped, savage animal.

At the same time someone shouted from the bridge, "There!" Then all the lights found the crouched figure. He jumped and I saw him as clear as if it were daylight.

"Ayeeeeee!" He screamed a blood curdling cry that echoed down the river. The men on the bridge didn't know what to do. They stood transfixed, looking down at the mad man waving the pistol in the air. "Ayeeeeeeee!" He cried again. It was a cry of rage and pain, and it made my soul sick. The cry of a tormented man had come to the peaceful green mystery of my river, and the great *presence* of the river watched from the shadows and deep recesses, as I watched from where I crouched at the bank.

"Japanese sol'jer, Japanese sol'jer!" he cried, "I am wounded. Come help me—" he called to the men on the bridge. The rising mist of the river swirled in the beams of spotlights. It was like a horrible nightmare.

Suddenly he leaped up and ran splashing through the water towards me. The lights followed him. He grew bigger, I heard his panting, the water his feet kicked up splashed on my face, and I thought he would run over me. Then as quickly as he had sprinted in my direction he turned and disappeared again into the dark clumps of reeds in the river. The lights moved in all directions, but they couldn't find him. Some of the lights swept over me and I trembled with fear that I would be found out, or worse, that I would be mistaken for Lupito and shot.

"The crazy bastard got away!" someone shouted on the bridge.

"Ayeeeeee!" the scream sounded again. It was a cry that I did not understand, and I am sure the men on the bridge did not either. The man they hunted had slipped away from human understanding; he had become a wild animal, and they were afraid.

"Damn!" I heard them cursing themselves. Then a car with a siren and flashing red light came on the bridge. It was Vigil, the state policeman who patrolled our town.

"Chávez is dead!" I heard him shout. "He never had a chance. His brains blown out—" There was silence.

"We have to kill him!" Jason's father shouted. His voice was full of anger, rage and desperation.

"I have to deputize you—" Vigil started to say.

"The hell with deputizing!" Chávez shouted. "He killed my brother! ¡Está loco!" The men agreed with their silence.

"Have you spotted him?" Vigil asked.

"Just now we saw him, but we lost him—"

"He's down there," someone added.

"He is an animal! He has to be shot!" Chávez cried out.

"¡Sí!" the men agreed.

"Now wait a moment—" It was my father who spoke. I do not know what he said because of the shouting. In the meantime I searched the dark of the river for Lupito. I finally saw him. He was about forty feet away, crouched in the reeds as before. The muddy waters of the river lapped and gurgled savagely around him. Before the night had been only cool, now it turned cold and I shivered. I was torn between a fear that made my body tremble, and a desire to help the poor man. But I could not move, I could only watch like a chained spectator.

"Márez is right!" I heard a booming voice on the bridge. In the lights I could make out the figure of Narciso. There was only one man that big and with that voice in town. I knew that Narciso was one of the old people from Las Pasturas, and that he was a good friend to my father. I knew they often drank together on Saturdays, and once or twice he had been to our house.

"¡Por Dios, hombres!" he shouted, "let us act like men! That is not an animal down there, that is a man. Lupito. You all know Lupito. You know that the war made him sick—" But the men would not listen to Narciso. I guess it was because he was the town drunk, and they said he never did anything useful.

"Go back to your drinking and leave this job to men," one of them jeered at him.

"He killed the sheriff in cold blood," another added. I knew that the sheriff had been greatly admired.

"I am not drinking," Narciso persisted, "it is you men who are drunk for blood. You have lost your reason—"

"Reason!" Chávez countered. "What reason did he have for killing my brother. You know," he addressed the men, "my brother did no one harm. Tonight a mad animal crawled behind him and took his life. You call that reason! That animal has to be destroyed!"

"¡Sí! ¡Sí!" the men shouted in unison.

"At least let us try to talk to him," Narciso begged. I knew that it was hard for a man of the llano to beg.

"Yes," Vigil added, "perhaps he will give himself up—"

"Do you think he'll listen to talk! " Chávez jumped forward.
"He's down there, and he still has the pistol that killed my
brother! Go down and talk to him!" I could see Chávez shouting in Vigil's face, and Vigil said nothing. Chávez laughed. "This
is the only talk he will understand—" he turned and fired over
the railing of the bridge. His shots roared then whined away
down the river. I could hear the bullets make splashing noises in
the water.

"Wait!" Narciso shouted. He took Chávez' rifle and with
one hand held it up. Chávez struggled against him but Narciso
was too big and strong. "I will talk to him," Narciso said. He
pushed Chávez back. "I understand your sorrow Chávez," he
said, "but one killing is enough for tonight—" The men must
have been impressed by his sincerity because they stood back
and waited.

Narciso leaned over the concrete railing and shouted down
into the darkness. "Hey Lupito! It is me, Narciso. It is me,
hombre, your compadre. Listen my friend, a very bad business
has happened tonight, but if we act like men we can settle
it—Let me come down and talk to you, Lupito. Let me help
you—"

I looked at Lupito. He had been watching the action on the
bridge, but now as Narciso talked to him I saw his head slump
on his chest. He seemed to be thinking. I prayed that he would
listen to Narciso and that the angry and frustrated men on the
bridge would not commit mortal sin. The night was very quiet.
The men on the bridge awaited an answer. Only the lapping
water of the river made a sound.

" ¡Amigo!" Narciso shouted, "You know I am your friend,
I want to help you, hombre—" He laughed softly. "Hey, Lupito,
you remember just a few years ago, before you went to the war,
you remember the first time you came into the Eight Ball to
gamble a little. Remember how I taught you how Juan Botas
marked the aces with a little tobacco juice, and he thought you
were green, but you beat him!" He laughed again. "Those were
good times, Lupito, before the war came. Now we have this bad
business to settle. But we are friends who will help you—"

I saw Lupito's tense body shake. A low, sad mournful cry
tore itself from his throat and mixed into the lapping sound of
the waters of the river. His head shook slowly, and I guess he
must have been thinking and fighting between surrendering or

remaining free, and hunted. Then like a coiled spring he jumped up, his pistol aimed straight up. There was a flash of fire and the loud report of the pistol. But he had not fired at Narciso or at any of the men on the bridge! The spotlights found him.

"There's your answer!" Chávez shouted.

"He's firing! He's firing!" Another voice shouted. "He's crazy!"

Lupito's pistol sounded again. Still he was not aiming at the men on the bridge. He was shooting to draw their fire!

"Shoot! Shoot!" someone on the bridge called.

"No, no," I whispered through clenched lips. But it was too late for anything. The frightened men responded by aiming their rifles over the side of the bridge. One single shot sounded then a barrage followed it like the roar of a canon, like the rumble of thunder in a summer thunderstorm.

Many shots found their mark. I saw Lupito lifted off his feet and hurled backward by the bullets. But he got up and ran limping and crying towards the bank where I lay.

"Bless me—" I thought he cried, and the second volley of shots from the bridge sounded, but this time they sounded like a great whirling of wings, like pigeons swirling to roost on the church top. He fell forward then clawed and crawled out of the holy water of the river onto the bank in front of me. I wanted to reach out and help him, but I was frozen by my fear. He looked up at me and his face was bathed in water and flowing, hot blood, but it was also dark and peaceful as it slumped into the sand of the riverbank. He made a strange gurgling sound in his throat, then he was still. Up on the bridge a great shout went up. The men were already running to the end of the bridge to come down and claim the man whose dead hands dug into the soft, wet sand in front of me.

I turned and ran. The dark shadows of the river enveloped me as I raced for the safety of home. Branches whipped at my face and cut it, and vines and tree trunks caught at my feet and tripped me. In my headlong rush I disturbed sleeping birds and their shrill cries and slapping wings hit at my face. The horror of darkness had never been so complete as it was for me that night.

I had started praying to myself from the moment I heard the first shot and I never stopped praying until I reached home. Over and over through my mind ran the words of the Act of Contrition. I had not yet been to catechism nor had I made my first holy communion, but my mother had taught me the Act of

Contrition. It was to be said after one made his confession to the priest, and as the last prayer before death.

Did God listen? Would he hear? Had he seen my father on the bridge? And where was Lupito's soul winging to, or was it washing down the river to the fertile valley of my uncles' farms?

A priest could have saved Lupito. Oh why did my mother dream for me to be a priest! How would I ever wash away the stain of blood from the sweet waters of my river! I think at that time I began to cry because as I left the river brush and headed up the hills I heard my sobs for the first time.

It was also then that I heard the owl. Between my gasps for air and my sobs I stopped and listened for its song. My heart was pounding and my lungs hurt, but a calmness had come over the moonlit night when I heard the hooting of Ultima's owl. I stood still for a long time. I realized that the owl had been with me throughout the night. It had watched over all that had happened on the bridge. Suddenly the terrible, dark fear that had possessed me was gone.

I looked at the house that my father and my brothers had built on the juniper-patched hill; it was quiet and peaceful in the blue night. The sky sparkled with a million stars and the Virgin's horned moon, the moon of my mother's people, the moon of the Lunas. My mother would be praying for the soul of Lupito.

Again the owl sang, Ultima's spirit bathed me with its strong resolution. I turned and looked across the river. Some lights shone in the town. In the moonlight I could make out the tower of the church, the school house top, and way beyond the glistening of the town's water tank. I heard the soft wail of a siren and I knew the men would be pulling Lupito from the river.

The river's brown waters would be stained with blood, forever and ever and ever . . .

In the autumn I would have to go to the school in the town, and in a few years I would go to catechism lessons in the church. I shivered. My body began to hurt from the beating it had taken from the brush of the river. But what hurt more was that I had witnessed for the first time the death of a man.

— My father did not like the town or its way. When we had first moved from Las Pasturas we had lived in a rented house in the town. But every evening after work he had looked across the river to these barren, empty hills, and finally he had bought a couple of acres and began building our house. Everyone told him he was crazy, that the rocky, wild hill could sustain no life, and my mother was more than upset. She wanted to buy along the river where the land was fertile and there was water for the plants and trees. But my father won the fight to be close to his llano, because truthfully our hill was the beginning of the llano, from here it stretched away as far as the eye could see, to Las Pasturas and beyond.

The men of the town had murdered Lupito. But he had murdered the sheriff. They said the war had made him crazy. The prayers for Lupito mixed into prayers for my brothers. So many different thoughts raced through my mind that I felt dizzy, and very weary and sick. I ran the last of the way and slipped quietly into the house. I groped for the stair railing in the dark and felt a warm hand take mine. Startled, I looked up into Ultima's brown, wrinkled face.

"You knew!" I whispered. I understood that she did not want my mother to hear.

"Sí," she replied.

"And the owl—" I gasped. My mind searched for answers, but my body was so tired that my knees buckled and I fell forward. As small and thin as Ultima was she had the strength to lift me in her arms and carry me into her room. She placed me on her bed and then by the light of a small, flickering candle she mixed one of her herbs in a tin cup, held it over the flame to warm, then gave it to me to drink.

"They killed Lupito," I said as I gulped the medicine.

"I know," she nodded. She prepared a new potion and with this she washed the cuts on my face and feet.

"Will he go to hell?" I asked.

"That is not for us to say, Antonio. The war-sickness was not taken out of him, he did not know what he was doing—"

"And the men on the bridge, my father!"

"Men will do what they must do," she answered. She sat on the bed by my side. Her voice was soothing, and the drink she had given me made me sleepy. The wild, frightening excitement in my body began to die.

"The ways of men are strange, and hard to learn," I heard her say.

"Will I learn them?" I asked. I felt the weight on my eyelids.

"You will learn much, you will see much," I heard her far-away voice. I felt a blanket cover me. I felt safe in the warm sweetness of the room. Outside the owl sang its dark questioning to the night, and I slept.

But even into my deep sleep my dreams came. In my dream I saw my three brothers. I saw them as I remembered them before they went away to war, which seemed so very long ago. They stood by the house that we rented in town and they looked across the river at the hills of the llano.

Father says that the town steals our freedom; he says that we must build a castle across the river, on the lonely hill of the mockingbirds. I think it was León who spoke first, he was the eldest, and his voice always had a sad note to it. But in the dark mist of the dream I could not be sure.

His heart has been heavy since we came to the town, the second figure spoke, his forefathers were men of the sea, the Márez people, they were conquistadores, men whose freedom was unbounded.

It was Andrew who said that! It was Andrew! I was sure because his voice was husky like his thick and sturdy body.

Father says the freedom of the wild horse is in the Márez blood, and his gaze is always westward. His fathers before him were vaqueros, and so he expects us to be men of the llano. I was sure the third voice belonged to Eugene.

I longed to touch them. I was hungry for their company. Instead I spoke.

We must all gather around our father, I heard myself say. His dream is to ride westward in search of new adventure. He builds highways that stretch into the sun, and we must travel that road with him.

My brothers frowned. You are a Luna, they chanted in unison, you are to be a farmer-priest for mother!

The doves came to drink in the still pools of the river and their cry was mournful in the darkness of my dream.

My brothers laughed. You are but a baby, Tony, you are our mother's dream. Stay and sleep to the doves cou-rou while we cross the mighty River of the Carp to build our father's castle in the hills.

I must go! I cried to the three dark figures. I must lift the muddy waters of the river in blessing to our new home!

Along the river the tormented cry of a lonely goddess filled the valley. The winding wail made the blood of men run cold.

It is la llorona, my brothers cried in fear, the old witch who cries along the river banks and seeks the blood of boys and men to drink!

La llorona seeks the soul of Antonioooooooooo . . .

It is the soul of Lupito, they cried in fear, doomed to wander the river at night because the waters washed his soul away!

Lupito seeks his blessingggggggggg . . .

It is neither! I shouted. I swung the dark robe of the priest over my shoulders then lifted my hands in the air. The mist swirled around me and sparks flew when I spoke. It is the presence *of the river!*

Save us, my brothers cried and cowered at my words.

I spoke to the presence *of the river and it allowed my brothers to cross with their carpenter tools to build our castle on the hill.*

Behind us I heard my mother moan and cry because with each turning of the sun her son was growing old . . .

Tres

The day dawned, and already the time of youth was fleeing the house which the three giants of my dreams had built on the hill of juniper tree and yucca and mesquite bush. I felt the sun of the east rise and I heard its light crackle and groan and mix into the songs of the mockingbirds on the hill. I opened my eyes and the rays of light that dazzled through the dusty window of my room washed my face clean.

The sun was good. The men of the llano were men of the sun. The men of the farms along the river were men of the moon. But we were all children of the white sun.

There was a bitter taste in my mouth. I remembered the remedy Ultima had given me after my frightful flight from the river. I looked at my arms and I felt my face. I had received cuts from tree branches before and I knew that the next day the cuts were red with dry blood and that the welts were sore. But last night's cuts were only thin pink lines on my flesh, and there was no pain. There was a strange power in Ultima's medicine.

Where was Lupito's soul? He had killed the sheriff and so he had died with a mortal sin on his soul. He would go to hell. Or would God forgive him and grant him Purgatory, the lonely, hopeless resting place of those who were neither saved nor damned. But God didn't forgive anyone. Perhaps, like the dream said, the waters of the river had washed his soul away, and perhaps as the water seeped into the earth Lupito's soul would water the orchards of my uncles, and the bright red apples would. . . .

Or perhaps he was doomed to wander the river bottom forever, a bloody mate to la Llorona . . . and now when I walked alone along the river I would always have to turn and glance over my shoulder to catch a glimpse of a shadow—Lupito's soul, or la Llorona, or the *presence* of the river.

I lay back and watched the silent beams of light radiate in the colorful dust motes I had stirred up. I loved to watch the sun beams of each new morning enter the room. They made me feel fresh and clean and new. Each morning I seemed to awaken with new experiences and dreams strangely mixed into me. Today it was all the vivid images of what had happened at the bridge last night. I thought of Chávez, angered by the death of his brother, seeking the blood of revenge. I thought of Narciso, standing alone against the dark figures on the bridge. I thought of my father. I wondered if he had fired down on Lupito.

Now the men on the bridge walked the earth with the terrible burden of dark mortal sin on their souls, and hell was the only reward.

I heard my mother's footsteps in the kitchen. I heard the stove clang and I knew she was kindling last night's ashes.

"¡Gabriel!" she called. She always called my father first. "Get up. It is Sunday," then she muttered, "and oh such evil things that walked the earth last night—"

On Sunday morning I always stayed in bed and listened to their argument. They always quarreled on Sunday morning. There were two reasons for this: the first was that my father worked only half a day on Saturdays at the highway and so in the afternoon he drank with his friends at the Longhorn Saloon in town. If he drank too much he came home a bitter man, then he was at war with everyone. He cursed the weak-willed men of the town who did not understand the freedom a man of the llano must have, and he cursed the war for taking his sons away. And if there was very much anger in him he cursed my mother because she was the daughter of farmers and it was she who kept him shackled to one piece of land.

Then there was the thing about religion. My father was not a strong believer in religion. When he was drunk he called priests "women," and made fun of the long skirts they wore. I had heard a story told in whispers not meant for my ears that once, long ago, my father's father had taken a priest from the church and beaten him on the street for preaching against something my grandfather Márez had done. So it was not a good feeling my father had for priests. My mother said the Márez clan was full of freethinkers, which was a blasphemy to her, but my father only laughed.

Then there was the strange, whispered riddle of the first priest who went to El Puerto. The colony had first settled there under a land grant from the Mexican government, and the man who led the colonization was a priest, and he was a Luna. That is why my mother dreamed of me becoming a priest, because there had not been a Luna priest in the family for many years. My mother was a devout Catholic, and so she saw the salvation of the soul rooted in the Holy Mother Church, and she said the world would be saved if the people turned to the earth. A community of farmers ruled over by a priest, she firmly believed, was the true way of life.

Why two people as opposite as my father and my mother had married I do not know. Their blood and their ways had kept them at odds, and yet for all this, we were happy.

"Deborah!" she called, "Get up. Get Theresa cleaned and dressed! Ay, what a night it has been—" I heard her murmur prayers.

"Ay Dios," I heard my father groan as he walked into the kitchen.

The sun coming over the hill, the sounds of my father and mother in the kitchen, Ultima's shuffle in her room as she burned incense for the new day, my sisters rushing past my door, all this was as it had always been and it was good.

"¡Antonio!" my mother called just when I knew she would and I jumped out of bed. But today I was awakening with a new knowledge.

"There will be no breakfast this morning," my mother said as we gathered around her, "today we will all go to communion. Men walk the world as animals, and we must pray that they see God's light." And to my sisters she said, "Today you will offer up half of your communion for your brothers, that God bring them home safely, and half—for what happened last night."

"What happened last night?" Deborah asked. She was like

that. I shivered and wondered if she had heard me last night and
if she would tell on me.

"Never mind!" my mother said curtly, "just pray for the
dearly departed souls—"

Deborah agreed but I knew that at church she would inquire
and find out about the killing of the sheriff and Lupito. It was
strange that she should have to ask others when I, who had been
there and seen everything, stood next to her. Even now I could
hardly believe that I had been there. Had it been a dream? Or had
it been a dream within a dream, the kind that I often had and
which seemed so real?

I felt a soft hand on my head and turned and saw Ultima.
She looked down at me and that clear, bright power in her eyes
held me spellbound.

"How do you feel this morning, my Antonio?" she asked
and all I could do was nod my head.

"Buenos días le de Dios, Grande," my mother greeted her.
So did my father who was drinking coffee at the big chair he
kept by the stove.

"Antonio, mind your manners," my mother urged me. I had
not greeted Ultima properly.

"Ay, María Luna," Ultima interrupted, "you leave Antonio
alone, please. Last night was hard for many men," she said
mysteriously and went to the stove where my father poured her
some coffee. My father and Ultima were the only people I ever
knew that did not mind breaking their fast before communion.

"The men, yes," my mother acknowledged, "but my Tony is
only a boy, a baby yet." She placed her hands on my shoulders
and held me.

"Ay, but boys grow to be men," Ultima said as she sipped
the black, scalding coffee.

"Ay, how true," my mother said and clutched me tightly,
"and what a sin it is for a boy to grow into a man—"

It was a sin to grow up and be a man.

"It is no sin," my father spoke up, "only a fact of life."

"Ay, but life destroys the pureness God gives—"

"It does not destroy," my father was becoming irritated at
having to go to church and listen to a sermon too, "it builds up.
Everything he sees and does makes him a man—"

I saw Lupito murdered. I saw the men—

"Ay!" my mother cried, "if only he could become a priest.
That would save him! He would be always with God. Oh,

Gabriel," she beamed with joy, "just think the honor it would bring our family to have a priest— Perhaps today we should talk to Father Byrnes about it—"

"Be sensible!" my father stood up. "The boy has not even been through his catechism. And it is not the priest who will decide when the time comes, but Tony himself!" He stalked past me. The smell of gunpowder was on his clothes.

They say the devil smells of sulfur.

"It is true," Ultima added. My mother looked at them and then at me. Her eyes were sad.

"Go feed the animals, my Toñito," she pushed me away, "it is almost time for mass—"

I ran out and felt the first cool touch of early autumn in the air. Soon it would be time to go to my uncles' farms for the harvest. Soon it would be time to go to school. I looked across the river. The town seemed still asleep. A thin mist rose from the river. It blurred the trees and buildings of the town, it hid the church tower and the schoolhouse top.

Ya las campanas de la iglesia están doblando . . .

I wanted not to think anymore of what I had seen last night. I threw fresh alfalfa into the rabbits pen and changed their water. I opened the door and the cow bounded out, hungry for fresh grass. Today she would not be milked until the evening and she would be very heavy. I saw her run towards the highway, and I was glad that she did not wander towards the river where the grass was stained—

Por la sangre de Lupito, todos debemos de rogar,
Que Dios la saque de pena y la lleve a descansar . . .

I was afraid to think anymore. I saw the glistening of the railroad tracks and my eyes fastened on them. If I followed the tracks I would arrive at Las Pasturas, the land of my birth. Someday I would return and see the little village where the train stopped for water, where the grass was as high and green as the waves of the ocean, where the men rode horses and they laughed and cried at births, weddings, dances, and wakes.

"¡Anthony! ¡Antonioooooooo!" I thought it was the voice of my dreams and jumped, but it was my mother calling. Everyone was ready for mass. My mother and Ultima dressed in black because so many women of the town had lost sons or husbands in the war and they were in mourning. Those years it seemed that the whole town was in mourning, and it was very sad on Sundays to see the rows of black-dressed women walking in procession to church.

"Ay, what a night," my father groaned. Today two more families would be in mourning in the town of Guadalupe, and indirectly the far-off war of the Japanese and the Germans had come to claim two victims in New Mexico.

"Ven acá, Antonio," my mother scolded. She wet my dark hair and brushed it down. In spite of her dark clothing she smelled sweet and it made me feel better to be near her. I wished that I could always be near her, but that was impossible. The war had taken my brothers away, and so the school would take me away.

"Ready, mamá," Deborah called. She said that in school the teachers let them speak only in English. I wondered how I would be able to speak to the teachers.

"¡Gabriel!" my mother called.

"Sí, sí," my father groaned. I wondered how heavy last night's sin lay on his soul.

My mother took one last cursory glance at her brood then led the way up the goat path; we called the path from our home to the bridge the goat path because when we ran to meet our father after his day's work he said we looked like goats, cabron-citos, or cabritos. We must have made a strange procession, my mother leading the group with her swift, proud walk, Deborah and Theresa skipping around her, my father muttering and dragging behind, and finally Ultima and myself.

"Es una mujer que no ha pecado . . ." some would whisper of Ultima.

"La curandera," they would exchange nervous glances.

"Hechicera, bruja," I heard once.

"Why are you so thoughtful, Antonio?" Ultima asked. Usually I was picking up stones to have ready for stray rabbits that crossed our path, but today my thoughts kept my soul in a shroud.

"I was thinking of Lupito," I said. "My father was on the bridge," I added.

"That is so," she said simply.

"But, Ultima, how can he go to communion? How can he take God in his mouth and swallow him? Will God forgive his sin and be with him?" For a long time Ultima did not answer.

"A man of the llano," she said, "will not take the life of a llanero unless there is just cause. And I do not think your father fired at Lupito last night. And more important, mi hijo, you must never judge who God forgives and who He doesn't—"

We walked together and I thought about what she had said. I knew she was right. "Ultima," I asked, "what was it you gave me to make me sleep last night? And did you carry me to my room?"

She laughed. "I am beginning to understand why your mother calls you the inquisitor," she said.

"But I want to know, there are so many things I want to know," I insisted.

"A curandera cannot give away her secrets," she said, "but if a person really wants to know, then he will listen and see and be patient. Knowledge comes slowly—"

I walked along, thinking about what she had said. When we came to the bridge my mother hurried the girls across, but my father paused to look over the railing. I looked too. What happened down there was like a dream, so far away. The brown waters of the River of the Carp wound their way southward to the orchards of my uncles.

We crossed the bridge and turned right. The dirt road followed the high cliff of the river on this side. It wound into the cluster of houses around the church then kept going, following the river to El Puerto. To our left began the houses and buildings of the town. All seemed to turn towards the Main Street of town, except one. This house, a large, rambling gray stucco with a picket fence surrounding the weedy grounds, stood away from the street, perched on a ledge that dropped fifty feet down into the river below.

A long time ago the house had belonged to a very respectable family but they had moved into town after the waters of the river began to cut into the cliff below them. Now the house belonged to a woman named Rosie. I knew that Rosie was evil, not evil like a witch, but evil in other ways. Once the priest had preached in Spanish against the women who lived in Rosie's house and so I knew that her place was bad. Also, my mother admonished us to bow our heads when we passed in front of the house.

The bell of the church began to ring, *una mujer con un diente, que llama a toda la gente.* The bell called the people to six o'clock mass.

But no. Today it was not just telling us that in five minutes mass would begin, today it was crying the knell of Lupito.

"¡Ay!" I heard my mother cry and saw her cross her forehead.

La campana de la iglesia está doblando . . .

The church bell tolled and drew to it the widows in black, the lonely, faithful women who came to pray for their men.

Arrímense vivos y difuntos
Aquí estamos todos juntos . . .

The church rose up from the dust of the road, huge brown granite blocks rose skyward to hold the bell tower and the cross of Christ. It was the biggest building I had ever seen in all my life. Now the people gathered at its doors like ants, asking questions and passing on rumors about what happened last night. My father went to talk to the men, but my mother and Ultima stood apart with the women with whom they exchanged formal greetings. I went around the side of the church where I knew the boys from town hung around until mass began.

Most of the kids were older than I. They were in the second or third grade at school. I knew most of them by name, not because I talked with them, but because after many Sundays of observing them I had learned who they were and a little bit about their characteristics. I knew that when I went to school in the fall I would get to know them well, I was only sad because they would be a year ahead of me and I already felt close to them.

"My ole man saw Lupito do it!" Ernie pointed his thumb in Abel's face. I knew Ernie liked to brag.

"Bullshit!" Horse cried out. They called him Horse because his face looked like the face of a horse, and he was always stomping at the ground.

"¡Chingada! Dah bastard neber have a chance! Puggggggh!" Bones exploded like a pistol. He grabbed at the top of his head and toppled on the dust of the street. His eyes rolled wildly. Bones was even crazier than Horse.

"I went to the river this morning," Samuel said softly. "There was blood on the sand—" No one heard him. I knew he lived across the river like I did, but he lived upriver where there were a few houses just past the railroad bridge.

"I'll race you! I'll race you!" The Vitamin Kid pawed ner-

vously at the ground. I never knew his real name, everyone just
called him the Vitamin Kid, even the teachers at school. He
could run, oh how he could run! Not even Bones in high gear
or Horse at full gallop could outrun the Vitamin Kid. He was
like the wind.

"Bullshit!" Horse cleared his throat and let fly a frog. Then
Florence cleared his throat and spit a nice wad that beat Horse's
by five feet at least.

"Heh. He beat you, damn he beat you," Abel laughed. Abel
was very small, even smaller than I, and he should never have
teased Horse. If there was one thing Horse loved to do, that was
to wrestle. His long arms reached out, caught Abel before he
could move away, and flipped him easily into the air. Abel
landed hard on the ground.

"Cabrón," he whimpered.

"Did he beat me?" Horse asked as he stood over Abel.

"No," Abel cried. He got up slowly, faking a broken leg,
then when he was out of Horse's reach he called, "he beat you,
fucker, he beat you! Yah-yah-ya-yah!"

"My ole man was right in the cafe when it happened," Ernie
continued. Ernie always wanted to be the center of interest.
"He said Lupito just walked in real slow, walked up right behind the sheriff who was biting into a piece of cherry pie, put
the pistol to the back of the sheriff's head—"

"Bullshit!" Horse neighed loudly. "Hey, Florence, top this
one!" Again he cleared his throat and spit.

"Nah," Florence grinned. He was tall and thin, with curly
blonde hair that fell to his shoulders. I had never seen anyone
like him, so white and speaking Spanish. He reminded me of
one of the golden angel heads with wings that hovered at the
feet of the Virgin in her pictures.

"Cherry pie? Aghhhhhh!"

"—And there were brains and blood all over the damned
place. On the table, on the floor, even on the ceiling, and his
eyes were open as he fell, and before he hit the floor Lupito was
out the door—"

"Bullshit." "Damn." " ¡Chingada!"

"He'll go to hell," Lloyd said in his girl's voice, "it's the law
that he go to hell for what he did."

"Everybody from Los Jaros goes to hell," Florence laughed.
Los Jaros was what they called the neighborhood across the
tracks, and Horse and Bones and Abel and Florence were from
there.

"You're going to hell, Florence, because you don't believe in God!" Horse shouted.

"Los vatos de Los Jaros are tough!" Bones gurgled. He wiped his thumbs on his nose and a green snot dangled there.

"Damn." "Chingada."

"Come on Florence, let's wrestle," Horse said. He was still angry about the spitting contest.

"You can't wrestle before mass, it'a a sin," Lloyd cut in.

"Bullshit," Horse said and he turned to pounce on Lloyd, but as he did he saw me for the first time. He looked at me for a long time then he called me. "Hey kid, come here."

They watched me with interest as I walked towards the Horse. I did not want to wrestle with Horse; he was tougher and bigger than I. But my father had often said that a man of the llano does not run from a fight.

"Who'z dat?" "Don't know." "Chingada."

The Horse reached for my neck, but I knew about his favorite trick and ducked. I went low and came up yanking at his left leg. With a hard pull I flipped the Horse on his back.

"¡Hiii-jo-lah!" "¡Ah la veca!" "Did'jew see that, the kid threw the Horse!" Everyone laughed at Horse in the dust.

He got up slowly, his wild eyes never leaving me; he wiped the seat of his pants and came towards me. I braced myself and stood my ground. I knew I was in for a whipping. The Horse came up to me very slowly until his face was close to mine. His dark, wild eyes held me hypnotically, and I could hear the deep sounds a horse makes inside his chest when he is ready to buck. Saliva curled around the edges of his mouth and spittle threads hung down and glistened like spider threads in the sun. He chomped his teeth and I could smell his bad breath.

I thought the Horse was going to rear up and paw and stomp me into the ground, and I guess the other kids did too because they were very quiet. But instead of attacking me the Horse let out a wild, shocking cry that sent me reeling backward.

"Whaggggggggh!" He brayed. "The little runt actually threw me, he threw me?" He laughed. "What's your name, kid?"

The other kids breathed easier. The Horse was not going to commit murder.

"Anthony Márez," I replied, "Antonio Juan Márez y Luna," I added in respect to my mother.

"Damn." "Chingada."

"Hey, you Andrew's brother?" Horse asked. I nodded yes,

"Well, put 'er there—" I shook my head no. I knew that Horse couldn't resist throwing anyone who held out his hand. It was just his nature.

"Smart kid," Bones laughed.

"Shut up!" Horse glared at him. "Okay, kid, I mean Anthony, you are a smart kid. The last guy that threw me was a big fifth grader, you hear—"

"I didn't mean to," I said. Everyone laughed.

"I know you didn't," Horse smiled, "and you're too small to fight. That's why I'm going to let you get away with it. But don't think you can do it again, understand!" The message was as much for me as for the rest of the gang, because we all nodded.

They all gathered around me and asked me where I lived and about school. They were good friends, even though they sometimes said bad words, and that day I became a part of their gang.

Then Abel, who had been pissing against the church wall, called out that mass was starting and we all rushed to get the premium pews at the very back of the church.

Cuatro

There is a time in the last few days of summer when the ripeness of autumn fills the air, and time is quiet and mellow. I lived that time fully, strangely aware of a new world opening up and taking shape for me. In the mornings, before it was too hot, Ultima and I walked in the hills of the llano, gathering the wild herbs and roots for her medicines. We roamed the entire countryside and up and down the river. I carried a small shovel with which to dig, and she carried a gunny sack in which to gather our magic harvest.

"¡Ay!" she would cry when she spotted a plant or root she needed, "what luck we are in today to find la yerba del manso!"

Then she would lead me to the plant her owl-eyes had found and ask me to observe where the plant grew and how its leaves looked. "Now touch it," she would say. The leaves were smooth and light green.

For Ultima, even the plants had a spirit, and before I dug she made me speak to the plant and tell it why we pulled it from its home in the earth. "You that grow well here in the arroyo by the dampness of the river, we lift you to make good medicine," Ultima intoned softly and I found myself repeating after her.

Then I would carefully dig out the plant, taking care not to let the steel of the shovel touch the tender roots. Of all the plants we gathered none was endowed with so much magic as the yerba del manso. It could cure burns, sores, piles, colic in babies, bleeding dysentary and even rheumatism. I knew this plant from long ago because my mother, who was surely not a curandera, often used it.

Ultima's soft hands would carefully lift the plant and examine it. She would take a pinch and taste its quality. Then she took the same pinch and put it into a little black bag tied to a sash around her waist. She told me that the dry contents of the bag contained a pinch of every plant she had ever gathered since she began her training as a curandera many years ago.

"Long ago," she would smile, "long before you were a dream, long before the train came to Las Pasturas, before the Lunas came to their valley, before the great Coronado built his bridge—" Then her voice would trail off and my thoughts would be lost in the labyrinth of a time and history I did not know.

We wandered on and found some orégano, and we gathered plenty because this was not only a cure for coughs and fever but a spice my mother used for beans and meat. We were also lucky to find some oshá, because this plant grows better in the mountains. It is like la yerba del manso, a cure for everything. It cures coughs or colds, cuts and bruises, rheumatism and stomach troubles, and my father once said the old sheepherders used it to keep poisonous snakes away from their bedrolls by sprinkling them with oshá powder. It was with a mixture of oshá that Ultima washed my face and arms and feet the night Lupito was killed.

In the hills Ultima was happy. There was a nobility to her walk that lent a grace to the small figure. I watched her carefully and imitated her walk, and when I did I found that I was no longer lost in the enormous landscape of hills and sky. I was a very important part of the teeming life of the llano and the river.

"¡Mira! Qué suerte, tunas," Ultima cried with joy and pointed to the ripe-red prickly pears of the nopal. "Run and gather some and we will eat them in the shade by the river." I ran to the cactus and gathered a shovelfull of the succulent, seedy pears. Then we sat in the shade of the álamos of the river and peeled the tunas very carefully because even on their skin they have fuzz spots that make your fingers and tongue itch. We sat and ate and felt refreshed.

The river was silent and brooding. The *presence* was watching over us. I wondered about Lupito's soul.

"It is almost time to go to my uncles' farms in El Puerto and gather the harvest," I said.

"Ay," Ultima nodded and looked to the south.

"Do you know my uncles, the Lunas?" I asked.

"Of course, child," she replied, "your grandfather and I are old friends. I know his sons. I lived in El Puerto, many years ago—"

"Ultima," I asked, "why are they so strange and quiet? And why are my father's people so loud and wild?"

She answered. "It is the blood of the Lunas to be quiet, for only a quiet man can learn the secrets of the earth that are necessary for planting— They are quiet like the moon— And it is the blood of the Márez to be wild, like the ocean from which they take their name, and the spaces of the llano that have become their home."

I waited, then said. "Now we have come to live near the river, and yet near the llano. I love them both, and yet I am of neither. I wonder which life I will choose?"

"Ay, hijito," she chuckled, "do not trouble yourself with those thoughts. You have plenty of time to find yourself—"

"But I am growing," I said, "every day I grow older—"

"True," she replied softly. She understood that as I grew I would have to choose to be my mother's priest or my father's son.

We were silent for a long time, lost in memories that the murmur of the mourning wind carried across the treetops. Cotton from the trees drifted lazily in the heavy air. The silence spoke, not with harsh sounds, but softly to the rhythm of our blood.

"What is it?" I asked, for I was still afraid.

"It is the *presence* of the river," Ultima answered.

I held my breath and looked at the giant, gnarled cottonwood trees that surrounded us. Somewhere a bird cried, and up on the hill the tinkling sound of a cowbell rang. The *presence* was immense, lifeless, yet throbbing with its secret message.

"Can it speak?" I asked and drew closer to Ultima.

"If you listen carefully—" she whispered.

"Can you speak to it?" I asked, and the whirling, haunting sound touched us.

"Ay, my child," Ultima smiled and touched my head, "you want to know so much—"

And the *presence* was gone.

"Come, it is time to start homeward." She rose and with the sack over her shoulder hobbled up the hill. I followed. I knew that if she did not answer my question that that part of life was not yet ready to reveal itself to me. But I was no longer afraid of the *presence* of the river.

We circled homeward. On the way back we found some manzanilla. Ultima told me that when my brother León was born that his mollera was sunken in, and that she had cured him with manzanilla.

She spoke to me of the common herbs and medicines we shared with the Indians of the Rio del Norte. She spoke of the ancient medicines of other tribes, the Aztecas, Mayas, and even of those in the old, old country, the Moors. But I did not listen, I was thinking of my brothers León, and Andrew, and Eugene.

When we arrived home we put the plants on the roof of the chicken shed to dry in the white sun. I placed small rocks on them so the wind wouldn't blow them away. There were some plants that Ultima could not obtain in the llano or the river, but many people came to seek cures from her and they brought in exchange other herbs and roots. Especially prized were those plants that were from the mountains.

When we had finished we went in to eat. The hot beans flavored with chicos and green chile were muy sabrosos. I was so hungry that I ate three whole tortillas. My mother was a good cook and we were happy as we ate. Ultima told her of the orégano we found and that pleased her.

"The time of the harvest is here," she said, "it is time to go to my brothers' farms. Juan has sent word that they are expecting us."

Every autumn we made a pilgrimage to El Puerto where my grandfather and uncles lived. There we helped gather the harvest and brought my mother's share home with us.

"He says there is much corn, and ay, such sweet corn my brothers raise!" she went on. "And there is plenty of red chile for making ristras, and fruit, ay! The apples of the Lunas are known throughout the state!" My mother was very proud of her brothers, and when she started talking she went on and on. Ultima nodded courteously but I slipped out of the kitchen.

The day was warm at noonday, not lazy and droning like July but mellow with late August. I went to Jasón's house and we played together all afternoon. We talked about Lupito's death, but I did not tell Jasón what I had seen. Then I went to

My mother had a beautiful statue of la Virgen de Guadalupe

the river and cut the tall, green alfalfa that grew wild and carried the bundle home so that I would have a few days of food
laid in for the rabbits.

Late in the afternoon my father came whistling up the goat
path, striding home from the flaming-orange sun, and we ran to
meet him. "Cabritos!" he called, "cabroncitos!" And he swung
Theresa and Deborah on his shoulders while I walked beside
him carrying his lunch pail.

After supper we always prayed the rosary. The dishes were
quickly done then we gathered in the sala where my mother
kept her altar. My mother had a beautiful statue of la Virgen de
Guadalupe. It was nearly two feet high. She was dressed in a
long, flowing blue gown, and she stood on the horned moon.
About her feet were the winged heads of angels, the babes of
Limbo. She wore a crown on her head because she was the
queen of heaven. There was no one I loved more than the
Virgin.

We all knew the story of how the Virgin had presented herself to the little Indian boy in Mexico and about the miracles
she had wrought. My mother said the Virgin was the saint of
our land, and although there were many other good saints, I
loved none as dearly as the Virgin. It was hard to say the rosary
because you had to kneel for as long as the prayers lasted, but I
did not mind because while my mother prayed I fastened my
eyes on the statue of the Virgin until I thought that I was
looking at a real person, the mother of God, the last relief of all
sinners.

God was not always forgiving. He made laws to follow and if
you broke them you were punished. The Virgin always forgave.

God had power. He spoke and the thunder echoed through
the skies.

The Virgin was full of a quiet, peaceful love.

My mother lit the candles for the brown madonna and we
knelt. "I believe in God the Father Almighty—" she began.

He created you. He could strike you dead. God moved the
hands that killed Lupito.

"Hail Mary, full of grace—"

But He was a giant man, and she was a woman. She could go
to Him and ask Him to forgive you. Her voice was sweet and
gentle and with the help of her Son they could persuade the
powerful Father to change His mind.

On one of the Virgin's feet there was a place where the

plaster had chipped and exposed the pure-white plaster. Her soul was without blemish. She had been born without sin. The rest of us were born steeped in sin, the sin of our fathers that Baptism and Confirmation began to wash away. But it was not until communion—it was not until we finally took God into our mouth and swallowed Him—that we were free of that sin and free of the punishment of hell.

My mother and Ultima sang some prayers, part of a novena we had promised for the safe delivery of my brothers. It was sad to hear their plaintive voices in that candle-lit room. And when the praying was finally done my mother arose and kissed the Virgin's feet then blew out the candles. We walked out of la sala rubbing our stiff knees. The candle-wick smoke lingered like incense in the dark room.

I trudged up the steps to my room. The song of Ultima's owl quickly brought sleep, and my dreams.

Virgen de Guadalupe, I heard my mother cry, return my sons to me.

Your sons will return safely, a gentle voice answered.

Mother of God, make my fourth son a priest.

And I saw the Virgin draped in the gown of night standing on the bright, horned moon of autumn, and she was in mourning for the fourth son.

"Mother of God!" I screamed in the dark, then I felt Ultima's hand on my forehead and I could sleep again.

Cinco

" ¡Antonioooooooo!" I awoke.

"Who?"

" ¡Antonioooooo! Wake up. Your uncle Pedro is here—"

I dressed and raced downstairs. Today was the day we went to El Puerto. My uncle had come for us. Of all my uncles I loved my uncle Pedro the most.

"Hey, Tony!" His embrace lifted me to the ceiling and his smile brought me safely down. "Ready to pick apples?" he asked.

"Sí, tío," I replied. I liked my uncle Pedro because he was the easiest one to understand. The rest of my uncles were very gentle and kind, but they were very quiet. They spoke very little. My mother said their communication was with the earth. She said they spoke to the earth with their hands. They used words mostly when each one in his own way walked through his field or orchard at night and spoke to the growing plants.

My uncle Pedro had lost his wife long before I was born and he had no children. I felt good with him. Also, of all my uncles, my father could talk only to my uncle Pedro.

"Antonio!" my mother called, "hurry and feed the animals! Make sure they have enough water! You know your

44

father will forget them while we are away!" I gulped the oatmeal she had prepared and ran out to feed the animals.

"Deborah!" my mother was calling, "are the bags packed? Is Theresa ready?" Although El Puerto was only ten miles down the valley, this trip was the only one we ever took and it meant a great deal to her. It was the only time during the year when she was with her brothers, then she was a Luna again.

My uncle Pedro loaded the bags on his truck while my mother ran around counting a hundred things that she was sure my father would forget to do while we were away. Of course, it never happened that way, but that is how she was.

"¡Vamos! ¡Vamos!" my uncle called and we clamored aboard. It was the first time Ultima would go with us. We sat quietly in the back of the truck with the bags and did not speak. I was too excited to talk.

The truck lurched down the goat path, over the bridge and swung south towards El Puerto. I watched carefully all that we left behind. We passed Rosie's house and at the clothesline right at the edge of the cliff there was a young girl hanging out brightly colored garments. She was soon lost in the furrow of dust the truck raised. We passed the church and crossed our foreheads, then we passed the El Rito bridge and far towards the river's side I could see the green water of the dam.

The air was fresh and the sun bright. The road wound along the edge of the river. At times the road cut into the cliffs made by the mesas that rose from the river valley, then the river was far below. There was much to see on such a trip, and almost before we had started it was over. I could hear my mother's joyful cry from the cab of the truck.

"There! There is El Puerto de los Lunas!" The road dropped into the flat valley and revealed the adobe houses of the peaceful village. "There!" she cried, "There is the church of my Baptism!"

The dusty road passed in front of the church, then past Tenorio's Bar and into the cluster of mud houses with rusted tin roofs. Each house had a small flower garden in front and a corral for animals at the back. A few dogs gave chase to the truck and in front of one house two small girls played, but for the most part the village was quiet—the men were in the fields working.

At the end of the dusty road was my grandfather's house. Beyond that the road dipped towards the bridge that crossed the river. My grandfather's house was the biggest one in the village, and it was rightly so, because after all the village had been largely settled by the Lunas. The first stop we made was at his house. It was unthinkable that we stop anywhere else before seeing him. Later we would go and stay with my uncle Juan because it was his turn that my mother's family visit with his and it would slight his honor if she didn't, but for now we had to greet our grandfather.

"Mind your manners," my mother cautioned us as we got down. My uncle led the way and we followed. In the cool, dark room which was the heart of the house my grandfather sat and waited. His name was Prudencio. He was old and bearded, but when he spoke or walked I felt the dignity of his many years and wisdom.

"Ay, papá," my mother cried when she saw him. She rushed into his arms and cried her joy out on his shoulders. This was expected and we waited quietly until she finished telling him how happy she was to see him. Then came our greetings. In turn we walked up, took his ancient, calloused hand and wished him a good day. Finally, Ultima greeted him.

"Prudencio," she said simply and they embraced.

"It is good to have you with us again, Ultima. We welcome you, our house is your house." He said our house because a couple of my uncles had built their houses against his until the original house spread into a long house with many of my cousins living in it.

"And Gabriel?" he asked.

"He is fine, and he sends you greetings," my mother said.

"And your sons, León, Andrés, Eugenio?"

"The letters say they are fine," and her eyes were full of tears, "but almost every day there is a tolling of the bells for a son that is lost to the war—"

"Take faith in God, my child," my grandfather said and he held her close, "He will return them safely. The war is terrible, the wars have always been terrible. They take the boys away from the fields and orchards where they should be, they give them guns and tell them to kill each other. It is against the will of God." He shook his head and knitted his eyebrows. I thought God must look that way when He is angry.

"And you heard about Lupito—" my mother said.

"A sad thing, a tragedy," my grandfather nodded. "This war of the Germans and the Japanese is reaching into all of us. Even into the refuge of the Valle de los Luna it reaches, we have just finished burying one of the boys of Santos Estevan. There is much evil running loose in the world—" They had turned towards the kitchen where they would drink coffee and eat sweet breads until it was time to go to my uncle Juan's.

We always enjoyed our stay at El Puerto. It was a world where people were happy, working, helping each other. The ripeness of the harvest piled around the mud houses and lent life and color to the songs of the women. Green chile was roasted and dried, and red chile was tied into colorful ristras. Apples piled high, some lent their aroma to the air from where they dried in the sun on the lean-to roofs and others as they bubbled into jellies and jams. At night we sat around the fireplace and ate baked apples spiced with sugar and cinammon and listened to the cuentos, the old stories of the people.

Late at night sleep dragged us away from the stories to a cozy bed.

"In that one there is hope," I heard my uncle Juan say to my mother. I knew he talked about me.

"Ay, Juan," my mother whispered, "I pray that he will take the vows, that a priest will return to guide the Lunas—"

"We will see," my uncle said. "After his first communion you must send him to us. He must stay with us a summer, he must learn our ways—before he is lost, like the others—"

I knew he meant my three brothers.

Across the river in the grove of trees the witches danced. In the form of balls of fire they danced with the Devil.

The chilled wind blew around the corners of the houses nestled in the dark valley, brooding, singing of the old blood which was mine.

Then the owl cried, it sang to the million stars that dotted the dark-blue sky, the Virgin's gown. All was watched over, all was cared for. I slept.

Seis

On the first day of school I awoke with a sick feeling in my stomach. It did not hurt, it just made me feel weak. The sun did not sing as it came over the hill. Today I would take the goat path and trek into town for years and years of schooling. For the first time I would be away from the protection of my mother. I was excited and sad about it.

I heard my mother enter her kitchen, her realm in the castle the giants had built. I heard her make the fire grow and sing with the kindling she fed to it.

Then I heard my father groan. " ¡Ay Dios, otro día! Another day and more miles of that cursed highway to patch! And for whom? For me that I might travel west! Ay no, that highway is not for the poor man, it is for the tourist—ay, María, we should have gone to California when we were young, when my sons were boys—"

He was sad. The breakfast dishes rattled.

"Today is Antonio's first day at school," she said.

"Huh! Another expense. In California, they say, the land flows with milk and honey—"

"Any land will flow with milk and honey if it is worked with honest hands!" my mother retorted. "Look at what my brothers have done with the bottomland of El Puerto—"

"Ay, mujer, always your brothers! On this hill only rocks grow!"

"Ay! And whose fault is it that we bought a worthless hill! No, you couldn't buy fertile land along the river, you had to buy this piece of, of—"

"Of the llano," my father finished.

"Yes!"

"It is beautiful," he said with satisfaction.

"It is worthless! Look how hard we worked on the garden all summer, and for what? Two baskets of chile and one of corn! Bah!"

"There is freedom here."

"Try putting that in the lunch pails of your children!"

"Tony goes to school today, huh?" he said.

"Yes. And you must talk to him."

"He will be all right."

"He must know the value of his education," she insisted. "He must know what he can become."

"A priest."

"Yes."

"For your brothers." His voice was cold.

"You leave my brothers out of this! They are honorable men. They have always treated you with respect. They were the first colonizers of the Llano Estacado. It was the Lunas who carried the charter from the Mexican government to settle the valley. That took courage—"

"Led by the priest," my father interrupted. I listened intently. I did not yet know the full story of the first Luna priest.

"What? What did you say? Do not dare to mention blasphemy where the children can hear, Gabriel Márez!" She scolded him and chased him out of the kitchen. "Go feed the animals! Give Tony a few minutes extra sleep!" I heard him laugh as he went out.

"My poor baby," she whispered, and then I heard her praying. I heard Deborah and Theresa getting up. They were excited about school because they had already been there. They dressed and ran downstairs to wash.

I heard Ultima enter the kitchen. She said good morning to my mother and turned to help prepare breakfast. Her sound in the kitchen gave me the courage I needed to leap out of bed and into the freshly pressed clothes my mother had readied for me. The new shoes felt strange to feet that had run bare for almost seven years.

"Ay! My man of learning!" my mother smiled when I entered the kitchen. She swept me in her arms and before I knew it she was crying on my shoulder. "My baby will be gone today," she sobbed.

"He will be all right," Ultima said. "The sons must leave the sides of their mothers," she said almost sternly and pulled my mother gently.

"Yes, Grande," my mother nodded, "it's just that he is so small—the last one to leave me—" I thought she would cry all over again. "Go and wash, and comb," she said simply.

I scrubbed my face until it was red. I wet my black hair and combed it. I looked at my dark face in the mirror.

Jasón had said there were secrets in the letters. What did he mean?

"Antoniooooo! Come and eat."

"Tony goes to school, Tony goes to school!" Theresa cried.

"Hush! He shall be a scholar," my mother smiled and served me first. I tried to eat but the food stuck to the roof of my mouth.

"Remember you are a Luna—"

"And a Márez," my father interrupted her. He came in from feeding the animals.

Deborah and Theresa sat aside and divided the school supplies they had bought in town the day before. Each got a Red Chief tablet, crayons, and pencils. I got nothing. "We are ready, mamá!" they cried.

Jasón had said look at the letter carefully, draw it on the tablet, or on the sand of the playground. You will see, it has magic.

"You are to bring honor to your family," my mother cautioned. "Do nothing that will bring disrespect on our good name."

I looked at Ultima. Her magic. The magic of Jasón's Indian. They could not save me now.

"Go immediately to Miss Maestas. Tell her you are my boy. She knows my family. Hasn't she taught them all? Deborah, take him to Miss Maestas."

"Gosh, okay, let's go!"

"Ay! What good does an education do them," my father filled his coffee cup, "they only learn to speak like Indians. Gosh, okay, what kind of words are those?"

"An education will make him a scholar, like—like the old Luna priest."

"A scholar already, on his first day of school!"

"Yes!" my mother retorted. "You know the signs at his birth were good. You remember, Grande, you offered him all the objects of life when he was just a baby, and what did he choose, the pen and the paper—"

"True," Ultima agreed.

"¡Bueno! ¡Bueno!" my father gave in to them. "If that is what he is to be then it is so. A man cannot struggle against his own fate. In my own day we were given no schooling. Only the ricos could afford school. Me, my father gave me a saddle blanket and a wild pony when I was ten. There is your life, he said, and he pointed to the llano. So the llano was my school, it was my teacher, it was my first love—"

"It is time to go, mamá," Deborah interrupted.

"Ay, but those were beautiful years," my father continued. "The llano was still virgin, there was grass as high as the stirrups of a grown horse, there was rain—and then the tejano came and built his fences, the railroad came, the roads—it was like a bad wave of the ocean covering all that was good—"

"Yes, it is time, Gabriel," my mother said, and I noticed she touched him gently.

"Yes," my father answered, "so it is. Be respectful to your teachers," he said to us. "And you, Antonio," he smiled, "suerte." It made me feel good. Like a man.

"Wait!" My mother held Deborah and Theresa back, "we must have a blessing. Grande, please bless my children." She made us kneel with her in front of Ultima. "And especially bless my Antonio, that all may go well for him and that he may be a man of great learning—"

Even my father knelt for the blessing. Huddled in the kitchen we bowed our heads. There was no sound.

"En el nombre del Padre, del Hijo, y el Espíritu Santo—"

I felt Ultima's hand on my head and at the same time I felt a great force, like a whirlwind, swirl about me. I looked up in fright, thinking the wind would knock me off my knees. Ultima's bright eyes held me still.

In the summer the dust devils of the llano are numerous. They come from nowhere, made by the heat of hell they carry with them the evil spirit of a devil, they lift sand and papers in their path. It is bad luck to let one of these small whirlwinds strike you. But it is easy to ward off the dust devil, it is easy to make it change its path and skirt around you. The power of God is so great. All you have to do is to lift up your right hand

and cross your right thumb over your first finger in the form of the cross. No evil can challenge that cross, and the swirling dust with the devil inside must turn away from you.

Once I did not make the sign of the cross on purpose. I challenged the wind to strike me. The twister struck with such force that it knocked me off my feet and left me trembling on the ground. I had never felt such fear before, because as the whirlwind blew its debris around me the gushing wind seemed to call my name:

Antonioooooooooooooooo . . .

Then it was gone, and its evil was left imprinted on my soul.

"¡Antonio!"

"What?"

"Do you feel well? Are you all right?" It was my mother speaking.

But how could the blessing of Ultima be like the whirlwind? Was the power of good and evil the same?

"You may stand up now." My mother helped me to my feet. Deborah and Theresa were already out the door. The blessing was done. I stumbled to my feet, picked up my sack lunch, and started towards the door.

"Tell me, Grande, please," my mother begged.

"María!" my father said sternly.

"Oh, please tell me what my son will be," my mother glanced anxiously from me to Ultima.

"He will be a man of learning," Ultima said sadly.

"¡Madre de Dios!" my mother cried and crossed herself. She turned to me and shouted, "Go! Go!"

I looked at the three of them standing there, and I felt that I was seeing them for the last time: Ultima in her wisdom, my mother in her dream, and my father in his rebellion.

"¡Adios!" I cried and ran out. I followed the two she-goats hopping up the path ahead of me. They sang and I brayed into the morning air, and the pebbles of the path rang as we raced with time towards the bridge. Behind me I heard my mother cry my name.

At the big juniper tree where the hill sloped to the bridge I heard Ultima's owl sing. I knew it was her owl because it was singing in daylight. High at the top by a clump of the ripe blue berries of the juniper I saw it. Its bright eyes looked down on me and it cried, whoooo, whoooo. I took confidence from its song, and wiping the tears from my eyes I raced towards the bridge, the link to town.

I was almost halfway across the bridge when someone called "Race!" I turned and saw a small, thin figure start racing towards me from the far end of the bridge. I recognized the Vitamin Kid.

Race? He was crazy! I was almost half way across. "Race!" I called, and ran. I found out that morning that no one had ever beaten the Vitamin Kid across the bridge, his bridge. I was a good runner and I ran as hard as I could, but just before I reached the other side the clatter of hoofbeats passed me by, the Kid smiled a "Hi Tony," and snorting and leaving a trail of saliva threads in the air, he was gone.

No one knew the Vitamin Kid's real name, no one knew where he lived. He seemed older than the rest of the kids he went to school with. He never stopped long enough to talk, he was always on the run, a blur of speed.

I walked slowly after I crossed the bridge, partly because I was tired and partly because of the dread of school. I walked past Rosie's house, turned, and passed in front of the Longhorn Saloon. When I got to Main Street I was astounded. It seemed as if a million kids were shoutingruntingpushingcrying their way to school. For a long time I was held hypnotized by the thundering herd, then with a cry of resolution exploding from my throat I rushed into the melee.

Somehow I got to the schoolgrounds, but I was lost. The school was larger than I had expected. Its huge, yawning doors were menacing. I looked for Deborah and Theresa, but every face I saw was strange. I looked again at the doors of the sacred halls but I was too afraid to enter. My mother had said to go to Miss Maestas, but I did not know where to begin to find her. I had come to the town, and I had come to school, and I was very lost and afraid in the nervous, excited swarm of kids.

It was then that I felt a hand on my shoulder. I turned and looked into the eyes of a strange red-haired boy. He spoke English, a foreign tongue.

"First grade," was all I could answer. He smiled and took my hand, and with him I entered school. The building was cavernous and dark. It had strange, unfamiliar smells and sounds that seemed to gurgle from its belly. There was a big hall and many rooms, and many mothers with children passed in and out of the rooms.

I wished for my mother, but I put away the thought because I knew I was expected to become a man. A radiator snapped with steam and I jumped. The red-haired boy laughed and led

me into one of the rooms. This room was brighter than the hall.
So it was like this that I entered school.

Miss Maestas was a kind woman. She thanked the boy whose
name was Red for bringing me in then asked my name. I told
her I did not speak English.

"¿Cómo te llamas?" she asked.

"Antonio Márez," I replied. I told her my mother said I
should see her, and that my mother sent her regards.

She smiled. "Anthony Márez," she wrote in a book. I drew
closer to look at the letters formed by her pen. "Do you want
to learn to write?" she asked.

"Yes," I answered.

"Good," she smiled.

I wanted to ask her immediately about the magic in the
letters, but that would be rude and so I was quiet. I was fascinated by the black letters that formed on the paper and made
my name. Miss Maestas gave me a crayon and some paper and I
sat in the corner and worked at copying my name over and
over. She was very busy the rest of the day with the other
children that came to the room. Many cried when their mothers
left, and one wet his pants. I sat in my corner alone and wrote.
By noon I could write my name, and when Miss Maestas discovered that she was very pleased.

She took me to the front of the room and spoke to the other
boys and girls. She pointed at me but I did not understand her.
Then the other boys and girls laughed and pointed at me. I did
not feel so good. Thereafter I kept away from the groups as
much as I could and worked alone. I worked hard. I listened to
the strange sounds. I learned new names, new words.

At noon we opened our lunches to eat. Miss Maestas left the
room and a high school girl came and sat at the desk while we
ate. My mother had packed a small jar of hot beans and some
good, green chile wrapped in tortillas. When the other children
saw my lunch they laughed and pointed again. Even the high
school girl laughed. They showed me their sandwiches which
were made of bread. Again I did not feel well.

I gathered my lunch and slipped out of the room. The
strangeness of the school and the other children made me very
sad. I did not understand them. I sneaked around the back of
the school building, and standing against the wall I tried to eat.
But I couldn't. A huge lump seemed to form in my throat and
tears came to my eyes. I yearned for my mother, and at the

same time I understood that she had sent me to this place where I was an outcast. I had tried hard to learn and they had laughed at me, I had opened my lunch to eat and again they had laughed and pointed at me.

The pain and sadness seemed to spread to my soul, and I felt for the first time what the grown-ups call, la tristesa de la vida. I wanted to run away, to hide, to run and never come back, never see anyone again. But I knew that if I did I would shame my family name, that my mother's dream would crumble. I knew I had to grow up and be a man, but oh it was so very hard.

But no, I was not alone. Down the wall near the corner I saw two other boys who had sneaked out of the room. They were George and Willy. They were big boys, I knew they were from the farms of Delia. We banded together and in our union found strength. We found a few others who were like us, different in language and custom, and a part of our loneliness was gone. When the winter set in we moved into the auditorium and there, although many a meal was eaten in complete silence, we felt we belonged. We struggled against the feeling of loneliness that gnawed at our souls and we overcame it; that feeling I never shared again with anyone, not even with Horse and Bones, or the Kid and Samuel, or Cico or Jasón.

Siete

Finally the war was over. At school the teachers gathered in the hall and talked excitedly, and some hugged each other. Our Miss Maestas came in and told us the war was over, and she was happy, but the little kids just went on writing the magic letters in their tablets. From my corner I smiled. My three brothers would be coming home, and I yearned for them.

Andrew wrote. They were coming from the lands of the east to meet in a place called San Diego. They wanted to come home together; they had gone to war together.

"¡Jesús, María Purísima!" my mother cried, "Blessed Virgen de Guadalupe, thank you for your intercession! Blessed St. Anthony, Holy San Martín, Ay Dios mío, gracias a San Cristóbal!" She thanked every saint she knew for her sons' safe delivery from war. She read the letter over and over and cried on it. When my father came home he had to pry the letter from her hand. By then it was falling apart with her tears, and the magic letters were stained and faded.

"We must pray," she beamed with joy although her eyes were red with crying. She lit many candles for the Virgin and she allowed Ultima to burn sweet incense at the foot of the Virgin's statue. Then we prayed. We prayed rosary after rosary, until the monotonous sound of prayers blended into the blur of flickering altar candles.

We prayed until our faith passed into an exhaustion that numbed us to sleep. The first to fall asleep was Theresa, and my father quietly got up and took her to bed. Then Deborah nodded and toppled. And I, who wanted to endure to please my mother, was next. I felt my father's strong arms carrying me out, and my last glimpse was that of my mother and Ultima kneeling obediently at the foot of the Virgin, praying their thanks.

I do not know how long they prayed. I only know that my soul floated with the holiness of prayer into the sky of dreams. The mist swirled around me. I was at the river, and I heard someone calling my name.

Antonioooooo, the voice called, Tony, Tonieeeeeeee . . .

Oh, my Antonio, the sound echoed down the valley.

Here! I replied. I peered into the dark mist but I could see no one. I only heard the lapping of the muddy waters of the river.

Antonio-forooooooooous, the voice teased, like my brothers used to tease me.

Here! I called. Here by the catfish hole where you taught me to fish. Here by the tall reeds where the blood of Lupito washes into the river. The thick mist swirled in gray eddies and curled about the trees. They looked like giant, spectral figures.

Toni-rooooo . . . Toni-reel-oooooo, the voices called. Oh, our sweet baby, we are coming home to you. We who had been beyond the land of our father's dream; we who have been beyond the ocean where the sun sets; we who have traveled west until we were in the east, we are coming home to you.

Me! My lost brothers.

Give us your hand, our sweet brother. Give us your saving hand.

We are the giants who are dying . . .

We have seen the land of the golden carp . . .

Then there was a loud crashing of branches behind me and I turned and saw the three dark figures looming over me.

"Aghhhhhhhh! *My brothers!" I screamed.* I bolted up and found myself in bed. My body was wet with sweat, and my lips were trembling. I felt a heavy sorrow gagging my heart and it was hard to breathe. Outside I heard the owl cry in alarm.

Someone was coming up the goat path. I jumped into my pants
and raced out into the cold night.

There! Just coming over the slope of the hill were three dark
figures.

"Andrew! León! Eugene!" I cried and ran barefeet up the
moonlit path.

"Hey, Tony!" they shouted and raced towards me, and in
one sweep I was gathered into the arms of the giants of my
dreams.

"Hey, Tony, how are you?" "Man, you're big!" "Hey, you
in school? How's mamá?" Then with me on Andrew's shoulders
they raced towards the house where there was already a light
shining in the kitchen window.

"¡Mis hijos!" my mother shouted and ran to embrace them.
It was a wild, exciting reunion. My mother called their names
over and over and ran from one to the other, holding him and
kissing him. My father shook their hands and gave each one the
abrazo. They had to kneel for Ultima's blessing of safe return.
Each one took turns picking up Deborah, Theresa or me and
dancing around the kitchen floor with us. They brought us gifts.

My father opened a bottle of whiskey and they all drank as
men, and my mother and Ultima set about to making dinner. I
had never experienced such happiness as the homecoming of my
brothers.

Then in the middle of her cooking my mother sat and cried,
and we all stood by quietly. She cried for a long time, and no
one, not even Ultima, made a move to touch her. Her body
heaved with choking sobs. She needed to cry. We waited.

"Thank God for your safe delivery," she said and stood up.
"Now we must pray."

"María," my father complained, "but we have prayed all
night!"

Nevertheless we had to kneel for one more prayer. Then she
went back to preparing food and we knew she was happy, and
everyone sat for the first time and there was quiet.

"Tell me about California!" my father begged.

"We were only there a few months," Andrew said shyly.

"Tell me about the war?"

"It was all right," León shrugged.

"Like hell," Gene scowled. He pulled away from us and sat
by himself. My mother said he was like that, a loner, a man who
did not like to show his feelings. We all understood that.

"Eugene, shame, in front of Ultima," my mother said.

"Perdón," Gene muttered.

"Did you see the vineyards?" my father asked. The whiskey made his face red. He was excited and eager now that his sons had returned. The dream of moving west was revived.

"Ay Dios, it was so hard without you," my mother said from the table.

"It will be all right now," Andrew reassured her. I remembered she said he was the one most like her.

"I would give anything to move to California right now!" my father exclaimed and banged his fist on the table. His eyes were wild with joy as he searched the eyes of his sons.

"Gabriel! They have just returned—" my mother said.

"Well," my father shrugged, "I don't mean tonight, maybe in a month or two, right boys?" My brothers glanced nervously at each other and nodded.

"¡León! ¡Oh my León!" my mother cried unexpectedly and went to León and held him. León simply looked up at her with his sad eyes. "Oh, you are so thin!"

We got used to her unexpected outbursts. We ate and listened while my father and mother asked a hundred questions. Then fatigue and its brother sleep came for us, and we stumbled off to warm beds while in the kitchen the questioning of the sons who had returned continued into the early morning.

My three brothers were back and our household was complete. My mother cared for them like a mother hen cares for her chicks, even though the hawk of war has flown away. My father was happy and full of life, regenerated by talk of the coming summer and moving to California. And I was busy at school, driven by the desire to make mine the magic of letters and numbers. I struggled and stumbled, but with the help of Miss Maestas I began to unravel the mystery of the letters.

Miss Maestas sent a note to my mother telling her that I was progressing very well and my mother was happy that a man of learning was once again to be delivered to the Lunas.

Ocho

The lime-green of spring came one night and touched the river trees. Dark buds appeared on branches, and it seemed that the same sleeping sap that fed them began to churn through my brothers. I sensed their restlessness, and I began to understand why the blood of spring is called *the bad blood*. It was bad not because it brought growth, that was good, but because it raised from dark interiors the restless, wild urges that lay sleeping all winter. It revealed hidden desires to the light of the new warm sun.

My brothers had spent the winter sleeping during the day and in town at night. They were like turgid animals who did things mechanically. I saw them only in the evening when they rose to clean up and eat. Then they were gone. I heard in whispers that they were wasting their service money in the back room of the Eight Ball Pool Hall. My mother worried about them almost as much as she had when they were at war, but she said nothing. As long as they were back she was happy.

My father increased his pleas that they plan a future with him in California, but they only nodded. They did not hear their father. They were like lost men who went and came and said nothing.

I thought that perhaps it was their way of forgetting the war, because we knew the war-sickness was in them. León had shown the sickness most. Sometimes at night he howled and cried like a wild animal . . .

And I remembered Lupito at the river . . .

Then my mother had to go to him and hold him like a baby until he could sleep again. It wasn't until he began to have long talks with Ultima and she gave him a remedy that he got better. His eyes were still sad, as they had always been, but there was a gleam of hope for the future in them and he could rest nights. So I thought perhaps they were all sick with the war and trying to forget it.

But with spring they became more restless. The money they had mustered out with was gone, and they had signed notes in town and gotten into trouble. It made my mother sad, and it slowly killed my father's dream. One warm afternoon while I fed the rabbits they talked, and I listened.

"We have to get the hell out'a here," Eugene said nervously, "this hick town is killing me!" Although he was the youngest he had always been the leader.

"Yeah. It's hell to have seen half the world then come back to this," León nodded across the river to the small town of Guadalupe. He always took his cues from Gene even though he was the oldest of the three.

"It's that Márez blood itching," Andrew laughed. Andrew listened to them, but he would not necessarily be led by Gene. Andrew liked to be his own man.

It was true, I thought, it is the Márez blood in us that touches us with the urge to wander. Like the restless, seeking sea.

"I don't care what it is, Andy!" Eugene shot back, "I just feel tied down here! I can't breathe!"

"And papá is still talking about California," León said dreamily.

"That's a bunch of bullshit!" Gene spit. "He knows damn well mamá would never move—"

"And that we won't go with him," Andrew finished.

Eugene scowled. "That's right! We won't! He doesn't realize we're grown men now. Hell, we fought a war! He had his time to run around, now he's getting old, and he still has the kids to think about. Why should we be tied down to him?"

Andrew and León looked at Gene and they knew he was speaking the truth. The war had changed them. Now they needed to lead their own lives.

"Yeah," Andrew said softly.

"It's either California, or going to work on the highway with him—" León thought aloud.

"Bullshit!" Gene exclaimed. "Why does it have to be just those two choices! Man, I've been thinking. If we got together we could move to Las Vegas, Santa Fe, maybe even Albuquerque. There's work there, we could rent—"

Andrew and León were looking at their brother intently. His forwardness and audacity often caught them off guard.

"Man, we could save up, buy a car, women—"

"Yeah, Gene," León nodded.

"It'd be great," Andrew agreed.

"We could go to Denver, Frisco, hell the sky's the limit!" His voice quavered. His excitement carried to his brothers.

"Gene, you've got beautiful ideas!" León beamed. He was proud of his brother. He himself would never have dared to think so far.

"Well let's not just sit around and talk about it, let's do it! Let's cut out! Move!"

"I can see the action now," León rubbed his hands, "money, booze, women—"

"Yeah! You're my boy!" Gene socked him.

"What about the folks?" It was Andrew who asked. They were quiet momentarily.

"Hell, Andy, they're doing okay," Gene said. "Ain't the old man working steady. We'll send them money when we can—"

"I didn't mean that," Andrew said.

"What?" I waited. I knew what he meant.

"I mean papá's dream about moving to California, and mamá wanting us to settle along the valley—" he said. They looked at each other uneasily. All their lives they had lived with the dreams of their father and mother haunting them, like they haunted me.

"Hell, Andy," Gene said softly, "we can't build our lives on their dreams. We're men, Andy, we're not boys any longer. We can't be tied down to old dreams—"

"Yeah," Andrew answered, "I guess inside I know you're right." I felt very sad when he said that. I did not want to lose my brothers again.

"And, they still have Tony," Gene said and looked at me. "Tony will be her priest," he laughed.

"Tony will be her farmer," León added.

"And her dream will be complete and we will be free!" Gene shouted.

"Yahoooooooo!" They jumped and shouted with joy. They danced and wrestled each other, and they rolled on the ground like wild animals, shouting and laughing.

"What'da yah say, Tony, you goin' be her priest!" "Bless us, Tony!" They knelt on the ground and raised their arms up and then down towards me. I grew frightened at their wild actions, but I found enough strength to shout at them.

"I will bless you!" I cried and made the sign of the cross, like I had done in the dream.

"You little bastard!" they laughed. They grabbed me, took off my pants and took turns spanking me. Then they tossed me on the roof of the chicken coop.

"This calls for a celebration!" Gene shouted.

"Yeah!"

"I will bless you!" I cried down at the three, giant figures, but they took no heed of me.

"Hey! We'll have to say goodbye to the girls at Rosie's!" Gene laughed and they both socked Andrew on the shoulder. Andrew grinned.

I remembered when we took our cow to Serrano's bull. It was a cold, misty Saturday. When the bull smelled the cow he jumped his pasture fence and came towards the truck. He circled us, snorting and pawing at the ground. I was very frightened. Finally we could open the tailgate of the truck and let the cow out. Immediately the massive weight of the bull was on her, humping her down, my father and Serrano were laughing and slapping their knees. They laughed until their eyes watered. Then they took turns drinking from a whiskey bottle, and they lowered their voices and talked about the girls at Rosie's.

"Whoopeeeee!" They shouted. They were like wild bulls running down the goat path towards town.

"See you Toni-eeeeee...." they called. And their dark outlines were lost in the setting sun.

I got down and put my pants on. It hurt where they had spanked me. I didn't know whether to cry or laugh with them. There was an empty feeling inside, not because they spanked me, but because they would be gone again.

They would be lost again.

I remembered when they built our home. They were like giants then. Would they always be lost to me?

I wanted to cry after them, I bless you.

Nueve

In the dark mist of my dreams I saw my brothers. *The three dark figures silently beckoned me to follow them. They led me over the goat path, across the bridge, to the house of the sinful women. We walked across the well-worn path in silence. The door to Rosie's house opened and I caught a glimpse of the women who lived there. There was smoke in the air, sweet from the fragrance of perfume, and there was laughing. My brothers pointed for me to enter.*

A young woman laughed gaily. She bowed and the soft flesh of her breasts hung loose and curved like cow udders.

When my mother washed her long, black hair she tucked in the collar of her blouse and I could see her shoulders and the pink flesh of her throat. The water wet her blouse and the thin cotton fabric clung around the curve of her breasts.

No! I shouted in my dream, I cannot enter, I cannot think those thoughts. I am to be a priest.

My brothers laughed and pushed me aside. Do not enter, I cried. It is written on the waters of the river that you shall lose your souls to hell if you enter!

Bah! Eugene scowled, you beat your breast like a holy-roller, but you too will find your way here. You are a Márez! he shouted and entered.

Even priests are men, León smiled, and every man is de-
livered of woman, and must be fulfilled by a woman. And he
entered.

Andrew, I begged to the last figure, do not enter.

Andrew laughed. He paused at the gaily lit door and said, I
will make a deal with you my little brother, I will wait and not
enter until you lose your innocence.

But innocence is forever, I cried.

You are innocent when you do not know, my mother cried,
but already you know too much about the flesh and blood of
the Márez men.

You are innocent until you understand, the priest of the
church said, and you will understand good and evil when the
communion is placed in your mouth and God fills your body.

Oh, where is the innocence I must never lose, I cried into the
bleak landscape in which I found myself. And in the swirling
smoke a flash of lightning struck and out of the thunder a dark
figure stepped forth. It was Ultima, and she pointed west, west
to Las Pasturas, the land of my birth.

She spoke. There in the land of the dancing plains and roll-
ing hills, there in the land which is the eagle's by day and the
owl's by night is innocence. There where the lonely wind of the
llano sang to the lovers' feat of your birth, there in those hills is
your innocence.

But that was long ago, I called. I sought more answers, but
she was gone, evaporated into a loud noise.

I opened my eyes and heard the commotion downstairs.

"We have to go! We have to go!" An excited voice called. It
was Eugene. I jumped to the door and peeked into the kitchen.
My mother was crying.

"But why?" my father asked. "You can find work here. I
can get you on a highway crew until summer, then we can—"

"We don't want to work on the highway!" Eugene exploded.
They were arguing about leaving and he was carrying the brunt
of the argument. I thought he must be drunk to talk to my
father like that. My father was small and thin compared to my
brothers, but he was strong. I knew he could still break any one
of them in two if he wanted.

But he was not mad. He knew he was losing them, and he
shrunk back.

"Eugenio!" my mother pleaded, "Watch your language! Do
not defy your father!"

Now it was my brother's turn to shrink back. Eugene mumbled an apology. They knew that it was within the power of the father to curse his sons, and ay! a curse laid on a disobedient son or daughter was irrevocable. I knew the stories of many bad sons and daughters who had angered their parents to the point of the disowning curse. Ay, those poor children had met the very devil himself or the earth had opened in their path and swallowed them. In any case the cursed children were never heard of again.

I saw my mother make the sign of the cross and I too prayed for Eugene.

"What is it you want?" my mother sobbed. "You have been gone so long, and now that you have just returned you want to leave again—"

"And what about California," my father sighed.

"We don't want to make you sad, mamá," León went to her and put his arm around her, "we just want to live our own lives."

"We don't want to go to California," Eugene said emphatically. "We just want to be on our own, move to Santa Fe and work—"

"You are forsaking me," my mother cried afresh.

"There will be no one left to help me move west—" my father whispered, and it seemed that a great load was placed on his shoulders.

"We are not forsaking you, mamá," Andrew said.

"We are men now, mamá," Gene said.

"Ay, Márez men," she said stoically and turned to my father. "The Márez blood draws them away from home and parents, Gabriel," she said. My father looked at her then bowed his head. The same wandering blood in his veins was in his sons. The restlessness of his blood had destroyed his dream, defeated him. He understood that now. It was very sad to see.

"You still have Tony," León said.

"Thanks be to God," my mother said, but there was no joy in her voice.

In the morning León and Eugene were gone, but Andrew remained. They had talked long into the night, and finally he had given up the idea of going with them. I think he did not like to follow their ways, and he wanted to please my mother. Then too he had been offered a job at Allen's Food Market and so the urge for adventure did not pull him away. I was glad. I had always felt close to Andrew and if I had to lose two of my brothers I was glad Andrew was not one of them.

That morning I walked to school with Andrew.

"Why didn't you go with León and Gene?" I asked.

"Ah, I got a job here, start today. So I figure I can do as well here as they do up in Vegas."

"Will you miss them?"

"Sure."

"I will too—"

"And I've been thinking a lot about finishing school—" he said.

"School?"

"Sure," he smiled, "why, you think I'm too old?"

"No," I said. I lied. I could not imagine this figure of my dreams in school.

"Sure," he went on, "I only had a few credits to go before León, Gene and me signed up—if there's one thing I learned in the army, it's that the guy with an education gets ahead. So I work and get some classes out of the way, get my diploma—"

We walked in silence. It was good what he said about learning. It made me feel good that I put so much effort into it.

"Do you have a girl?" I asked.

He looked at me sternly and I thought he was going to be mad. Then he smiled and said, "Ay chango, you ask too many questions! No I don't have a girl. Girls are only trouble when a man is young and wanting to get ahead. A girl wants to get married right away—"

"How will you get ahead?" I asked. "Will you become a farmer?"

"No," he chuckled.

"Will you become a priest?" I held my breath.

He laughed. Then he stopped, put his hand on my shoulder, and said, "Look, Tony, I know what you're thinking about. You're thinking about mamá and papá, you're thinking of their wishes—but it's too late for us, Tony. León, Gene, me, we can't become farmers or priests, we can't even go to California with papá like he wants."

"Why?" I asked.

"We just can't," he grimaced. "I don't know, maybe it's because the war made men out of us too fast, maybe it's because their dreams were never real to begin with—I guess if anyone is going to fit into their dreams it's going to have to be you, Tony. Just don't grow up too fast," he added.

I thought about what he said as we walked to the bridge. I wondered if I would grow up too fast, I yearned for knowledge and understanding and yet I wondered if it would make me lose my dreams. Andrew said it was up to me, and I wanted to be a good son, but the dreams of my mother were opposite the wishes of my father. She wanted a priest to watch over the farmers of the valley, he wanted a son to travel with him to the vineyards of California.

Oh, it was hard to grow up. I hoped that in a few years the taking of the first holy communion would bring me understanding.

"Race you across the bridge!" Andrew shouted. In a spurt we were off and running. We were halfway across when we heard the clobbering of hooves on the pavement and turned to catch a glimpse of the Vitamin Kid bearing down on us.

"Let's go!" Andrew urged me, and although I could keep up with Andrew we did not have enough wind to outdistance the Kid. The steady clippity-clop grew louder, the frothy smell of just-chewed weeds filled the air, and the Kid passed us by.

"Toni-eeee the giant killer—" he smiled and whizzed by.

"Never beat him!" Andrew gasped at the end of the bridge.

"Nobody, can, beat, him," I panted hard.

"I swear, he sleeps, under the bridge!" Andrew laughed. "Why did he, call you, the giant killer—"

"I don't know," I nodded. I thought of my brothers as giants. Now two were gone.

"Crazy little bastard!" Andrew nodded. His face was red from running and his eyes full of tears. "Someday you will beat him, Tony. Some day you will beat us all—" He waved and went off to work.

I did not feel that I could ever beat the Vitamin Kid, but Andrew must have had a reason for saying that. I looked across the bridge and Samuel was starting across. I waited for him and we walked to school together.

"Samuel," I asked, "where does the Kid live?"

"The Kid is my brother," Samuel said softly. I did not know if he was kidding or not, but we never talked about it again.

That year we waited for the world to end. Each day the rumor spread farther and wider until all the kids were looking at the calendar and waiting for the day. "It'll be in fire," one would say, "it'll be in water," another would argue. "It's in the Bible." "My father said." The days grew heavy and ominous. Nobody seemed to know except the kids that the world was coming to an end. During recess we gathered in the playground and talked about it. We talked about the signs we had seen; Bones even said he had talked to people from a ship from space. We looked at the clouds and waited. We prayed. Fear grew. Then the day came, and was gone, and it was kind of disappointing that the world didn't end. Then everybody just said, "see, I told you so."

And that year Bones had a wild fit and busted Willie's head open with a big jar of paste. It was too bad because after that not too many of us ate the sweet-tasting paste.

That year a pissing contest was held behind the school house, and Horse won, but the principal found out about it and all the pissers in the contest got spanked.

George got to burping in class. He could burp anytime he wanted to. He would just go "Auggghk!" Then he could do variations with it. "Augggh-pah-pah-pop!" He would do it in girls' ears and get socked every time. But he didn't mind, he was kinda crazy, like Bones.

And that year I learned to read and write. Miss Maestas was very pleased with me. On the last day of school she handed out report cards to the other kids but when it came to me she took me to the principal's office. He explained to me that I was a little older than the other kids in first grade and that my progress had been very good. Miss Maestas beamed. So instead of passing me from first to second he was passing me from first to third.

"What do you think of that?" he smiled.

"Thank you, sir," I said. I was very happy. My mother would be proud of me, and that meant that next year I would be in the same grade as the rest of the gang.

"Your mother will be very pleased," Miss Maestas said. She kissed my cheek.

"Yes," I said.

The principal handed me my report card and a piece of paper. "That will explain everything to your parents," he said. He shook my hand, like man to man, and he said "Good luck."

There was magic in the letters, and I had been eager to learn the secret.

"Thank you, sir," I said.

The rest of the day we were like goats held by hobbles. At the end of the day some of the mothers planned a party for our class, but I did not feel like staying because I still felt apart from them. And my mother would not be there. I thanked Miss Maestas for her help and when the last bell rang I ran home. The freedom of the summer raced with my footsteps as I worked my way through the sweaty, swarming mob of kids.

"School is over! School is over!" was on every tongue. The buses honked nervously for their kids. I waved and the farm kids waved back. We would see each other next fall. By the see-saws a fight had started, but I didn't want to waste time watching it.

"Whagggggggh!" The cry split the air. The vatos from Los Jaros ran by. I raced after them but cut off at Allen's, past the Longhorn Saloon, cut past Rosie's and to the bridge.

I started across the bridge and it was the first time I ever remember talking to it. I sang a song in my mind. Oh beautiful bridge, I cross you and leave the town, I cross towards the llano! I climb the hill, I race over the goat path, and I am home! I did not feel it was a silly song, I only felt happy.

"Toni-eeeeee . . ." hoof beats clattered on the concrete and the hatchet face of the Kid passed me by.

"Pass?"

"Yeah!" And he was gone. At the far end of the bridge he passed Samuel. "Samuel!" I called. He turned and waited for me. "I passed, did you?"

"Oh yes," he smiled, "those teachers keep passing us right along," he said. Samuel was only in the third grade, but he always seemed wise and old when he talked, kind of like my grandfather.

"But I passed to the third grade, next year I'll be in class with you!" I bragged.

"Good," he said, "let's go fishing."

"Now?"

"Sure."

Usually I only thought of fishing on weekends, but it was true that school was over. The first runoff was just subsiding in the river. There should be a lot of hungry catfish waiting for us.

"No line," I said.

"I have some," he said.

I thought of my mother. I always went straight home after

school, but today I had something to celebrate. I was growing up and becoming a man and suddenly I realized that I could make decisions.

"Sure," I said. We turned right towards the railroad bridge. I never came up this way. Farther up were the cliffs where Jasón's Indian lived. We passed under the dark shadow of the gigantic railroad bridge.

"There is evil here," Samual said. He pointed to a clear plastic balloon beside the path. I did not know why that was evil.

"Heeee-heee-haaaah-haaaaaagh!" Frightening, wild laughter filled the air. I froze in my tracks. I thought that surely here in the dark shadow of this bridge la llorna lurked.

"Ay!" I cried. I must have jumped because Samuel put his hand on my shoulder and smiled. He pointed up. I looked up at the black girders of the huge bridge and saw a figure scamper precariously from perch to perch. I thought it was the Kid.

"Is he crazy?" I asked Samuel.

Samuel only smiled. "He is my brother," he answered. He led me out of the shadow of the bridge and far away from it. We walked to the bank of the river where Samuel had some line and hooks hidden. We cut some tamarisk branches for poles and dug worms for bait.

"You fish a lot?" I asked.

"I have always been a fisherman," he answered, "as long as I can remember—"

"You fish," he said.

"Yes. I learned to fish with my brothers when I was very little. Then they went to war and I couldn't fish anymore. Then Ultima came—" I paused.

"I know," he said.

"So last summer I fished. Sometimes with Jasón."

"You have a lot to learn—"

"Yes," I answered.

The afternoon sun was warm on the sand. The muddy waters after-the-flood churned listlessly south, and out of the deep hole by the rock in front of us the catfish came. They were biting good for the first fishing of summer. We caught plenty of channel catfish and a few small yellow-bellies.

"Have you ever fished for the carp of the river?"

The river was full of big, brown carp. It was called the River of the Carp. Everybody knew it was bad luck to fish for the big carp that the summer floods washed downstream. After every flood, when the swirling angry waters of the river subsided, the big fish could be seen fighting their way back upstream. It had always been so.

The waters would subside very fast and in places the water would be so low that, as the carp swam back upstream, the backs of the fish would raise a furrow in the water. Sometimes the townspeople came to stand on the bridge and watch the struggle as the carp splashed their way back to the pools from which the flood had uprooted them. Some of the town kids, not knowing it was bad luck to catch the carp, would scoop them out of the low waters and toss the fish upon the sand bars. There the poor carp would flop until they dried out and died, then later the crows would swoop down and eat them.

Some people in town would even buy the carp for a nickel and eat the fish! That was very bad. Why, I did not know.

It was a beautiful sight to behold, the struggle of the carp to regain his abode before the river dried to a trickle and trapped him in strange pools of water. What was beautiful about it was that you knew that against all the odds some of the carp made it back and raised their families, because every year the drama was repeated.

"No," I answered, "I do not fish for carp. It is bad luck."

"Do you know why?" he asked and raised an eyebrow.

"No," I said and held my breath. I felt I sat on the banks of an undiscovered river whose churning, muddied waters carried many secrets.

"I will tell you a story," Samuel said after a long silence, "a story that was told to my father by Jasón's Indian—"

I listened breathlessly. The lapping of the water was like the tide of time sounding on my soul.

"A long time ago, when the earth was young and only wandering tribes touched the virgin grasslands and drank from the pure streams, a strange people came to this land. They were sent to this valley by their gods. They had wandered lost for many years but never had they given up faith in their gods, and so they were finally rewarded. This fertile valley was to be their home. There were plenty of animals to eat, strange trees that bore sweet fruit, sweet water to drink and for their fields of maíz—"

"Were they Indians?" I asked when he paused.

"They were *the people*," he answered simply and went on.

"There was only one thing that was withheld from them, and that was the fish called the carp. This fish made his home in the waters of the river, and he was sacred to the gods. For a long time the people were happy. Then came the forty years of the sun-without-rain, and crops withered and died, the game was killed, and the people went hungry. To stay alive they finally caught the carp of the river and ate them."

I shivered. I had never heard a story like this one. It was getting late and I thought of my mother.

"The gods were very angry. They were going to kill all of the people for their sin. But one kind god who truly loved the people argued against it, and the other gods were so moved by his love that they relented from killing the people. Instead, they turned the people into carp and made them live forever in the waters of the river—"

The setting sun glistened on the brown waters of the river and turned them to bronze.

"It is a sin to catch them," Samuel said, "it is a worse offense to eat them. They are a part of *the people.*" He pointed towards the middle of the river where two huge back fins rose out of the water and splashed upstream.

"And if you eat one," I whispered, "you might be punished like they were punished."

"I don't know," Samuel said. He rose and took my fishing line.

"Is that all the story?" I asked.

He divided the catfish we had caught and gave me my share on a small string. "No, there is more," he said. He glanced around as if to make sure we were alone. "Do you know about the golden carp?" he asked in a whisper.

"No," I shook my head.

"When the gods had turned the people into carp, the one kind god who loved the people grew very sad. The river was full of dangers to the new fish. So he went to the other gods and told them that he chose to be turned into a carp and swim in the river where he could take care of his people. The gods agreed. But because he was a god they made him very big and colored him the color of gold. And they made him the lord of all the waters of the valley."

"The golden carp," I said to myself, "a new god?" I could not believe this strange story, and yet I could not disbelieve Samuel. "Is the golden carp still here?"

"Yes," Samuel answered. His voice was strong with faith. It made me shiver, not because it was cold but because the roots of everything I had ever believed in seemed shaken. If the golden carp was a god, who was the man on the cross? The Virgin? Was my mother praying to the wrong God?

"Where?" I wanted to know.

"It is very late," Samuel said. "You have learned a lot today. This summer Cico will find you and take you to the golden carp—" And with a swish of branches he disappeared into the dusk.

"Samuel!" I called. Only silence. I had heard Cico's name mentioned before. He was a town boy, but he didn't hang out with them. They said he spent all his time along the river, fishing. I turned homeward in the gathering dusk, full of wonder at the strange story Samuel had told me.

"Toni-eeee!" someone called. I broke into a run and didn't stop until I got home.

When I got home my mother was very angry with me. I had never been late before. " ¡Nuestra Señora de Guadalupe! I have been crazy with worry about you!" she cried. I showed her my promotion and her feelings changed quickly. "Grande, Deborah, Theresa! Come quick! Tony has been promoted two grades! Oh I knew he would be a man of learning, maybe a priest!" She crossed herself and sobbed as she held me tightly.

Ultima was very happy too. "This one learns as much in one day as most do in a year," she smiled. I wondered if she knew about the golden carp.

"We must pray to the Virgin," my mother said, and although Deborah objected, saying nobody prayed for a grade promotion, my mother gathered us around the Virgin's altar.

My father arrived home late from work and was hungry. We were still praying and supper was late. He was angry.

Diez

The summer came and burned me brown with its energy, and the llano and the river filled me with their beauty. The story of the golden carp continued to haunt my dreams. I went to Samuel's house but it was boarded up. A neighbor, an old lady, told me that Samuel and his father had taken a job sheepherding for the rest of the summer. My only other avenue to the golden carp would be Cico, so every day I fished along the river, and watched and waited.

Andrew worked all day so I did not see him much, but it was reassuring at least to have him home. León and Gene hardly ever wrote. Ultima and I worked in the garden every morning, struggling against the llano to rescue good earth in which to plant. We spoke little, but we shared a great deal. In the afternoons I was free to roam along the river or in the blazing hills of the llano.

My father was dejected about his sons leaving and he drank more than before. And my mother also was unhappy. That was because one of her brothers, my uncle Lucas, was sick. I heard them whispering at night that my uncle had been bewitched, a bruja had put a curse on him. He had been sick all winter and he had not recovered with the coming of spring. Now he was on his deathbed.

My other uncles had tried everything to cure their youngest brother. But the doctor in town and even the great doctor in Las Vegas had been powerless to cure him. Even the holy priest at El Puerto had been asked to exorcise el encanto, the curse, and he had failed. It was truly the work of a bruja that was slowly killing my uncle!

I heard them say late at night, when they thought I was asleep, that my uncle Lucas had seen a group of witches do their evil dance for el Diablo, and that is why he had been cursed. In the end it was decided to hire the help of a curandera, and they came to Ultima for help.

It was a beautiful morning when the yucca buds were opening and the mocking birds were singing on the hill that my uncle Pedro drove up. I ran to meet him.

"Antonio," he shook my hand and hugged me, as was the custom.

"Buenos días le de Dios, tío," I answered. We walked into the house where my mother and Ultima greeted him.

"How is my papá?" she asked and served him coffee. My uncle Pedro had come to seek the help of Ultima and we all knew it, but there was a prescribed ceremony they had to go through.

"He is well, he sends his love," my uncle said and looked at Ultima.

"And my brother Lucas?"

"Ay," my uncle shrugged despairingly, "he is worse than when you saw him last. We are at the end of our rope, we do not know what to do—"

"My poor brother Lucas," my mother cried, "that this should happen to the youngest! He has such skill in his hands, his gift with the care and grafting of trees is unsurpassed." They both sighed. "Have you consulted a specialist?" she asked.

"Even to the great doctor in Las Vegas we took him, to no avail," my uncle said.

"Did you go to the priest?" my mother asked.

"The priest came and blessed the house, but you know that priest at El Puerto, he does not want to pit his power against those brujas! He washes his hands of the whole matter."

My uncle spoke as if he knew the witches who cursed Lucas. And I also wondered, why doesn't the priest fight against the evil of the brujas. He has the power of God, the Virgin, and all the saints of the Holy Mother Church behind him.

He dismounted and crept up to a clearing. . .

"Is there no one we can turn to!" my mother exclaimed. She and my uncle glanced at Ultima who had remained quiet and listened to their talk. Now she stood up and faced my uncle.

"Ay, Pedro Luna, you are like an old lady who sits and talks and wastes valuable time—"

"You will go," he smiled triumphantly.

"¡Gracias a Dios!" my mother cried. She ran to Ultima and hugged her.

"I will go with one understanding," Ultima cautioned. She raised her finger and pointed at both of them. The gaze of her clear eyes held them transfixed. "You must understand that when anybody, bruja or curandera, priest or sinner, tampers with the fate of a man that sometimes a chain of events is set into motion over which no one will have ultimate control. You must be willing to accept this responsibility."

My uncle looked at my mother. Their immediate concern was to save Lucas from the jaws of death, for that they would accept any responsibility.

"I will accept that responsibility on behalf of all my brothers," my uncle Pedro intoned.

"And I accept your help on behalf of my family," my mother added.

"Very well," Ultima nodded, "I will go and cure your brother." She went out of the kitchen to prepare the herbs and oils she would need to affect her cure. As she passed me she whispered, "Be ready Juan—"

I did not understand what she meant. Juan was my middle name, but it was never used.

"Ave María Purísima," my mother said and slumped into a chair, "she will cure Lucas."

"The curse is deep and strong," my uncle brooded.

"Ultima is stronger," my mother said, "I have seen her work miracles. She learned from the greatest healer of all time, the flying man from Las Pasturas—"

"Ay," my uncle nodded. Even he acknowledged the great power of that ancient one from Las Pasturas.

"But tell me, who laid the evil curse?" my mother asked.

"It was the daughters of Tenorio," my uncle said.

"Ay! Those evil brujas!" My mother crossed her forehead and I followed suit. It was not wise to mention the names of witches without warding off their evil with the sign of the holy cross.

"Ay, Lucas told papá the story after he took sick, but it is not until now, that we have to resort to a curandera, that our father made the story known to us. It was in the bad month of February that Lucas crossed the river to look for a few stray milk cows that had wandered away. He met Manuelito, Alfredo's boy, you know the one that married the lame girl. Anyway, Manuelito told him he had seen the cows moving towards the bend of the river, where the cottonwoods make a thick bosque, the evil place."

Again my mother made the sign of the cross.

"Manuelito said he tried to turn the cows back, but they were already too near that evil place, and he was afraid. He tried to warn Lucas to stay away from that place. Dusk was falling and there were evil signs in the air, the owls were crying to the early horned moon—"

" ¡Ay, Dios mío!" my mother exclaimed.

"But Lucas did not take Manuelito's warning to wait until the next morning, and besides our papá, Manuelito was the last person Lucas spoke to. Ay, that Lucas is so thick-headed, and so full of courage, he spurred his horse into the brush of the evil place—" He paused for my mother to serve him fresh coffee.

"I still remember when we were children, watching the evil fires dance in that same place," my mother said.

"Ay," my uncle agreed. "And that is what Lucas saw that night, except he was not sitting across the river like we used to. He dismounted and crept up to a clearing from where the light of the fireballs shone. He drew near and saw that it was no natural fire he witnessed, but rather the dance of the witches. They bounded among the trees, but their fire did not burn the dry brush—"

" ¡Ave María Purísima!" my mother cried.

I had heard many stories of people who had seen the bright balls of fire. These fireballs were brujas on their way to their meeting places. There, it was said, they conducted the Black Mass in honor of the devil, and the devil appeared and danced with them.

Ay, and there were many other forms the witches took. Sometimes they traveled as coyotes or owls! Only last summer the story was told that at Cuervo a rancher had shot a coyote. He and his sons had followed the trail of blood to the house of an old woman of the village. There they found the old woman dead of a gunshot wound. The rancher swore that he had etched

a cross on his bullet, and that proved that the old woman was a
witch, and so he was let free. Under the old law there was no
penalty for killing a witch.

"When he was up close," my uncle continued, "Lucas saw
that the fireballs began to acquire a form. Three women dressed
in black appeared. They made a fire in the center of the clearing. One produced a pot and another an old rooster. They beheaded the rooster and poured its blood into the pot. Then they
began to cook it, throwing in many other things while they
danced and chanted their incantations. Lucas did not say what
it was they cooked, but he said it made the most awful stench
he had ever smelled—"

"The Black Mass!" my mother gasped.

"Sí," my uncle nodded. He paused to light a cigarette and
refill his cup of coffee. "Lucas said they poured sulfur on the
coals of the fire and that the flames rose up in devilish fashion.
It must have been a sight to turn the blood cold, the dreariness
of the wind and the cold night, the spot of ground so evil and so
far from Christian help—"

"Yes, yes," my mother urged, "and then what happened?"
The story had held us both spellbound.

"Well, you know Lucas. He could see the evil one himself
and not be convinced. He thought the three witches were three
old dirty women who deserved a Christian lashing, tongue or
otherwise, so he stepped forth from behind the tree that hid
him and he challenged them!"

"No!" my mother gasped.

"Sí," my uncle nodded. "And if I know Lucas, he probably
said something like: Hie, you ugly brujas, prepare to meet a
Christian soul!"

I was astounded at the courage of my uncle Lucas. No one in
his right mind would confront the cohorts of the devil!

"It was then that he recognized the Trementina sisters,
Tenorio's three girls—"

"¡Ay Dios mío!" my mother cried.

"Ay, they have always been rumored to be brujas. They
were very angry to be caught performing their devilish mass. He
said they screamed like furies and were upon him, attacking him
like wild animals—but he did the right thing. While he was behind the tree he had taken two dead branches and quickly tied
them together with a shoe lace. He made a rude cross with the
two sticks. Now he held up the holy cross in the face of those

evil women and cried out, "Jesús, María, y José!" At the sight
of the cross and at the sound of those holy words the three
sisters fell to the ground in a fit of agony and pain. They rolled
on the ground like wounded animals until he lowered the cross.
Then they picked themselves up and fled into the darkness,
cursing him as they went.

"Everything was silent then. Only Lucas remained by the
light of the dying fire at that cursed spot. He found his frightened horse by the river, mounted it, and returned home. He
told the story only to papá, who admonished him not to repeat
it. But within the week Lucas was stricken. He speaks only to
mutter of the revenge the Trementina sisters took on him for
discovering their secret ceremony. The rest of the time his
mouth is clamped so tight he cannot eat. He wastes away. He is
dying—"

They were silent for a long time, each one thinking about
the evil thing that befell their brother.

"But didn't you go to Tenorio?" my mother asked.

"Papá was against it. He would not believe in this witchcraft
thing. But Juan and Pablo and myself went to Tenorio and
confronted him, but we could not charge him with anything
because we had no proof. He only laughed at us and told us he
was within his right to shoot us if we made an accusation
against him without proof. And he had his ring of coyotes
around him in the saloon. He said he had witnesses if we tried
anything, and so we had to leave. He laughed at us."

"Ay, he is an evil man," my mother shuddered.

"Evil begets evil," my uncle said. "His wife was known to
make clay dolls and prick them with needles. She made many
people of the valley sick, some died from her curses. She paid
for her sins, but not before she delivered three brujas to carry
on her work in our peaceful valley—"

"I am ready," Ultima interrupted.

I turned to see her standing, watching us. She carried only
her small black satchel. She was dressed in black and her head
scarf crossed over her face so that only her bright eyes shone.
She bore herself with dignity, and although she was very small
she was ready to do battle with all the terrible evil about which
I had just heard.

"Grande," my mother went to her and hugged her, "it is
such a difficult task we ask you to do, but you are our last
hope."

Ultima remained motionless. "Evil is not easy to destroy," she said, "one needs all the help one can get." She looked at me and her gaze made me step forward. "The boy will have to go with me," she whispered.

"What?" My mother was startled.

"Antonio must go with me. I have need of him," Ultima repeated softly.

"I will go," I said.

"But why?" my mother asked.

My uncle answered the question. "He is a Juan—"

"Ay."

"And he has strong Luna blood—"

"Ave María Purísima," my mother muttered.

"It must be so if you want your brother cured," Ultima decreed.

My mother looked at her brother. My uncle only shrugged. "Whatever you say, Grande," my mother said. "It will be good for Anthony to see his uncles—"

"He does not go to visit," Ultima said solemnly.

"I will prepare some clothing—"

"He must go as he is," Ultima said. She turned to me. "Do you want to help your uncle, Antonio?" she asked.

"Yes," I replied.

"It will be hard," she said.

"I do not mind," I answered, "I want to help."

"And if people say you walk in the footsteps of a curandera, will you be ashamed?"

"No, I will be proud, Ultima," I said emphatically.

She smiled. "Come, we waste precious time—" My uncle and I followed her outside and into the truck. Thus began our strange trip.

"Adiós," my mother called, " ¡Cuidado! ¡Saludos a papá, y a todos! ¡Adiós!"

" ¡Adiós!" I called. I turned and waved goodbye.

The drive to El Puerto was always a pleasant one, but today it was filled with strange portents. Across the river where lonely farms dotted the hills, whirlwinds and dust devils darkened the horizon. I had never seen anything like it, we seemed to travel a sea of calmness but all around the sky darkened. And when we arrived at the village we saw the horned day-moon fixed exactly between the two dark mesas at the southern end of the valley!

"The moon of the Lunas," my uncle remarked, breaking the silence of the entire trip.

"It is a good sign," Ultima nodded. "That is why they call this place El Puerto de la Luna," she said to me, "because this valley is the door through which the moon of each month passes on its journey from the east to the west—"

So it was fitting that these people, the Lunas, came to settle in this valley. They planted their crops and cared for their animals according to the cycles of the moon. They lived their lives, sang their songs, and died under the changing moon. The moon was their goddess.

But why was the weather so strange today? And why had Ultima brought me? I wanted to help, but how was I to help? Just because my name was Juan? And what was it about my innocent Luna blood that was to help lift the curse from my uncle? I did not know then, but I was to find out.

A dust trail followed the truck down the dusty street. It was deathly quiet in El Puerto. Not even the dogs barked at the truck. And the men of the village were not working in the fields, they clung together in groups at the adobe corners of houses and whispered to each other as we drove by. My uncle drove straight to my grandfather's house. No one came to the truck for a long time and my uncle grew nervous. Women in black passed silently in and out of the house. We waited.

Finally my grandfather appeared. He walked slowly across the dirt patio and greeted Ultima. "Médica," he said, "I have a son who is dying."

"Abuelo," she answered, "I have a cure for your son."

He smiled and reached through the open window to touch her hand. "It is like the old days," he said.

"Ay, we still have the power to fight this evil," she nodded.

"I will pay you in silver if you save my son's life," he said. He seemed unaware of me or my uncle. It seemed a ceremony they performed.

"Forty dollars to cheat la muerte," she mumbled.

"Agreed," he responded. He looked around to the nearby houses where, through parted curtains, curious eyes watched. "The people of the pueblo are nervous. It has been many years since a curandera came to cure—"

"Farmers should be farming," Ultima said simply. "Now, I have work to do." She stepped out of the truck.

"What will you need?" my grandfather asked.

"You know," she said. "A small room, bedsheets, water, stove, atole to eat—"

"I will prepare everything myself," he said.

"There are women already mourning in the house," Ultima said and gathered her shawl around her head, "get rid of them."

"As you say," my grandfather answered. I do not think he liked to empty his house of his sons' wives, but he knew that when a curandera was working a cure she was in charge.

"There will be animals sniffing around the house at night, the coyotes will howl at your door—inform your sons that no shots are to be fired. I will deal with those who come to spoil the cure myself—"

My grandfather nodded. "Will you enter my house now?" he asked.

"No. I must first speak to Tenorio. Is he in his dog hole, that place he calls a saloon?" she asked. My grandfather said yes. "I will speak to him," Ultima said, "I will first try to reason with him. He must know that those who tamper with fate are often swallowed by their own contrivance—"

"I will send Pedro and Juan with you," my grandfather began, but she interrupted him.

"Since when does a curandera need help to deal with dogs," she retorted. "Come, Antonio," she called and started down the street. I scurried after her.

"The boy is necessary?" my grandfather called.

"He is necessary," she answered. "You are not afraid, are you Antonio?" she asked me.

"No," I answered and took her hand. Many hidden eyes followed our progress up the dusty, vacant street. The saloon was at the end of the street, and opposite the church.

It was a small, run-down adobe house with a sign over the entrance. The sign said the saloon belonged to Tenorio Trementina. This man who doubled as the villagers' barber on Saturdays had a heart as black as the pit of hell!

Ultima did not seem to fear him, nor the evil powers of his three daughters. Without hesitation she pushed her way through the doorway, and I followed in her wake. There were four men huddled around one of the few tables. Three turned and looked at Ultima with surprise written in their eyes. They had not expected her to come into this place of evil. The fourth one kept his back to us, but I saw his hunched shoulders tremble.

"I seek Tenorio!" Ultima announced. Her voice was strong and confident. She stood tall, with a nobleness to her stature that I had seen often when we walked on the llano. She was not afraid, and so I tried to stand like her and put my fears out of my heart.

"What do you want bruja!" the man who would not face us snarled.

"Give me your face," Ultima demanded. "Have you not the strength to face an old woman? Why do you keep your back to me?"

The thin, hunched body jumped up and spun around. I think I jumped at the sight of his face. It was thin and drawn, with tufts of beard growing on it. The eyes were dark and narrow. An evil glint emanated from them. The thin lips trembled when he snarled, "Because you are a bruja!" Spots of saliva curled at the edges of the mouth.

Ultima laughed. "Ay, Tenorio," she said, "you are as ugly as your dark soul." It was true, I had never seen an uglier man.

"¡Toma!" Tenorio shouted. He crossed his fingers and held the sign of the cross in front of Ultima's face. She did not budge. Tenorio gasped and drew back, and his three cronies pushed their chairs to the floor and backed away. They knew that the sign of the cross would work against any bruja, but it had not worked against Ultima. Either she was not a bruja, or to their way of thinking, she had powers that belonged to the Devil himself.

"I am a curandera," Ultima said softly, "and I have come to lift a curse. It is your daughters who do evil that are the brujas—"

"You lie, vieja!" He shouted. I thought he would attack Ultima, but his gnarled body only trembled with anger. He could not find the courage to touch her.

"Tenorio!" It was Ultima who now spoke sternly, "you are a fool if you do not heed my words. I did not need to come to you, but I did. Listen to my words of reason. Tell your daughters to lift the curse—"

"Lies!" He screamed as if in pain. He turned to the three men he had depended upon to act as witnesses, but they did not protest on his behalf. They nervously glanced at each other and then at Ultima.

"I know when and where the curse was laid," Ultima continued. "I know when Lucas came to your shop for a drink and to have his hair clipped by your evil shears. I know that your daughters gathered the cut hair, and with that they worked their evil work!"

It was more than the three men could stand. They were frightened. They lowered their eyes to avert Tenorio's gaze and scurried for the door. The door banged shut. A strange, dark whirlwind swept through the dusty street and cried mournfully around the corner of the saloon. The storm which had been around us broke and the rising dust seemed to shut off the light of the sun. It grew dark in the room.

"¡Ay bruja!" Tenorio threatened with his fist, "for what you have said to shame my daughters and my good name in front of those men, I will see you dead!" His voice was harsh and ominous. His evil eyes glared at Ultima.

"I do not fear your threats, Tenorio," Ultima said calmly. "You well know, my powers were given to me by el hombre volador—"

At the mention of this great healer from Las Pasturas Tenorio drew back as if slapped in the face by an invisible power.

"I thought I could reason with you," Ultima continued, "I thought you would understand the powers at work and how they can wreck the destinies of many lives—but I see it is useless. Your daughters will not lift the curse, and so I must work the magic beyond evil, the magic that endures forever—"

"And my three daughters?" Tenorio cried.

"They chose to tamper with fate," Ultima answered. "Pity the consequence—" She took my hand and we walked out into the street. The choking dust was so thick that it shut out the sun. I was used to the dust storms of early spring, but this one in the middle of summer was unnatural. The wind moaned and cried, and in the middle of the sky the sun was a blood-red dot. I put one hand to my eyes and with the other I gripped Ultima tightly as we struggled against the wind.

I was thinking about the evil Tenorio and how Ultima had made him cower when I heard the hoofbeats. If I had been alone I would have paid no heed to them, so concerned was I with finding some direction in the strange duststorm. But Ultima was more alert than I. With a nimble sidestep and a pull she jerked me from the path of the black horse and rider that went crashing by us. The rider that had almost run us down disappeared into the swirling dust.

"Tenorio!" Ultima shouted in my ear. "He is hurrying home to warn his daughters. Beware of his horse," she added, "he has trained it to trample and kill—" I realized how close I had been to injury or death.

As we approached my grandfather's house there was a lull in the storm. The sky remained dark around us, but the clouds of dust abated somewhat. The women who were already in mourning for my uncle Lucas took this opportunity to place their mantas over their faces and to scurry to their homes before the hellish storm raised its head again. It was very strange to see the women in black hurrying out of the house and into the howling storm. It was like seeing death leaving a body.

We hurried into the house. The door slammed behind us. In the dark my grandfather was waiting. "I grew worried," he said.

"Is everything ready?" Ultima asked.

"As you ordered," he said and led us through the dark, quiet rooms of the house. The flickering lantern he held cast our dancing shadows on the smooth, clean adobe walls. I had never seen the house quiet and empty like it was today. Always there were my uncles and aunts and cousins to greet. Now it was like a quiet tomb.

Far in the deep recesses of the long house we came to a small room. My grandfather stood at the door and motioned. We entered the simple room. It had a dirt floor packed down from many water sprinklings, and its walls were smooth-plastered adobe. But the good clean earth of the room did not wash away or filter the strong smell of death in the room. The wooden bed in the room held the shrunken body of my dying uncle Lucas. He was sheathed in white and I thought he was already dead. He did not seem to breathe. His eyes were two dark pits, and the thin parchment of yellow skin clung to his bony face like dry paper.

Ultima went to him and touched his forehead. "Lucas," she whispered. There was no answer.

"He has been like this for weeks now," my grandfather said, "beyond hope." There were tears in his eyes.

"Life is never beyond hope," Ultima nodded.

"Ay," my grandfather agreed. He straightened his stooped shoulders. "I have brought everything you ordered," he nodded towards the small stove and pile of wood. There was clean linen on the chair next to the stove, and on the shelf there was water, atole meal, sugar, milk, kerosene, and other things. "The men have been instructed about the animals, the women in mourning have been sent away—I will wait outside the room, if you need anything I will be waiting—"

"There must be no interference," Ultima said. She was already removing her shawl and rolling up her sleeves.

"I understand," my grandfather said. "His life is in your hands." He turned and walked out, closing the door after him.

"Antonio, make a fire," Ultima commanded. She lit the kerosene lantern while I made the fire, then she burned some sweet incense. With the crackling warmth of the fire and the smell of purifying incense the room seemed less of a sepulchre. Outside the storm roared and dark night came.

We warmed water in a large basin and Ultima bathed my uncle. He was like a rag doll in her hands. I felt great pity for my uncle. He was the youngest of my uncles, and I always remembered him full of life and bravado. Now his body was a thin skeleton held together by dry skin, and on the face was written the pain of the curse. At first the sight of him made me sick, but as I helped Ultima I forgot about that and I took courage.

"Will he live?" I asked her while she covered him with fresh sheets.

"They let him go too long," she said, "it will be a difficult battle—"

"But why didn't they call you sooner?" I asked.

"The church would not allow your grandfather to let me use my powers. The church was afraid that—" She did not finish, but I knew what she would have said. The priest at El Puerto did not want the people to place much faith in the powers of la curandera. He wanted the mercy and faith of the church to be the villagers only guiding light.

Would the magic of Ultima be stronger than all the powers of the saints and the Holy Mother Church? I wondered.

Ultima prepared her first remedy. She mixed kerosene and water and carefully warmed the bowl on the stove. She took many herbs and roots from her black bag and mixed them into the warm oily water. She muttered as she stirred her mixture and I did not catch all of what she said, but I did hear her say, "the curse of the Trementinas shall bend and fly in their faces. We shall test the young blood of the Lunas against the old blood of the past—"

When she was done she cooled the remedy, then with my help we lifted my uncle and forced the mixture down his throat. He groaned in pain and convulsed as if he wanted to throw up the medicine. It was encouraging to see signs of life in him, but it was difficult to get him to keep the medicine down.

"Drink, Lucas," she coaxed him, and when he clamped his teeth shut she pried them open and made him drink. Howls of pain filled the small room. It was very frightening, but at length we got the medicine down. Then we covered him because he began sweating and shivering at the same time. His dark eyes looked at us like a captured animal. Then finally they closed and the fatigue made him sleep.

"Ay," Ultima said, "we have begun our cure." She turned and looked at me and I could tell she was tired. "Are you hungry?" she smiled.

"No," I replied. I had not eaten since breakfast, but the things that had happened had made me forget my hunger.

"Still, we had better eat," she said, "it might be the last meal we will have for a few days. They had his fresh clipped hair to work with, the curse is very strong and his strength is gone. Lay your blankets there and make yourself a bed while I fix us some atole."

I spread the blankets close to the wall and near the stove while Ultima prepared the atole. My grandfather had brought sugar and cream and two loaves of fresh bread so we had a good meal.

"This is good," I said. I looked at my uncle. He was sleeping peacefully. The fever had not lasted long.

"There is much good in blue corn meal," she smiled. "The Indians hold it sacred, and why not, on the day that we can get Lucas to eat a bowl of atole then he shall be cured. Is that not sacred?"

I agreed. "How long will it take?" I asked.

"A day or two—"

"When we were in Tenorio's bar, you were not afraid of him. And here, you were not afraid to enter where death lurks—"

"Are you afraid?" she asked in turn. She put her bowl aside and stared into my eyes.

"No," I said.

"Why?"

"I don't know," I said.

"I will tell you why," she smiled, "it is because good is always stronger than evil. Always remember that, Antonio. The smallest bit of good can stand against all the powers of evil in the world and it will emerge triumphant. There is no need to fear men like Tenorio."

I nodded. "And his daughters?"

"They are women who are too ugly to make men happy," she answered, "and so they spend their time reading in the Black Book and practicing their evil deeds on poor, unsuspecting people. Instead of working, they spend their nights holding their black masses and dancing for the devil in the darkness of the river. But they are amateurs, Antonio," Ultima shook her head slowly, "they have no power like the power of a good curandera. In a few days they will be wishing they had never sold their souls to the devil—"

The cry of hungry coyotes sounded outside. Their laughter-cry sounded directly outside the small window of the room. I shivered. Their claws scratched at the adobe walls of the house. I looked anxiously at Ultima but she held her hand up in a sign for me to listen. We waited, listening to the howling wind and the cries of the pack scratching at our wall.

Then I heard it. It was the call of Ultima's owl. "O-oooo-ooo," it shrieked into the wind, dove and pounced on the coyotes. Her sharp claws found flesh because the evil laughter of the coyotes changed to cries of pain.

Ultima laughed. "Oh those Trementina girls will be cut and bruised tomorrow," she said. "But I have much work to do," she spoke to herself now. She tucked me into the blankets and then burned more incense in the room. I huddled against the wall so I could see everything she did. I was tired now, but I could not sleep.

The power of the doctors and the power of the church had failed to cure my uncle. Now everyone depended on Ultima's magic. Was it possible that there was more power in Ultima's magic than in the priest?

My eyelids grew very heavy, but they would not close completely. Instead of sleep I slipped into a deep stupor. My gaze fixed on my poor uncle and I could not tear my glance away. I was aware of what happened in the room, but my senses did not seem to respond to commands. Instead I remained in that waking dream.

I saw Ultima make some medicine for my uncle, and when she forced it down his throat and his face showed pain, my body too felt the pain. I could almost taste the oily hot liquid. I saw his convulsions and my body too was seized with aching cramps. I felt my body wet with sweat. I tried to call to Ultima but there was no voice, I tried to move but there was no movement. I suffered the spasms of pain my uncle suffered, and these alternated with feelings of elation and power. When the pain passed a wave of energy seemed to sweep through my body. Still, I could not move. And I could not take my eyes from my uncle. I felt that somehow we were going through the same cure, but I could not explain it. I tried to pray, but no words filled my mind, only the closeness I shared with my uncle remained. He was across the room from me, but our bodies did not seem separated by the distance. We dissolved into each other, and we shared a common struggle against the evil within, which fought to repulse Ultima's magic.

Time ceased to exist. Ultima came and went. The moaning of the wind and the cries of the animals outside mixed into the thin smoke of incense and the fragrance of piñón wood burning in the stove. At one time Ultima was gone a long time. She disappeared. I heard the owl singing outside, and I heard its whirling wings. I saw its wise face and fluttering wings at the window—then Ultima was by me. Her feet were wet with the clay-earth of the valley.

"The owl—" I managed to mutter.

"All is well," Ultima answered. She touched my forehead and the terrible strain I felt seemed lifted from my shoulders. "There is no fever," Ultima whispered to me, "you are strong. The blood of the Lunas is very thick in you—"

Her hand was cool, like the fresh air of a summer night.

My uncle groaned and thrashed about in his bed. "Good," Ultima said, "we have beaten the death spirit, now all that remains is to have him vomit the evil spirit—"

She went to the stove and prepared a fresh remedy. This one did not smell like the first one, it was more pungent. I saw her use vials of oil she had not used before, and I saw that some of the roots she used were fresh with wet earth. And for the first time she seemed to sing her prayers instead of muttering them.

When she had finished mixing her herbs she let the small bowl simmer on the stove, then she took from her black bag a large lump of fresh, black clay. She turned off the kerosene lantern and lit a candle. Then she sat by the candlelight and sang as she worked the wet clay. She broke it in three pieces, and she worked each one carefully. For a long time she sat and molded the clay. When she was through I saw that she had molded three dolls. They were lifelike, but I did not recognize the likeness of the clay dolls as anyone I knew. Then she took the warm melted wax from the candle and covered the clay dolls with it so they took on the color of flesh. When they had cooled she dressed the three dolls with scraps of cloth which she took from her black bag.

When she was done she stood the three dolls around the light of the flickering candle, and I saw three women. Then Ultima spoke to the three women.

"You have done evil," she sang,
"But good is stronger than evil,
"And what you sought to do will undo you . . ."

She lifted the three dolls and held them to my sick uncle's mouth, and when he breathed on them they seemed to squirm in her hands.

I shuddered to see those clay dolls take life.

Then she took three pins, and after dipping them into the new remedy on the stove, she stuck a pin into each doll. Then she put them away. She took the remaining remedy and made my uncle drink it. It must have been very strong medicine because he screamed as she forced it down. The strong smell filled the room, and even I felt the searing liquid.

After that I could rest. My eyelids closed. My stiff muscles relaxed and I slid from my sitting position and snuggled down into my blankets. I felt Ultima's gentle hands covering me and that is all I remember. I slept, and no dreams came.

When I awoke I was very weak and hungry. "Ultima," I called. She came to my side and helped me sit up.

"Ay mi Antonito," she teased, "what a sleepy head you are. How do you feel?"

"Hungry," I said weakly.

"I have a bowl of fresh atole waiting for you," she grinned. She washed my hands and face with a damp cloth and then she brought the basin for me to pee in while she finished preparing the hot cereal. The acrid smell of the dark-yellow pee blended into the fragrance of the cereal. I felt better after I sat down again.

"How is my uncle Lucas?" I asked. He seemed to be sleeping peacefully. Before he did not seem to breathe, but now his chest heaved with the breath of life and the pallor was gone from his face.

"He will be well," Ultima said. She handed me the bowl of blue atole. I ate but I could not hold the food down at first. I gagged and Ultima held a cloth before me into which I vomited a poisonous green bile. My nose and eyes burned when I threw up but I felt better.

"Will I be all right?" I asked as she cleaned away the mess.

"Yes," she smiled. She threw the dirty rags in a gunny sack at the far end of the room. "Try again," she said. I did and this time I did not vomit. The atole and the bread were good. I ate and felt renewed.

"Is there anything you want me to do?" I asked after I had eaten.

"Just rest," she said, "our work here is almost done—"

It was at that moment that my uncle sat up in bed. It was a fearful sight and one I never want to see again. It was like seeing a dead person rise, for the white sheet was wet with sweat and it clung to his thin body. He screamed the tortured cry of an animal in pain.

"Ai-eeeeeeeeee!" The cry tore through contorted lips that dripped with frothy saliva. His eyes opened wide in their dark pits, and his thin, skeletal arms flailed the air before him as if he were striking at the furies of hell.

"Au-gggggggggh! Ai-eeee!" He cried in pain. Ultima was immediately at his side, holding him so that he would not tumble from the bed. His body convulsed with the spasms of a madman, and his face contorted with pain.

"Let the evil come out!" Ultima cried in his ear.

"¡Dios mío!" were his first words, and with those words the evil was wrenched from his interior. Green bile poured from his mouth, and finally he vomited a huge ball of hair. It fell to the floor, hot and steaming and wiggling like live snakes.

It was his hair with which they had worked the evil!

"Ay!" Ultima cried triumphantly and with clean linen she swept up the evil, living ball of hair. "This will be burned, by the tree where the witches dance—" she sang and swiftly put the evil load into the sack. She tied the sack securely and then came back to my uncle. He was holding the side of the bed, his thin fingers clutching the wood tightly as if he were afraid to slip back into the evil spell. He was very weak and sweating, but he was well. I could see in his eyes that he knew he was a man again, a man returned from a living hell.

Ultima helped him lie down. She washed him and then fed him his first meal in weeks. He ate like a starved animal. He vomited once, but that was only because his stomach had been so empty and so sick. I could only watch from where I sat.

After that my uncle slept, and Ultima readied her things for departure. Our work was done. When she was ready she went to the door and called my grandfather.

"Your son lives, old man," she said. She undid her rolled sleeves and buttoned them.

My grandfather bowed his head. "May I send the word to those who wait?" he asked.

"Of course," Ultima nodded, "We are ready to leave."

"Pedro!" my grandfather called. Then my grandfather came into the room. He walked towards the bed cautiously, as if he were not sure what to expect.

Lucas moaned and opened his eyes. "Papá," he said. My grandfather gathered his son in his arms and cried. "Thanks be to God!"

Aunts and uncles and cousins began to fill the house, and there was a great deal of excitement. The story of the cure spread quickly through El Puerto. My uncles began to pour into the room to greet their brother. I looked at Ultima and knew that she wanted to get out of the commotion as quickly as possible.

"Do not tire him too much at first," Ultima said. She looked at Lucas, who gazed around with curious but happy eyes.

"Gracias por mi vida," he said to Ultima. Then all my uncles stood and said gracias. My grandfather stepped forward and handed Ultima the purse of silver which was required by custom.

"I can never repay you for returning my son from death," he said.

Ultima took the purse. "Perhaps someday the men of El Puerto will save my life—" she answered. "Come Antonio," she motioned. She clutched her black bag and the gunny sack that had to be burned. We pressed through the curious, anxious crowd and they parted to let us pass.

"¡La curandera!" someone exclaimed. Some women bowed their heads, others made the sign of the cross. "Es una mujer que no ha pecado," another whispered. "Hechicera." "Bruja—"

"No!" one of my aunts contested the last word. She knelt by Ultima's path and touched the hem of her dress as she passed by.

"Es sin pecado," was the last I heard, then we were outside. My uncle Pedro led us to his truck.

He held the door open for Ultima and said, "gracias." She nodded and we got in. He started the truck and turned on the lights. The two headlights cut slices into the lonely night.

"Do you know the grove of trees where Lucas saw the brujas dance?" Ultima asked.

"Sí," my uncle said.

"Take us there," Ultima said.

My uncle Pedro sighed and shrugged. "You have performed a miracle," he said, "were it not for that I would not visit that cursed spot for all the money in the world—" The truck leaped forward. We crossed the ancient wooden bridge and turned right. The truck bounced along the cow path. On either side of us the dark brush of the bosque closed in.

Finally we came to the end of the rutty trail. My uncle stopped the truck. We seemed swamped by the thick brush of the river. Strange bird cries cut into the swampy night air. "We can go no farther," my uncle said. "The clearing of the witches is straight ahead."

"Wait here," Ultima said. She shouldered the sack that contained all the dirty linen and the evil ball of hair. She disappeared into the thick brush.

"Ay, what courage that old woman has!" my uncle exclaimed. I felt him shiver next to me, and I saw him make the sign of the cross to ward off the evil of this forsaken ground. Around us the trees rose like giant skeletons. They had no green on them, but were bare and white.

"Uncle," I asked, "how long were we in the room with my uncle Lucas?"

"Three days," he answered. "Do you feel well, Tony?" he rubbed my head. Next to Ultima it seemed the first human contact I had felt in a long time.

"Yes," I answered.

Up ahead we saw a fire burst out. It was Ultima burning the evil load of the sack exactly where the three witches had danced when my uncle saw them. A trace of the smell of sulfur touched the foul, damp air. Again my uncle crossed himself.

"We are indebted to her forever," he said, "for saving the life of my brother. Ay, what courage to approach the evil place alone!" he added.

The burst of flames in the bush died down and smouldered to ashes. We waited for Ultima. It was very quiet in the cab of truck. There was a knock and we were startled by Ultima's brown face at the window. She got in and said to my uncle, "our work is done. Now take us home, for we are tired and must sleep."

Once

"Hey Toni-eeeeee. Huloooooo Antonioforous!"

A voice called.

At first I thought I was dreaming. I was fishing, and sitting on a rock; the sun beating on my back had made me sleepy. I had been thinking how Ultima's medicine had cured my uncle and how he was well and could work again. I had been thinking how the medicine of the doctors and of the priest had failed. In my mind I could not understand how the power of God could fail. But it had.

"Toni-eeeeee!" the voice called again.

I opened my eyes and peered into the green brush of the river. Silently, like a deer, the figure of Cico emerged. He was barefoot, he made no noise. He moved to the rock and squatted in front of me. I guess it was then that he decided to trust me with the secret of the golden carp.

"Cico?" I said. He nodded his dark, freckled face.

"Samuel told you about the golden carp," he said.

"Yes," I replied.

"Have you ever fished for carp?" he asked. "Here in the river, or anywhere?"

"No," I shook my head. I felt as if I was making a solemn oath.

"Do you want to see the golden carp?" he whispered.

"I have hoped to see him all summer," I said breathlessly.

"Do you believe the golden carp is a god?" he asked.

The commandment of the Lord said, Thou shalt have no other gods before me . . .

I could not lie. I knew he would find the lie in my eyes if I did. But maybe there were other gods? Why had the power of God failed to cure my uncle?

"I am a Catholic," I stuttered, "I can believe only in the God of the church—" I looked down. I was sorry because now he would not take me to see the golden carp. For a long time Cico did not speak.

"At least you are truthful, Tony," he said. He stood up. The quiet waters of the river washed gently southward. "We have never taken a non-believer to see him," he said solemnly.

"But I want to believe," I looked up and pleaded, "it's just that I have to believe in Him?" I pointed across the river to where the cross of the church showed above the tree tops.

"Perhaps—" he mused for a long time. "Will you make an oath?" he asked.

"Yes," I answered. But the commandment said, Thou shalt not take the Lord's name in vain.

"Swear by the cross of the church that you will never hunt or kill a carp." He pointed to the cross. I had never sworn on the cross before. I knew that if you broke your oath it was the biggest sin a man could commit, because God was witness to the swearing on his name. But I would keep my promise! I would never break my oath!

"I swear," I said.

"Come!" Cico was off, wading across the river. I followed. I had waded across that river many times, but I never felt an urgency like today. I was excited about seeing the magical golden carp.

"The golden carp will be swimming down the creek today," Cico whispered. We scrambled up the bank and through the thick brush. We climbed the steep hill to the town and headed towards the school. I never came up this street to go to school and so the houses were not familiar to me. We paused at one place.

"Do you know who lives there?" Cico pointed at a green arbor. There was a fence with green vines on it, and many trees. Every house in town had trees but I had never seen a place so green. It was thick like some of the jungles I saw in the movies in town.

"No," I said. We drew closer and peered through the dense curtain of green that surrounded a small adobe hut.

"Narciso," Cico whispered.

Narciso had been on the bridge the night Lupito was murdered. He had tried to reason with the men, he had tried to save Lupito's life. He had been called a drunk.

"My father and my mother know him," I said. I could not take my eyes from the garden that surrounded the small house. Every kind of fruit and vegetable I knew seemed to grow in the garden, and there was even more abundance here than on my uncles' farms.

"I know," Cico said, "they are from the llano—"

"I have never seen such a place," I whispered. Even the air of the garden was sweet to smell.

"The garden of Narciso," Cico said with reverence, "is envied by all— Would you like to taste its fruits?"

"We can't," I said. It was a sin to take anything without permission.

"Narciso is my friend," Cico said. He reached through the green wall and a secret latch opened an ivy-laden door. We walked into the garden. Cico closed the door behind him and said, "Narciso is in jail. The sheriff found him drunk."

I was fascinated by the garden. I forgot about seeing the golden carp. The air was cool and clear, not dusty and hot like the street. Somewhere I heard the sound of gurgling water.

"Somewhere here there is a spring," Cico said, "I don't know where. That is what makes the garden so green. That and the magic of Narciso—"

I was bewildered by the garden. Everywhere I looked there were fruit-laden trees and rows and rows of vegetables. I knew the earth was fruitful because I had seen my uncles make it bear in abundance; but I never realized it could be like this! The ground was soft to walk on. The fragrance of sun-dazzling flowers was deep, and soft, and beautiful.

"The garden of Narciso," I whispered.

"Narciso is my friend," Cico intoned. He pulled some carrots from the soft, dark earth and we sat down to eat.

"I cannot," I said. It was silent and peaceful in the garden. I felt that someone was watching us.

"It is all right," Cico said.

And although I did not feel good about it, I ate the golden carrot. I had never eaten anything sweeter or juicier in my life.

"Why does Narciso drink?" I asked.

"To forget," Cico answered.

"Does he know about the golden carp?" I asked.

"The magic people all know about the coming day of the golden carp," Cico answered. His bright eyes twinkled. "Do you know how Narciso plants?" he asked.

"No," I answered. I had always thought farmers were sober men. I could not imagine a drunk man planting and reaping such fruits!

"By the light of the moon," Cico whispered.

"Like my uncles, the Lunas—"

"In the spring Narciso gets drunk," Cico continued. "He stays drunk until the bad blood of spring is washed away. Then the moon of planting comes over the elm trees and shines on the horde of last year's seeds— It is then that he gathers the seeds and plants. He dances as he plants, and he sings. He scatters the seeds by moonlight, and they fall and grow— The garden is like Narciso, it is drunk."

"My father knows Narciso," I said. The story Cico had told me was fascinating. It seemed that the more I knew about people the more I knew about the strange magic hidden in their hearts.

"In this town, everybody knows everybody," Cico said.

"Do you know everyone?" I asked.

"Uh-huh," he nodded.

"You know Jasón's Indian?"

"Yes."

"Do you know Ultima?" I asked.

"I know about her cure," he said. "It was good. Come on now, let's be on our way. The golden carp will be swimming soon—"

We slipped out of the coolness of the garden into the hot, dusty street. On the east side of the school building was a barren playground with a basketball goal. The gang was playing basketball in the hot sun.

"Does the gang know about the golden carp?" I asked as we approached the group.

"Only Samuel," Cico said, "only Samuel can be trusted."

"Why do you trust me?" I asked. He paused and looked at me.

"Because you are a fisherman," he said. "There are no rules on who we trust, Tony, there is just a feeling. The Indian told Samuel the story; Narciso told me; now we tell you. I have a feeling someone, maybe Ultima, would have told you. We all share—"

"Hey!" Ernie called, "you guys want to play!" They ran towards us.

"Nah," Cico said. He turned away. He did not face them.

"Hi, Tony," they greeted me.

"Hey, you guys headed for Blue Lake? Let's go swimming," Florence suggested.

"It's too hot to play," Horse griped. He was dripping with sweat.

"Hey, Tony, is it true what they say? Is there a bruja at your house?" Ernie asked.

" ¡A bruja!" " ¡Chingada!" " ¡A la veca!"

"No," I said simply.

"My father said she cursed someone and three days later that person changed into a frog—"

"Hey! Is that the old lady that goes to church with your family!" Bones shrieked.

"Let's go," Cico said.

"Knock it off, you guys, are we going to play or not!" Red pleaded. Ernie spun the basketball on his finger. He was standing close to me and grinning as the ball spun.

"Hey, Tony, can you make the ball disappear?" He laughed. The others laughed too.

"Hey, Tony, do some magic!" Horse threw a hold around my neck and locked me into his half-nelson.

"Yeah!" Ernie shouted in my face. I did not know why he hated me.

"Leave him alone, Horse," Red said.

"Stay out of it, Red," Ernie shouted, "you're a Protestant. You don't know about the brujas!"

"They turn to owls and fly at night," Abel shouted.

"You have to kill them with a bullet marked with a cross," Lloyd added. "It's the law."

"Do magic," Horse grunted in my ear. His half-nelson was tight now. My stomach felt sick.

"Voodoo!" Ernie spun the ball in my face.

"Okay!" I cried. It must have scared Horse because he let loose and jumped back. They were all still, watching me.

The heat and what I had heard made me sick. I bent over, wretched and vomited. The yellow froth and juice of the carrots splattered at their feet.

"Jesuschriss!" " ¡Chingada!" " ¡Puta!" " ¡A la madre!"

"Come on," Cico said. We took advantage of their surprise and ran. We were over the hill, past the last few houses, and at Blue Lake before they recovered from the astonishment I saw in their faces. We stopped to rest and laugh.

"That was great, Tony," Cico gasped, "that really put Ernie in his place—"

"Yeah," I nodded. I felt better after vomiting and running. I felt better about taking the carrots, but I did not feel good about what they had said about Ultima.

"Why are they like that?" I asked Cico. We skirted Blue Lake and worked our way through the tall, golden grass to the creek.

"I don't know," Cico answered, "except that people, grownups and kids, seem to want to hurt each other—and it's worse when they're in a group."

We walked on in silence. I had never been this far before so the land interested me. I knew that the waters of el Rito flowed from springs in the dark hills. I knew that those hills cradled the mysterious Hidden Lakes, but I had never been there. The creek flowed around the town, crossed beneath the bridge to El Puerto, then turned towards the river. There was a small reservoir there, and where the water emptied into the river the watercress grew thick and green. Ultima and I had visited the place in search of roots and herbs.

The water of el Rito was clear and clean. It was not muddy like the water of the river. We followed the footpath along the creek until we came to a thicket of brush and trees. The trail skirted around the bosque.

Cico paused and looked around. He pretended to be removing a splinter from his foot, but he was cautiously scanning the trail and the grass around us. I was sure we were alone; the last people we had seen were the swimmers at the Blue Lake a few miles back. Cico pointed to the path.

"The fishermen follow the trail around the brush," he whispered, "they hit the creek again just below the pond that's hidden in here." He squirmed into the thicket on hands and knees, and I followed. After a while we could stand up again and follow the creek to a place where an old beaver dam made a large pond.

It was a beautiful spot. The pond was dark and clear, and the water trickled and gurgled over the top of the dam. There was plenty of grass along the bank, and on all sides the tall brush and trees rose to shut off the world.

Cico pointed. "The golden carp will come through there." The cool waters of the creek came out of a dark, shadowy grotto of overhanging thicket, then flowed about thirty feet before they entered the large pond. Cico reached into a clump of grass and brought out a long, thin salt cedar branch with a spear at the end. The razor-sharp steel glistened in the sun. The other end of the spear had a nylon cord attached to it for retrieving.

"I fish for the black bass of the pond," Cico said. He took a position on a high clump of grass at the edge of the bank and motioned for me to sit by the bank, but away from him.

"How can you see him?" I asked. The waters of the pool were clear and pure, but dark from their depth and shadows of the surrounding brush. The sun was crystaline white in the clear, blue sky, but still there was the darkness of shadows in this sacred spot.

"The golden carp will scare him up," Cico whispered. "The black bass thinks he can be king of the fish, but all he wants is to eat them. The black bass is a killer. But the real king is the golden carp, Tony. He does not eat his own kind—"

Cico's eyes remained glued on the dark waters. His body was motionless, like a spring awaiting release. We had been whispering since we arrived at the pond, why I didn't know, except that it was just one of those places where one can communicate only in whispers, like church.

We sat for a long time, waiting for the golden carp. It was very pleasant to sit in the warm sunshine and watch the pure waters drift by. The drone of the summer insects and grasshoppers made me sleepy. The lush green of the grass was cool, and beneath the grass was the dark earth, patient, waiting . . .

To the northeast two hawks circled endlessly in the clear sky. There must be something dead on the road to Tucumcari, I thought.

Then the golden carp came. Cico pointed and I turned to where the stream came out of the dark grotto of overhanging tree branches. At first I thought I must be dreaming. I had expected to see a carp the size of a river carp, perhaps a little bigger and slightly orange instead of brown. I rubbed my eyes and watched in astonishment.

"Behold the golden carp, Lord of the waters—" I turned and saw Cico standing, his spear held across his chest as if in acknowledgement of the presence of a ruler.

The huge, beautiful form glided through the blue waters. I could not believe its size. It was bigger than me! And bright orange! The sunlight glistened off his golden scales. He glided down the creek with a couple of smaller carp following, but they were like minnows compared to him.

"The golden carp," I whispered in awe. I could not have been more entranced if I had seen the Virgin, or God Himself. The golden carp had seen me. It made a wide sweep, its back making ripples in the dark water. I could have reached out into the water and touched the holy fish!

"He knows you are a friend," Cico whispered.

Then the golden carp swam by Cico and disappeared into the darkness of the pond. I felt my body trembling as I saw the bright golden form disappear. I knew I had witnessed a miraculous thing, the appearance of a pagan god, a thing as miraculous as the curing of my uncle Lucas. And I thought, the power of God failed where Ultima's worked; and then a sudden illumination of beauty and understanding flashed through my mind. This is what I had expected God to do at my first holy communion! If God was witness to my beholding of the golden carp then I had sinned! I clasped my hands and was about to pray to the heavens when the waters of the pond exploded.

I turned in time to see Cico hurl his spear at the monstrous black bass that had broken the surface of the waters. The evil mouth of the black bass was open and red. Its eyes were glazed with hate as it hung in the air surrounded by churning water and a million diamond droplets of water. The spear whistled through the air, but the aim was low. The huge tail swished and contemptuously flipped it aside. Then the black form dropped into the foaming waters.

"Missed," Cico groaned. He retrieved his line slowly.

I nodded my head. "I can't believe what I have seen," I heard myself say, "are all the fish that big here—"

"No," Cico smiled, "they catch two and three pounders below the beaver dam, the black bass must weigh close to twenty—" He threw his spear and line behind the clump of grass and came to sit by me. "Come on, let's put our feet in the water. The golden carp will be returning—"

"Are you sorry you missed?" I asked as we slid our feet into the cool water.

Behold the golden carp . . .

"No," Cico said, "it's just a game."

The orange of the golden carp appeared at the edge of the pond. As he came out of the darkness of the pond the sun caught his shiny scales and the light reflected orange and yellow and red. He swam very close to our feet. His body was round and smooth in the clear water. We watched in silence at the beauty and grandeur of the great fish. Out of the corners of my eyes I saw Cico hold his hand to his breast as the golden carp glided by. Then with a switch of his powerful tail the golden carp disappeared into the shadowy water under the thicket.

I shook my head. "What will happen to the golden carp?"

"What do you mean?" Cico asked.

"There are many men who fish here—"

Cico smiled. "They can't see him, Tony, they can't see him. I know every man from Guadalupe who fishes, and there ain't a one who has ever mentioned seeing the golden carp. So I guess the grown-ups can't see him—"

"The Indian, Narciso, Ultima—"

"They're different, Tony. Like Samuel, and me, and you—"

"I see," I said. I did not know what that difference was, but I did feel a strange brotherhood with Cico. We shared a secret that would always bind us.

"Where does the golden carp go?" I asked and nodded upstream.

"He swims upstream to the lakes of the mermaid, the Hidden Lakes—"

"The mermaid?" I questioned him.

"There are two deep, hidden lakes up in the hills," he continued, "they feed the creek. Some people say those lakes have no bottom. There's good fishing, but very few people go there. There's something strange about those lakes, like they are haunted. There's a strange power, it seems to watch you—"

"Like the *presence* of the river?" I asked softly. Cico looked at me and nodded.

"You've felt it," he said.

"Yes."

"Then you understand. But this thing at the lakes is stronger, or maybe not stronger, it just seems to want you more. The time I was there—I climbed to one of the overhanging cliffs, and I just sat there, watching the fish in the clear water—I didn't know about the power then, I was just thinking how good the fishing would be, when I began to hear strange music. It came

from far away. It was a low, lonely murmuring, maybe like
something a sad girl would sing. I looked around, but I was
alone. I looked over the ledge of the cliff and the singing
seemed to be coming from the water, and it seemed to be
calling me—"

I was spellbound with Cico's whispered story. If I had not
seen the golden carp perhaps I would not have believed him.
But I had seen too much today to doubt him.

"I swear, Tony, the music was pulling me into the dark
waters below! The only thing that saved me from plunging into
the lake was the golden carp. He appeared and the music
stopped. Only then could I tear myself away from that place.
Man, I ran! Oh how I ran! I had never been afraid before, but I
was afraid then. And it wasn't that the singing was evil, it was
just that it called for me to join it. One more step and I'da
stepped over the ledge and drowned in the waters of the lake—"

I waited a long time before I asked the next question. I
waited for him to finish reliving his experience. "Did you see
the mermaid?"

"No," he answered.

"Who is she?" I whispered.

"No one knows. A deserted woman—or just the wind singing
around the edges of those cliffs. No one really knows. It just
calls people to it—"

"Who?"

He looked at me carefully. His eyes were clear and bright,
like Ultima's, and there were lines of age already showing.

"Last summer the mermaid took a shepherd. He was a man
from Méjico, new here and working for a ranch beyond the
hills. He had not heard the story about the lakes. He brought his
sheep to water there, and he heard the singing. He made it back
to town and even swore that he had seen the mermaid. He said
it was a woman, resting on the water and singing a lonely song.
She was half woman and half fish— He said the song made him
want to wade out to the middle of the lake to help her, but his
fear had made him run. He told everyone the story, but no one
believed him. He ended up getting drunk in town and swearing
he would prove his story by going back to the lakes and bringing back the mer-woman. He never returned. A week later the
flock was found near the lakes. He had vanished—"

"Do you think the mermaid took him?" I asked.

"I don't know, Tony," Cico said and knit his brow, "there's

a lot of things I don't know. But never go to the Hidden Lakes alone, Tony, never. It's not safe."

I nodded that I would honor his warning. "It is so strange," I said, "the things that happen. The things that I have seen, or heard about."

"Yes," he agreed.

"These things of the water, the mermaid, the golden carp. They are strange. There is so much water around the town, the river, the creek, the lakes—"

Cico leaned back and stared into the bright sky. "This whole land was once covered by a sea, a long time ago—"

"My name means sea," I pondered aloud.

"Hey, that's right," he said, "Márez means sea, it means you came from the ocean, Tony Márez arisen from the sea—"

"My father says our blood is restless, like the sea—"

"That is beautiful," he said. He laughed. "You know, this land belonged to the fish before it belonged to us. I have no doubt about the prophecy of the golden carp. He will come to rule again!"

"What do you mean?" I asked.

"What do I mean?" Cico asked quizzically, "I mean that the golden carp will come to rule again. Didn't Samuel tell you?"

"No," I shook my head.

"Well he told you about the people who killed the carp of the river and were punished by being turned into fish themselves. After that happened, many years later, a new people came to live in this valley. And they were no better than the first inhabitants, in fact they were worse. They sinned a lot, they sinned against each other, and they sinned against the legends they knew. And so the golden carp sent them a prophecy. He said that the sins of the people would weigh so heavy upon the land that in the end the whole town would collapse and be swallowed by water—"

I must have whistled in exclamation and sighed.

"Tony," Cico said, "this whole town is sitting over a deep, underground lake! Everybody knows that. Look." He drew on the sand with a stick. "Here's the river. The creek flows up here and curves into the river. The Hidden Lakes complete the other border. See?"

I nodded. The town was surrounded by water. It was frightening to know that! "The whole town!" I whispered in amazement.

"Yup," Cico said, "the whole town. The golden carp has warned us that the land cannot take the weight of the sins—the land will finally sink!"

"But you live in town!" I exclaimed.

He smiled and stood up. "The golden carp is my god, Tony. He will rule the new waters. I will be happy to be with my god—"

It was unbelievable, and yet it made a wild kind of sense! All the pieces fitted!

"Do the people of the town know?" I asked anxiously.

"They know," he nodded, "and they keep on sinning."

"But it's not fair to those who don't sin!" I countered.

"Tony," Cico said softly, "all men sin."

I had no answer to that. My own mother had said that losing your innocence and becoming a man was learning to sin. I felt weak and powerless in the knowledge of the impending doom.

"When will it happen?" I asked.

"No one knows," Cico answered. "It could be today, tomorrow, a week, a hundred years—but it will happen."

"What can we do?" I asked. I heard my voice tremble.

"Sin against no one," Cico answered.

I walked away from that haven which held the pond and the swimming waters of the golden carp feeling a great weight in my heart. I was saddened by what I had learned. I had seen beauty, but the beauty had burdened me with responsibility. Cico wanted to fish at the dam, but I was not in the mood for it. I thanked him for letting me see the golden carp, crossed the river, and trudged up the hill homeward.

I thought about telling everyone in town to stop their sinning, or drown and die. But they would not believe me. How could I preach to the whole town, I was only a boy. They would not listen. They would say I was crazy, or bewitched by Ultima's magic.

I went home and thought about what I had seen and the story Cico told. I went to Ultima and told her the story. She said nothing. She only smiled. It was as if she knew the story and found nothing fantastic or impending in it. "I would have told you the story myself," she nodded wisely, "but it is better that you hear the legend from someone your own age . . ."

"Am I to believe the story?" I asked. I was worried.

"Antonio," she said calmly and placed her hand on my shoulder, "I cannot tell you what to believe. Your father and your mother can tell you, because you are their blood, but I cannot. As you grow into manhood you must find your own truths—"

That night in my dreams I walked by the shore of a great lake. A bewitching melody filled the air. It was the song of the mer-woman! I looked into the dark depths of the lake and saw the golden carp, and all around him were the people he had saved. On the bleached shores of the lake the carcasses of sinners rotted.

Then a huge golden moon came down from the heavens and settled on the surface of the calm waters. I looked towards the enchanting light, expecting to see the Virgin of Guadalupe, but in her place I saw my mother!

Mother, I cried, you are saved! We are all saved!

Yes, my Antonio, she smiled, we who were baptized in the water of the moon which was made holy by our Holy Mother the Church are saved.

Lies! my father shouted, Antonio was not baptized in the holy water of the moon, but in the salt water of the sea!

I turned and saw him standing on the corpse-strewn shore. I felt a searing pain spread through my body.

Oh please tell me which is the water that runs through my veins, I moaned; oh please tell me which is the water that washes my burning eyes!

It is the sweet water of the moon, my mother crooned softly, it is the water the Church chooses to make holy and place in its font. It is the water of your baptism.

Lies, lies, my father laughed, through your body runs the salt water of the oceans. It is that water which makes you Márez and not Luna. It is the water that binds you to the pagan god of Cico, the golden carp!

Oh, I cried, please tell me. The agony of pain was more than I could bear. The excruciating pain broke and I sweated blood.

There was a howling wind as the moon rose and its powers pulled at the still waters of the lake. Thunder split the air and the lightning bursts illuminated the churning, frothy tempest. The ghosts stood and walked upon the shore.

The lake seemed to respond with rage and fury. It cracked with the laughter of madness as it inflicted death upon the people. I thought the end had come to everything. The cosmic struggle of the two forces would destroy everything!

The doom which Cico had predicted was upon us! I clasped

my hands and knelt to pray. The terrifying end was near. Then I heard a voice speak above the sound of the storm. I looked up and saw Ultima.

Cease! she cried to the raging powers, and the power from the heavens and the power from the earth obeyed her. The storm abated.

Stand, Antonio, she commanded, and I stood. You both know, she spoke to my father and my mother, that the sweet water of the moon which falls as rain is the same water that gathers into rivers and flows to fill the seas. Without the waters of the moon to replenish the oceans there would be no oceans. And the same salt waters of the oceans are drawn by the sun to the heavens, and in turn become again the waters of the moon. Without the sun there would be no waters formed to slake the dark earth's thirst.

The waters are one, Antonio. I looked into her bright, clear eyes and understood her truth.

You have been seeing only parts, she finished, and not looking beyond into the great cycle that binds us all.

Then there was peace in my dreams and I could rest.

Doce

Ultima's cure and the golden carp occupied my thoughts the rest of the summer. I was growing up and changing. I had plenty of time to be by myself and to think and feel the magic these events contained.

Things were quiet at home since the departure of León and Eugene. My father was drinking more than usual. It was because he felt that they had betrayed him. He would come home, black from the asphalt of the highway, wash himself out by the windmill, then spend the rest of the afternoon doing small, odd jobs around the rabbit pens. I didn't have to worry much about keeping the animals fed because he did all the work. He kept a bottle of whiskey out there and he drank until suppertime. I went to call him to supper one afternoon and I heard him muttering in the dusk.

"They have forsaken their father," he spoke to the gentle rabbits which gathered around his feet, "they have left me. Oh," he moaned, "it was not their fault. I am the fool! I should have known that the Márez blood in them would make them restless. It is the same blood that set me to wandering when I was young! Oh, I should have known. I was proud that they would show the true blood of the Márez, but little did I realize that same pride would make them desert me. Gone. We are all wanderers. And I am here alone—"

"¿Papá?" I called.

"¿Qué?" he turned. "Oh, it is you Antonito. It is time for supper, eh." He came to my side and placed his hand on my shoulder. "Perhaps it is true the Luna's blood will win out in the end," he said, "perhaps it is better that way—"

My mother, too, was very quiet. She tried to cheer herself by saying Andrew was still home, but Andrew worked all day and was usually in town at night. I only saw him for a few moments at breakfast and at suppertime. Mamá teased him that he had a girl in town and that soon she and papá would have to go and speak to the girl's parents, but Andrew remained silent. He would not be drawn into conversation. Of course my mother had Ultima to talk with during the day, and that was very good for her.

Ultima and I continued to search for plants and roots in the hills. I felt more attached to Ultima than to my own mother. Ultima told me the stories and legends of my ancestors. From her I learned the glory and the tragedy of the history of my people, and I came to understand how that history stirred in my blood.

I spent most of the long summer evenings in her room. We talked, stored the dry herbs, or played cards. One night I asked her about the three dolls on her shelf. The dolls were made of clay and shellacked with candle wax. They were clothed, and lifelike in appearance.

"They look familiar," I thought to myself.

"Do not touch them," she said. There were many things in Ultima's room that I instinctively knew I should not touch, but I could not understand why she was so blunt about the dolls.

"One of them must have been left in the sun," I said. I looked closely at one doll that sagged and bent over. The clay face seemed to be twisted with pain.

"Come here!" Ultima called me away from the dolls. I went and stood before her. Her clear stare fixed me to the spot and made me forget the dolls. "Do you know the man Tenorio?" she asked.

"Yes. He is the man who threatened you at El Puerto when we went to cure my uncle Lucas."

"He is a wicked man," she said. "When you are out alone,

One night I asked about three dolls she had

placed on her shelf.

fishing along the river, if you see this man Antonio, you are to keep away from him. Do you understand?"

"I understand," I nodded. She spoke very calmly and so I was not frightened.

"You are a good boy. Now come here. I have something for you." She took her scapular from around her neck. "Next spring you will start your catechism, and when you make your first communion you will receive your scapular. It will protect you from all evil. In the meantime, I want you to wear mine—" She took the thin string and placed it around my neck. I had seen my sisters' scapulars and knew that the bit of cloth at the end had a picture of the Virgin or St. Joseph on it, but this scapular held a small, flattened pouch. I smelled it and its fragrance was sweet.

"A small pouch of helpful herbs," Ultima smiled, "I have had that since I was a child. It will keep you safe."

"But what will you use?" I asked.

"Bah," she laughed, "I have many ways to keep me safe— Now promise you will tell no one about this." She tucked the scapular under my shirt.

"I promise," I answered.

Another thing I did that summer was to confirm Cico's story. I followed the line of water Cico said was drawn around the town, and it was true, the entire town was surrounded by water! Of course I did not go to the Hidden Lakes but I could see the obvious truth nevertheless. The town was ringed by the river, the creek, the lakes, and numerous other springs. I waited many an afternoon to catch sight of the beautiful golden carp as it swam by, and while I waited in the sun I pondered over his legend.

And there were good times too, gay times before the awful storm that broke over our house. When the people of Las Pasturas came to town for supplies, they always came to visit with my parents. When they came my father was happy, not only because they were his people, but because they were a happy people. They were always laughing, and the men's eyes were always bright with the sting of whiskey. Their talk was loud and excited, and there was a song in it. They even smelled different from the people of the town, or my uncles from El Puerto. My uncles were quiet and the odor around them was deep and quiet, like damp earth. The people from Las Pasturas were like the wind, and the fragrances they carried on their clothing shifted as the wind shifted.

The people from Las Pasturas always had stories to tell about the places where they had worked. Sometimes they talked about picking cotton in east Texas and about running whiskey into the cottonfields of dry counties. Sometimes they talked about picking broom corn, and as they talked and laughed I could see the rows of green broom corn and I could smell the sweet scent it left in their sweaty workclothes. Or they would speak about the potato fields of Colorado, and the tragedy that befell them there. They left a son in the dark earth of Colorado, crushed into the tilled earth by a spilled tractor. And then, even the grown men cried, but it was all right to cry, because it was fitting to grieve the death of a son.

But always the talk would return to stories of the old days in Las Pasturas. Always the talk turned to life on the llano. The first pioneers there were sheepherders. Then they imported herds of cattle from Mexico and became vaqueros. They became horsemen, caballeros, men whose daily life was wrapped up in the ritual of horsemanship. They were the first cowboys in a wild and desolate land which they took from the Indians.

Then the railroad came. The barbed wire came. The songs, the corridos became sad, and the meeting of the people from Texas with my forefathers was full of blood, murder, and tragedy. The people were uprooted. They looked around one day and found themselves closed in. The freedom of land and sky they had known was gone. Those people could not live without freedom and so they packed up and moved west. They became migrants.

My mother did not like the people of the llano. To her they were worthless drunkards, wanderers. She did not understand their tragedy, their search for the freedom that was now forever gone. My mother had lived in the llano many years when she married my father, but the valley and the river were too ingrained in her for her to change. She made only two lasting friends in Las Pasturas, Ultima, for whom she would lay down her life, and Narciso, whose drinking she tolerated because he had helped her when her twins were born.

It was late in the summer and we were all seated around the kitchen table making our plans to go to El Puerto for the harvest when my mother with strange premonition remembered Narciso. "He is a fool, and he is a drunkard, but he did help me in my hour of need—"

"Ah yes, that Narciso is a gentleman," my father winked and teased her.

"Bah!" my mother scoffed, and went on. "That man didn't sleep for three days, rushing around getting things for Ultima and me, and he never touched the bottle."

"Where was papá?" Deborah asked.

"Who knows. The railroad took him to places he never told me about," my mother answered angrily.

"I had to work," my father said simply, "I had to support your family—"

"Anyway," my mother changed the subject, "it has been a good summer at El Puerto. The harvest will be good, and it will be good to see my papá, and Lucas—" She turned and looked thankfully at Ultima.

"This calls for a drink of thanksgiving," my father smiled. He too wanted to preserve the good spirits and humor that were with us that night. He was standing when Narciso burst through the kitchen door. He came in without knocking and we all jumped from our seats. One minute the kitchen was soft and quiet and the next it was filled with the huge figure of Narciso. He was the biggest man I had ever seen. He wore a huge mustache and his hair flowed like a lion's mane. His eyes were wild and red as he stood over us, gasping and panting for breath; saliva dripped from his mouth. He looked like a huge, wounded monster. Deborah and Theresa screamed and ran behind my mother.

"Narciso!" my father exclaimed, "what is the matter?"

"Teh-Teh-norio!" Narciso gasped. He pointed at Ultima and ran and kneeled at her feet. He took her hand and kissed it.

"Narciso," Ultima smiled. She took his hand and made him stand.

"¿Qué pasa?" my father repeated.

"He is drunk!" my mother exclaimed anxiously. She clutched Deborah and Theresa.

"No! No!" Narciso insisted, "Tenorio!" he gasped and pointed to the kitchen door. "Grande, you must hide!" he pleaded with Ultima.

"You don't make sense," my father said. He took Narciso by the shoulders. "Sit down, catch your breath— María, send the children to bed."

My mother pushed us past Narciso, who sank into my father's chair. I didn't know what was happening, nobody seemed to know, but I was not about to miss the action simply because I was a child. My mother's first concern was to rush the frightened Deborah and Theresa up the stairs to their room. I held back and slipped into the darkness beneath the stairs. I huddled down and watched with anticipation the drama that unfolded as Narciso regained his composure and related his story.

"Grande must hide!" he insisted. "We must waste no time! Even now they come!"

"Why must I hide, Narciso?" Ultima asked calmly.

"Who is coming?" my mother added as she returned to the kitchen. She had not missed me and I was glad for it.

Narciso roared. "Oh my God!"

At that moment I heard Ultima's owl hoot a danger cry outside. There was someone out there. I looked at Ultima and saw her smile vanish. She held her head high, as if sniffing the wind, and the strength I had seen when she dealt with Tenorio at the bar filled her face. She, too, had heard the owl.

"We know nothing," my father said, "now make sense, hombre!"

"Today Tenorio's daughter, nay, his witch died. The small evil one died at El Puerto today—"

"What has that to do with us?" my father asked.

"¡Ay Dios!" Narciso cried and wrung his hands, "living on this cursed hill, away from town, you hear nothing! Tenorio has blamed la Grande for his daughter's death!" He pointed to Ultima.

"¡Ave María Purísima!" my mother cried. She went to Ultima and put her arms around her. "That is impossible!"

"You must take her away, hide her until this evil story is ended—"

Again I heard the owl cry, and I heard Ultima whisper, "it is too late—"

"Bah!" my father almost laughed, "Tenorio spreads rumors like an old woman. The next time I see him I will pull his dog-beard and make him wish he had never been born."

"It is not rumor," Narciso pleaded, "he has gathered his cronies around him at the bar, he has filled them with whiskey all day, and he has convinced them to burn a witch! They come on a witchhunt!"

"¡Ay!" my mother choked a sob and crossed her forehead.

I held my breath at what I heard. I could not believe that anyone could ever think that Ultima was a witch! She did only good. Again the owl cried. I turned and stared into the

darkness, but I could see nothing. Still I felt something or someone lurking in the shadows, else why should the owl cry?

"Who told you this wild story," my father demanded.

"Jesús Silva has come from El Puerto. I spoke to him just
minutes ago and came running to warn you! You know his
word is gold!" Narciso answered. My father nodded in agreement.

"¡Gabriel! What are we to do?" my mother cried.

"What proof does Tenorio have?" my father asked.

"Proof!" Narciso roared, he was now nearly out of his
mind with the deliberateness of my father, "he does not need
proof, hombre! He has filled the men with whiskey; he has
spread his poisonous vengeance into them!"

"We must flee!" my mother cried.

"No," Ultima cut in. She looked at my father and measured
him carefully with her intent gaze. "A man does not flee from
the truth," she said.

"Ay, Grande," Narciso moaned, "I am only thinking of
your welfare. One does not talk about the truth to men drunk
with whiskey and the smell of a lynching—"

"If he has no proof, then we need not be concerned with the
stories a wolf spreads," my father said.

"All right!" Narciso jumped up, "if it is proof you insist on
before you hide la Grande, I will tell you what Jesús told
me! Tenorio has told the men who would listen to him that he
found la Grande's stringed bag, you know the kind the curan-
deras wear around their neck, under the bed of his dead daughter!"

"It cannot be!" I jumped up and shouted. I rushed to my
father. "It could not be Ultima's, because I have it!" I tore open
my shirt and showed them the stringed scapular. And at the
same time we heard the loud report of a shot and running men
carrying burning torches surrounded our house.

"It is them! It is too late!" Narciso moaned and slumped
back into the chair. I saw my father look at his rifle on the
shelf, then dismissing it he walked calmly to the door. I followed closely behind him.

"¡Gabriel Márez!" an evil voice called from beyond the dancing light of the torches. My father stepped outside and I followed him. He was aware of me, but he did not send me back.
He was on his land and as such would not be shamed in front of
his son.

At first we could see only the flaring light of the piñón torches. Then our eyes grew accustomed to the dark and we could see the dark outlines of men, and their red, sweating faces by the light of their torches. Some of the men had drawn charcoal crosses on their foreheads. I trembled. I was afraid, but I vowed I would not let them take Ultima. I waited for my father to speak.

"¿Quién es?" my father asked. He spread his feet as if ready to fight.

"We have no quarrel with you, Márez!" the evil voice called out, "we only want the witch!"

My father's voice was tense with anger now. "Who speaks?" he asked loudly. There was no answer.

"Come, come!" my father repeated, almost shouting, "you know me! You call me by my name, you walk upon my land! I want to know who speaks!"

The men glanced nervously at each other. Two of them drew close to each other and whispered secretly. A third came from around the house and joined them. They had thought taking Ultima would be easy, but now they realized that my father would let no man invade his home.

"Our business here tonight is not with you, Márez," the voice of Tenorio squeaked in the dark. I recognized the voice from the bar at El Puerto.

"You walk on my land! That is my business!" my father shouted.

"We do not want to quarrel with you, Márez; it is the old witch we want. Give her to us and we will take her away. There will be no trouble. Besides, she is of no relation to you, and she stands accused of witchcraft—"

"Who accuses her?" my father asked sternly. He was forcing the men to identify themselves, and so the false courage the whiskey and the darkness had lent them was slipping away. In order to hold the men together Tenorio was forced to speak up.

"It is I, Tenorio Trementina, who accuses her!" he shouted and jumped forward so that I could plainly see his ugly face. "¡La mujer que no ha pecado es bruja, le juro a Dios!"

He did not have a chance to finish his accusation because my father reached out and grabbed him by the collar. Tenorio was not a small man, but with one hand my father jerked him off his feet and pulled the cringing figure forward.

"You are a cabrón," he said, almost calmly, into Tenorio's

evil, frightened face. "You are a whoring old woman!" With his left hand he grabbed at the tuft of hair that grew on Tenorio's chin and yanked it hard. Tenorio screamed in pain and rage. Then my father extended his arm and Tenorio went flying. He landed screaming in the dust, and then scrambling to his feet he ran to find refuge behind two of his coyotes.

"Wait, Márez!" one of the men shouted and jumped between my father and Tenorio. "We did not come to fight you! There is no man here that does not hold you in respect. But witchcraft is a serious accusation, you know that. We do not like this any better than you do, but the charge must be cleared up! This morning Tenorio's daughter died. He has proof that it is Ultima's curse that killed her—"

The rest of the men nodded and moved forward. Their faces were sullen. They all held hastily made crosses of green juniper and piñón branches. The light of the torches danced off crosses of pins and needles they had pinned on their coats and shirts. One man had even run needles through the skin of his lower lip so that no curse might enter him. Blood trickled down his lip and dropped from his chin.

"Is that you, Blas Montaño?" my father asked of the man who had just spoken.

"Sí," the man answered and bowed his head.

"Give us the witch!" Tenorio shouted from behind the safety of his men. He was raging with insult, but he would not approach my father.

"There is no witch here!" my father answered and crouched as if to await their attack.

"Tenorio has proof!" another man shouted.

"¡Chinga tu madre!" my father retorted. They were going to have to fight him to take Ultima, but there were too many for him! I thought of running for the rifle.

"Give us the bruja!" Tenorio shouted. He urged the men forward and they answered as a chorus, "Give us the witch!" "Give us the witch!" The man with the crossed needles on his lip waved his juniper cross towards the house. The others waved their torches back and forth as they slowly approached my father.

"Give us the witch!" "Give us the witch!" they chanted and moved forward, but my father held his ground. The hissing of the torches frightened me, but I took courage from my father. They were almost upon us when they suddenly stopped. The

screen door banged and Narciso stepped forward. Instead of a
bumbling drunkard there now stood in the path of the mob a
giant man. He held my father's rifle casually in his hands, as he
surveyed the mob.

"¿Qué pasa aquí?" his booming voice broke the tense silence. "Why are farmers out playing vigilantes when they should
be home, sitting before a warm fire, playing cards, counting the
rich harvest, eh? I know you men, I know you, Blas Montaño,
Manuelito, and you Cruz Sedillo—and I know you are not men
who need the cover of darkness to hide your deeds!"

The men glanced at each other. The man they considered the
town drunk had shamed them by pointing out the lowliness of
their deed. One man took a drink from a bottle he held and
tried to pass it on, but no one would take it. They were silent.

"You shame your good names by following this jodido
Tenorio!" Narciso continued.

"Aieeeee!" Tenorio groaned with rage and hate, but there
was nothing he dared to do.

"This cabrón has lost a daughter today, and for that El
Puerto can sleep easier now that her evil-doing is gone to hell
with her!"

"Animal!" Tenorio spit out.

"I may well be a beast," Narciso laughed, "but I am not a
fool!"

"We are not fools!" Blas shouted back, "we came on an
errand that is a law by custom. This man has proof that the
curandera Ultima is a witch, and if it is her curse that caused a
death then she must be punished!" The men around him nodded in agreement. I was mortally afraid that Narciso, like my
father, would anger the mob and we would be overrun. Then I
knew they would take Ultima and kill her.

Narciso's throat rumbled with laughter. "I do not question
your right to charge someone with witchcraft, it is so in custom.
But you are fools, fools for drinking the devil's whiskey!" and
he pointed at Tenorio, "and fools for following him across the
countryside in the middle of the night—"

"You have insulted me, and for that you will pay!" Tenorio
shouted and waved his fist, "and now he calls you fools!" he
turned to the men. "Enough of this talking. We came to take
the witch! Let it be done!"

"¡Sí!" the men nodded in agreement.

"Wait!" Narciso stopped them. "Yes, I called you fools,

but not to insult you. Listen my friends, you have already violated this man's land—you have come and created much bad blood when you could have done this simply. You have the right to charge someone with witchcraft, and to discover the truth of that charge there is a very simple test!" He reached forward and pulled the needles from the man's lip. "Are these needles holy?" he asked the man.

"Sí," the man answered, "blessed just last Sunday by the priest." He wiped the blood on his lip.

"I call you fools because you all know the test for a bruja, and yet you did not think to use it. It is simple. Take the holy needles and pin them to the door. Put them in so they are crossed—and in the name of God!" he roared, "you all know that a witch cannot walk through a door so marked by the sign of Christ!"

"¡Ay sí!" the men exclaimed. It was true.

"It is a true test," the man called Cruz Sedillo spoke. He took the needles from Narciso. "It is legal in our customs. I have seen it work."

"But we must all abide by the trial," Narciso said. He looked at my father. For the first time my father turned and looked at the kitchen door. In the light were the two huddled figures of my mother and Ultima. Then he glanced at Narciso. He placed his faith in his old friend.

"I will abide by the test," he said simply. I crossed my forehead. I had no doubt that Ultima could walk by the way of the holy cross. Now everyone turned and looked at Tenorio, for it was he who had accused Ultima.

"I will abide," he muttered. He had no other choice.

"I will place the needles," Cruz Sedillo said. He walked to the door and stuck the two needles in the form of a cross at the top of the door frame. Then he turned and spoke to the men. "It is true that no person of evil, no bruja, can walk through a door guarded by the sign of the Holy Cross. In my own lifetime I have seen a woman so judged, because her body burned with pain at the sight of the cross. So if Ultima cannot step through the threshold, then our work tonight has just begun. But if she crosses the threshold, then she can never again be accused of witchcraft—we call God as our witness," he finished and stepped back. All the men made the sign of the cross and murmured a prayer.

We all turned and looked at the door. The fire from the

torches was dying, and in fact some of the men had already dropped their smoldering torches to the ground. We could see Ultima plainly as she walked to the door.

"Who is it that accuses me?" she asked from behind the screen door. Her voice was very clear and powerful.

"Tenorio Trementina accuses you of being a witch!" Tenorio answered in a savage, hate-filled voice. He had stepped forward to shout his accusation, and as he did I heard Ultima's owl shriek in the dark. There was a rustling and whirling of wings above us, and all the men ducked and held their hands up to protect themselves from the attack. But the owl sought only one man, and it found him. It hurled itself on Tenorio, and the sharp talons gouged out one eye from the face of the evil man.

"Aieeeeeeeeeee!" he screamed in pain. "I am blinded! I am blinded!" In the dying light I saw blood spurt from the dark pit and bloody pulp that had once been an eye.

"¡Madre de Dios!" the men cried. They cringed in fear around the screaming, cursing Tenorio. They trembled and looked into the dark sky for the owl, but it was gone.

"¡Mira!" one of them cried. He pointed and they turned to see Ultima. She had walked through the door!

"It is proven!" Narciso cried.

Ultima took a step towards the men and they fell back. They could not understand why the owl had attacked Tenorio, they could not understand the power of Ultima. But she had walked through the door, and so the power of la curandera was good.

"It is proven," Cruz Sedillo said, "the woman is free of the accusation." He turned and walked to the hill where they had left their trucks and several of the men hurried after him. Two stayed to help Tenorio.

"Your evil bird has blinded me!" he cried. "For that I curse you! I will see you dead! And you, Narciso, I swear to kill you!" The men pulled him away. They disappeared out of the dim light of the sputtering torches and into the darkness.

"¡Grande!" It was my mother who now burst through the door. She put her arms around Ultima and led her back into the house.

"Ay, what a night," my father shrugged as he looked after the men who had slunk away. Up on the hill we heard their trucks start, then leave. "Someday I may have to kill that man," he said to himself.

"He needs killing," Narciso agreed.

"How can I thank you, old friend," my father said turning to Narciso.

"I owe la Grande my life," Narciso said, "and I owe you many favors, Márez. What are thanks among friends."

My father nodded. "Come, I need a drink—" They walked into the house. I followed, but paused at the door. A faint glitter caught my eye. I bent down and picked up the two needles that had been stuck to the top of the door frame. Whether someone had broken the cross they made, or whether they had fallen, I would never know.

Trece

We awakened late and hurried to pack for our trip to El Puerto. We did not talk about the awful thing that had happened that night, but I guess it was because of it that my father decided to go with us. We were excited because it was the first time he had made the trip and stayed. He went into town and arranged for a week's leave from his work on the highway. When he returned I heard him whisper to my mother about the talk in town.

"Tenorio is in the hospital, he has lost the eye—and they say the priest at El Puerto will not allow the dead daughter inside the church for her mass. There is no telling what will happen—"

"I am glad you are going with us, Gabriel," my mother answered.

I went outside. Someone, I guess my mother, had cleaned away the burnt torches and swept clean the patio. There was no trace of what had happened. The sun shone white and clean, and there was chill in the air. I ran to Jasón's and asked him to feed the animals for me while we were gone. When I returned my uncle Pedro was already there, helping to load our luggage.

"¡Antonio!" he greeted me with an abrazo. I returned the greeting and went off to find Ultima. I was worried about her.

But I found her busy at work, cleaning up the morning dishes. Everyone was busy doing something, and that helped us to forget the terror of the night before.

Deborah, Theresa, my mother and Ultima rode with my father. I rode with my uncle. We drove in silence and I had time to think. We drove past Rosie's house and I thought about the sins of the town and how the golden carp would punish the sinners. He would drown them in clear, blue water. Then we passed the church and I thought about God's punishment for sinners. He casts them in the burning pit of hell where they burn for eternity.

We passed over the bridge at el Rito and I remembered Cico's story of the people and the god who became a fish. But why had the new god, the golden carp, chosen also to punish people? The old God did it already. Drowning or burning, the punishment was all the same. The soul was lost, unsafe, unsure, suffering—why couldn't there be a god who would never punish his people, a god who would be forgiving all of the time? Perhaps the Virgin Mary was such a god? She had forgiven the people who killed her son. She always forgave. Perhaps the best god would be like a woman, because only women really knew how to forgive.

"You are quiet, Antonio," my uncle Pedro interrupted my thoughts, "are you thinking about last night?"

"No," I replied, "I am thinking about God."

" ¡Ay! Do not let me interrupt you."

"Why did you not come to warn us last night?" I asked. My uncle frowned.

"Well," he said finally, "your grandfather would not allow any of us to mix in what took place yesterday—"

"But Ultima cured my uncle Lucas! Isn't he grateful for that?"

"Of course he is!" he contended, "you just don't understand—"

"What?"

"Well, the village of El Puerto is small. We have lived there a long time, and we have lived in harmony with the good and the bad. We have not passed judgment on anyone." He nodded with some finality.

"But you allowed Tenorio to pass judgment on Ultima," I said, "and if it had not been for Narciso he would have carried out his judgment. Is that fair?"

My uncle started to answer, but held back. I saw his hands grip the steering wheel so hard that his knuckles turned white. For a long time he fidgeted, then he finally said, "It does not decrease my shame to say I was a coward last night. We all were. We took our father's wish as an excuse. Believe me, my faith is bound with that woman for saving Lucas. The next time, and God grant there isn't a next time, I will not shirk my duty to her." Then he turned and looked at me and reached out and touched my head. "I am glad you stood by your friend," he smiled, "that is what friends are for."

Yes, I had stood by Ultima. And so had my father, and Narciso, and the owl. We would all have slashed out, like the owl, to protect Ultima. It was not easy to forgive men like Tenorio. Perhaps that is why God could not forgive, He was too much like man.

There was a great deal of excitement when we arrived at El Puerto. Of course everyone in the village knew what had happened to Tenorio, and all were waiting for him to return to bury his daughter. We knew the priest would not let her be buried in the holy ground of the campo santo next to the church. But harvest time was a time for work and not for mitote. My uncles were farmers, men who took their only truth from the earth, and so by early afternoon we were out in the fields and orchards and the most important thing became the harvest.

It was good too, because it allowed us to forget what we did not want to remember. We returned from the first day of harvest by the first light of the moon as it came through the portal formed by the black mesas. After a heavy supper we settled in the room of my uncle Mateo, because he was the story teller. My mother and Ultima kept to themselves, tying the red chile into long, thick ristras. My aunts had been very cordial to Ultima. They treated her with respect because of what she had done for Lucas, but otherwise they kept their distance from her. I think Ultima liked it that way.

"Ay, it is a very bad thing what these Trementinas do," my uncle Mateo whispered. He glanced down the hall, but my grandfather had already retired. My grandfather would not allow any talk of witchcraft in his presence.

"I talked to Porfirio Baca today," my uncle Juan said, "and he said the two remaining sisters spent the day making her coffin."

"Ah!" my uncle Mateo signaled us to listen. "They were gathering cottonwood branches and weaving a coffin. That proves she was a bruja! A bruja cannot be buried in a casket made of pine or piñón or cedar."

"They say Tenorio returned today. He is blind in one eye."

"Yes," my uncle continued, "and tonight they will gather around the dead body and pray from their Black Book. Listen!"

We listened to the howl of the cold wind outside and could hear at intervals the bitter bark of a coyote. In the corral the penned animals milled nervously. Evil was in the autumn night air.

"They will burn sulfur instead of holy incense. They will sing and dance around her coffin, pulling at their hair and flesh. They will slay a rooster and spread his blood on their dead sister. Mark my word, when the Trementina bruja is brought in to church it will be in a basket woven of cottonwood branches, and her body will be smeared with blood—"

"But why do they do this?" someone whispered.

"For the devil," my uncle answered. "They do it so that the devil himself will come and sleep with the corpse before it is buried—"

"¡Mateo!" one of my aunts cautioned him. She pointed at the children.

"It is true!" he said.

"But why then will they bring her to church?" my uncle Juan's wife asked.

"Bah! Little do they care about church. That is only to keep up appearances," my uncle smiled.

"How is it you know all this?" she scoffed.

"Why, my sweet Oretea told me," he grinned and turned to his wife who sat beside him and patted her goodnaturedly. She looked at him and nodded in agreement. We laughed because we all knew that Oretea, my uncle Mateo's wife, had been deaf and dumb since birth.

Sleep came, and with it came my dream-fate which drew me to the witches' Black Mass. *I saw all, and it was exactly as my uncle had described it. Then my dream-fate drew me to the coffin. I peered in and to my horror I saw Ultima!*

I must have cried in my sleep, because I felt someone pick me up, and after that I felt warm and was at peace. When I awoke it was light outside. The house, which was normally alive and full of creaking, clattering sounds, was still, like a grave. I

jumped out of bed, dressed, and hurried outside. The people of
the village lined the street. They talked in excited, hushed whispers and craned their necks to look down the dusty street towards the bridge. Then I heard the creaking sound of a heavy,
horse-drawn wagon.

I spotted Ultima, standing alone on a rise of the ground
beside the house. I ran to her and held her hand. She seemed
oblivious to me. Her black shawl was drawn around her head
and face so that only her eyes remained uncovered. She
watched intently the funeral procession that came up the street
towards the church. Everyone was quiet. The still morning air
carried the creaking sound of the loaded wagon, and we could
hear the snorting mules and the squeaking of their harnesses as
they tugged and pulled the wagon carrying the body of the dead
woman. On the seat of the wagon sat two thin women dressed
in black. Black veils covered their faces, and as they passed in
front of Ultima they turned away.

On the bed of the wagon rested the casket. It was a basket
woven from pliant cottonwood branches, so that as the weight
of the body inside shifted the coffin seemed to groan. A strong,
rotting odor filled the air as the wagon passed by.

At the head of the procession rode Tenorio. He was dressed
in black and sat humped on his saddle. He wore a dark, wide-
brimmed hat pulled low to cover a black patch over his eye. His
spirited horse pranced nervously and tossed its head from side
to side.

The sky was blue and quiet. Our gazes followed the groaning
wagon down the dusty street, past the saloon, to the front of
the church. There the procession stopped and waited for the
priest to appear. When he came out of the church Tenorio
spoke to him and the priest answered. He held his arms out as if
to bar entrance to the church and nodded his head. He was
refusing the mass for the dead and holy burial in the campo
santo. The air grew tense. There was no telling what Tenorio
would do at this insult, but everyone knew he was crazy enough
to assault the priest.

But Tenorio was beaten. The entire village was witness to the
excommunication. The priest's refusal meant the church was
taking its stand and that the evil ways of the Trementinas were
known to all. Tenorio had not thought the priest would stand
against him. For a long time there was silence, then Tenorio
turned his horse and the procession came back down the street.

It was a basket woven out of pliant cottonwood branches.

He would have to bury his daughter in unholy ground, and without the saving grace of the mass her soul was doomed to perdition. But what hurt Tenorio most was that he would no longer be able to rally the townspeople around him; he would no longer be able to hold them through fear. If the priest, who had for so long been unwilling to condemn the Trementinas' doings, had taken a stand then surely that would lend courage to the villagers.

The sisters slumped in the seat of the wagon as they passed by, and their mournful cries were as much for themselves as for the fate of their sister. They had tampered with a man's fate and they now knew the consequences. Tenorio, too, leaned forward in his saddle. He had pulled his long, black coat around his thin body and huddled within it as if he hoped to escape the eyes of the villagers. Only when he passed in front of Ultima did he glance up, and in that swift glance his evil eye vowed his revenge on Ultima.

Everyone was subdued by what had occurred, but by afternoon the work of the harvest raised our spirits. Under the watchful eye of my grandfather the bounty of the fields and orchards was gathered. The loaded wagons moved between the fields and the village like ants scurrying to store their seeds. Green chile was roasted and set to dry. Red chile became huge ristras. The roofs of lean-toos were golden with slices of drying apples. The air was sweet with the aroma of boiling jellies and preserves and the laughter of the women. Corn was roasted to make chicos, blue corn was ground into meal, and the rest was stored for the animals.

Then as quietly as the green had slipped into the time of the river, the golden time of the harvest was completed. We had to return to Guadalupe. School was starting again.

" ¡Adiós! ¡Adiós!" we called to one another. It was then my uncle Juan took my father and mother aside and whispered the desires of my uncles.

"Antonio has worked well," he said stiffly, "he has the feel of the earth in his blood. We would be honored if you saw fit to allow him to spend a summer with us—the others," he said, "did not choose our way of life. So be it. But if Antonio is to know our way, we must initiate him next summer—" The rest of my uncles nodded at this brief speech. My uncles were not men of many words.

" ¡Oh, Gabriel!" my mother exclaimed, beaming with pride.

"We shall see," my father said. And we left.

Catorce

" ¡Adiós, Antonioooooooo . . ."

"Adiós, mamá, adiós, Ultima," I waved.

"You say the damnest things," Andrew laughed.

"Respect your teacher! Give my regards to Miss Maestas! Do not bring shame to our name." My mother's voice was distant now.

"Why?" I asked Andrew.

"I don't know," he answered as I followed his long strides up the goat path, "just the way you turn and wave goodbye to Grande and mamá—beats all."

"I always turn and look back," I said, falling into the measure of his walk. I was glad to be walking with him.

"Why?"

"I don't know—sometimes I get the feeling that I will come home, and it will all be changed. It won't be the same any more—" I could not tell him that I wanted the castle of the giants to stand forever, that I wanted the goat path and the hill to be for always. But I had misgivings, I was beginning to learn that things wouldn't always be the same.

"I know what you mean," he said as Deborah and Theresa passed us by like two wild goats, "when I came back from the army I felt it had changed. Everything seemed smaller."

"I'm glad you will be home," I said. I clutched my Red Chief tablet and my pencil. I was anxious to see the gang. I wondered how hard the third grade would be.

"Ah, I feel like an old man going to school, but it's the only way, Tony, the only way—"

At the bridge we met the Kid and Samuel. We raced across and as usual the brown, savage figure of the Kid left us behind. At the end of the bridge Andrew hung behind to catch his breath he said, and Samuel and I went on. We passed Rosie's house and headed towards the school. I told Samuel I had seen the golden carp that summer and he was very pleased.

"You might become one of us," he smiled his wise, contented smile.

"What did you do?" I asked. "I went for you, but you were gone."

"My father and I herded sheep on the Agua Negra ranch," he said. "You know, Tony," he added, "I think I will become a sheepherder."

"My mother wants me to become a farmer, or a priest," I said.

"There are rewards in caring for sheep, and there are rewards for tilling the soil, but the greatest calling is to be a priest," he said. "A priest is a man who cares for his people—"

"Yes."

"I heard about the evil thing they did to Ultima, the story of Tenorio's blinding was throughout the camps." He paused and looked at me. "You must be careful, the kids in town will not understand."

"I will," I said.

We reached the tumultuous playground and I told Samuel that I had to see Miss Maestas. He understood. I wanted to see Miss Maestas and deliver my mother's greetings before I got involved with the gang. Miss Maestas was busy with the first graders and so I did not stay long, but she was happy to see me and I was happy to see her. She hadn't changed much from last year.

Then I ran out and joined the gang at our spot on the playground. "Hi, Tony!" they called, and Horse threw me a pass. I caught it and passed it to Florence. "¡Chingada!"

Florence missed it and shagged. "¡Ah la veca!" "Butterfingers!"

"Who's your teacher, Tony?"

"Miss Harris or Miss Violet?"

"Don' know?"

"Miss Violet!" Bones cried out, "we all got Miss Violet! Chingada, I told you!"

"How do you know?" Lloyd asked.

"They give the dumb kids to Miss Violet—"

"All the dumb yellow birds! Yah, yah," Lloyd mimicked.

"Tony ain't dumb, he passed two grades!"

"He has a witch to help him," Ernie sneered.

Ernie was still after me. I still didn't know why.

"Miss Violet gives all her kids prunes on Fridays!"

"She gets even with our parents for having to guard us all week!" Everybody laughed.

"I ain't no dumb yellow bird!" Horse whinnied.

"Hey, Tony!" Ernie called, "is it true your brother's been whoring with the girls at Rosie's?"

"¡Ah la veca!" "¡Las putas!"

I did not know what the word whoring meant, but I knew Rosie's was a bad place. I did not answer.

"Knock it off," Red said, "why pick on Tony! Everybody in town goes to Rosie's!"

"Yeah-hhhhhhh," Bones howled, and his eyeballs rolled loose in their sockets, "including Ernie's old man!"

"¡Cabrón Bones!" Ernie glared, but he didn't jump Bones. It was stupid to jump Bones. Bones might kill you and not care.

"Ernie's old man!" Horse shouted and mounted Bones, and everybody laughed. "Hah, hah, hah!" Horse gasped.

"Very funny!" Ernie spit and swung to face me, "but at least we don't have a witch around our house!"

"Hey yeah! Tony's got a witch!" "I heard about it this summer!" "¡Chingada!" "¡Ah la veca!"

"Is that right, Tony?" Florence asked.

"She blinded a man!" Abel nodded vigorously.

"How?"

"Witchcraft—"

"Ah la verga—"

They were around me now, looking at me. The circle was tight and quiet. Around us the playground was one jarring, humming noise, but inside the circle it was quiet.

"Come on you guys!" Red said, "this is Tony's first year with us! Let's play ball! Come on, there ain't no such thing as witches—"

"There is if you're a Catholic!" Lloyd countered.

"Yeah," Horse agreed, "Red don't know nothing about anything. He's going to hell because he's not a Catholic!"

"Bullshit!" Red said.

"It's true," Lloyd said, "heaven is only for Catholics!"

"Not really—" Florence nodded, his angular figure rocking back and forth.

"Come on, Tony," Ernie said coming closer, "she is a witch, ain't she! They were going to burn her, huh!"

"They would have to drive a stake through her heart to make it legal," Lloyd said.

"She is not a witch, she is a good woman," I answered. I barely heard myself speak. Out of the corner of one eye I saw Samuel sitting on the seesaws.

"You calling me a liar!" Ernie shouted in my face. His saliva was hot and bitter. Someone said he only drank goat's milk because he was allergic to cow's milk.

"Yes!" I shouted in his face. I had felt like running away, but I remembered my father and Narciso standing firm for Ultima. I saw Ernie's eyes narrow and felt the vacuum created as everyone held his breath. Then Ernie's arms snapped out and the football he was holding hit me full on my face. I instinctively struck out and felt my fist land on his chin.

"Fight! Fight!" Horse shouted and jumped on me. I opened my watering eyes as I went down and saw Bones pile on top of Ernie. After that, it was a free-for-all. Everyone jumped into the swirling, thrashing pile. Curses and grunts and groans filled the air briefly, then a couple of the junior high teachers reached into the pile and pulled us out, one by one. No one was hurt and it was the first day of school, so they did not report us to the principal. They only laughed at us, and we laughed along with them. The bell rang and we ran to begin another year of school.

No one teased me about Ultima after that. If I had been willing to take on Ernie I guess they figured that I would fight anybody. It wasn't worth it. And besides, behind the force that Red and Samuel would lend me in a fight lay the powerful, unknown magic of Ultima.

The pleasant autumn days were all too quickly eroded by the winds of time. School settled into routine. As the cold settled over the llano and there was less to do on the farms and ranches, more and more of those kids came into school. The green of the river passed through a bright orange and turned brown. The trickle of water in the river bed was quiet, not singing as in the summer. The afternoons were gray and quiet, charged with the air of ripeness and belonging. There was a safe, secure welcome in opening the kitchen door and being greeted by the warm aroma of cooking, and my mother and Ultima.

Just before Christmas the snows and winds of the llano locked the land in an icy grip. After school the playgrounds were quickly deserted, and if you had to stay after school it was eerie and lonely to walk alone through the deserted streets. Snows alternated with the wind of the llano, the coldest wind of the world. The snows would melt then the wind would freeze the water into ice. Then the snows would come again. The river was completely frozen over. The great trees that lined the banks looked like giant snowmen huddling together for warmth. On the llano the cattlemen struggled to feed their herds. Many animals were lost, and the talk was always about the terrible cold of this winter that competed with other years lost in the memories of the old people.

The entire school looked forward eagerly to Christmas vacation. The two weeks would be a welcome relief from trudging back and forth to school. The last thing we looked forward to doing in school was the presentation of the play we had done in Miss Violet's room. Actually the girls had done the work, but we all took credit for it.

No one had expected the blizzard that blew in the night before we were to give our play. "¡Madre mía!" I heard my mother cry. I looked over frosty, frozen blankets and saw my small window entirely covered with ice. With the cold hugging me like death I dressed and ran steaming into the warm kitchen. "Look!" my mother said. She had cleaned a small spot on the icy window. I looked out and saw a white countryside, desolate except where ripples of blue broke the snowdrifts.

"The girls will not go to school today," she said to Ultima, "what's one day. Deborah, Theresa!" she called up the stairs, "stay in bed! The snow has covered the goat path!"

I heard squeals and giggles from upstairs.

"Will Tony go?" Andrew asked, walking to the stove and shivering, dressed to do battle with the snow drifts.

"I have to go," I answered, "the play is today—"

"It is not good," Ultima whispered. She did not mean the play, she meant something in the weather because I saw her raise her head slightly as if to sniff the scent of the wind outside.

"It's only one day, Tony," Andrew said, coming to sit at the breakfast table.

"It is good for him," my mother said. She served us bowls of steaming atole and hot tortillas. "If he is to be a priest, he should learn early about sacrifice—"

Andrew looked at me and I at him, but we didn't speak. Instead Andrew asked, "How about work at the highway? Has it opened up?"

"Ay no," my mother said, "the ground is frozen. Your father has been home two weeks—only the salt trucks are out."

"What's the play about, Tony?" Andrew asked.

"Christ," I said.

"What part do you play?"

"A shepherd."

"You think you should go to school?" he inquired. I knew he was concerned because the snow was so deep.

"Yes," I nodded.

"How about you, Andrés?" my mother asked, "I thought today was your day off at the store—"

"It is," Andrew answered, "just going to pick up my check."

"And see your girl," my mother smiled.

"No girl," Andrew frowned. "Come on, Tony," he rose and put on his jacket, "let's get going."

My mother tucked me into my jacket and put my wool cap on my head. "My man of learning," she smiled and kissed my forehead. "Que dios te bendiga."

"Gracias," I said. "Adiós, Ultima." I went to her and gave her my hand.

"Take care of the evil in the wind," she whispered and bent low to kiss my cheek. "Sí," I answered. I put my hand to my chest where I wore her scapular and she nodded.

"Come on!" Andrew called from the door. I ran after him and followed him down the goat path, trying to step in his footsteps where he broke the snow. The early morning sun was shining and everything was bright. It hurt my eyes to see so much whiteness. "Perhaps the blizzard will lift now . . ." Andrew puffed ahead of me. In the west the clouds were still dark, but I said nothing. It was slow walking through the thick snow, and by the time we got to the bridge our feet were wet, but it was not cold.

"There's the Kid." It was the first time I had ever seen the Kid standing still. He and Samuel had caught sight of us and were waiting.

"Race!" the Kid called as we came up.

"Not today," Andrew answered, "you're liable to break your neck on that ice." He nodded and we looked down the ice-covered sidewalk of the bridge. Cars had splashed ice water onto the sidewalk and overnight it had frozen solid. We had to pick our way carefully across the bridge. Still the Kid did not trust us. He walked just ahead of us, backwards, so that he could see us at all times.

"Did you hear about the fight last night?" Samuel asked. He walked quietly beside us. Our breath made plumes in the crisp, raw air. Down in the river the water, bushes, trees, everything was covered with ice. The sun from the east sparkled on everything and created a frozen fairyland.

"No," Andrew said. "Who?"

"Tenorio and Narciso—"

I listened carefully. I still remembered Tenorio's threat.

"Where?"

"At the Longhorn."

"Drunk?"

"Drinking—"

"Who told you?"

"My father was there. My father was drinking with Narciso," Samuel said, "then Tenorio came in from El Puerto. Tenorio was cursing la Grande, Ultima. Then he cursed Narciso in front of the men. But it wasn't until he cursed all of the people of Las Pasturas that Narciso got up and pulled that funny little beard that grows on Tenorio's face—"

"Ha!" Andrew laughed. "Serves that old bastard right!"

Samuel continued, "My father says it will not end at that—"

We reached the end of the bridge and the Kid jumped across. He had won the walking race.

"Where will it end?" I asked Samuel.

"It will only end when blood is spilled," Samuel said. "My father says that the blood of a man thickens with the desire for revenge, and if a man is to be complete again then he must let some of that thick blood flow—"

We stopped and it was very quiet. One car started across the bridge. It moved very slowly, its tires slipping on the ice. Up ahead a few of the gas station owners could be seen sweeping snow from their driveways. Everyone was hoping the blizzard had lifted. Everyone was sick of the cold.

"They are drunks with nothing better to do than argue like old women," Andrew laughed. "Perhaps your father would be right if he were talking of men."

"Drunks and devils are also men," Samuel countered.

"Ah!" Andrew puffed white steam, "you guys run on to school. See you tonight, Tony."

"See you," I waved. The Kid had already bolted away. I ran to keep up with Samuel.

The school house was quiet, like a tomb frozen over by winter. The buses didn't come in because of the blizzard, and even most of the town kids stayed home. But Horse and Bones and the rest of the gang from Los Jaros were there. They were the dumbest kids in school, but they never missed a single day. Hell could freeze over but they would still come marching across the tracks, wrestling, kicking at each other, stomping into the classrooms where they fidgeted nervously all day and made things miserable for their teachers.

"Where are the girls?" Bones sniffed the wind wildly and plunked into a frozen desk.

"They didn't come," I answered.

"Why?" " ¡Chingada!" "What about the play?"

"I don't know," I said and pointed to the hall where Miss Violet conferred with the other teachers who had come to school. They all wore their sweaters and shivered. Downstairs the furnace groaned and made the steam radiators ping, but it was still cold.

"No play, shit!" Abel moaned.

Miss Violet came in. "What did you say, Abel?"

"No play, shucks," Abel said.

"We can still have a play," Miss Violet sat down and we gathered around her, "if the boys play the parts—"

We all looked at each other. The girls had set up all the stuff in the auditorium; and they had, with Miss Violet's help, composed the story about the three wise men. Originally we just stood around and acted like shepherds, but now we would have to do everything because the girls stayed home.

"Yeahhhhhh!" Horse breathed on Miss Violet.

"The other teachers don't have much to do, with so many kids absent," she turned away from the inquisitive Horse, "and they would like to come to our play—"

"Aghhhh Nooooo," Bones growled.

"We have to read all the parts," Lloyd said. He was carefully picking at his nose.

"We could practice all morning," Miss Violet said. She looked at me.

"I think it's a great idea," Red nodded his head vigorously. He always tried to help the teacher.

"¡A la veca!"

"What does that mean?" Miss Violet asked.

"It means okay!"   *bonding, conspiracy*

So the rest of the morning we sat around reading the parts for the play. It was hard because the kids from Los Jaros couldn't read. After lunch we went to the auditorium for one quick practice before the other teachers came in with their classes. Being on stage scared us and some of the boys began to back down. Bones climbed up a stage rope and perched on a beam near the ceiling. He refused to come down and be in the play.

"Boooooooo-enz!" Miss Violet called, "come down!"

Bones snapped down at her like a cornered dog. "The play is for sissies!" he shouted.

Horse threw a chunk of a two-by-four at him and almost clobbered him. The board fell and hit the Kid and knocked him out cold. It was funny because although he turned white and was out, his legs kept going, like he was racing someone across the bridge. Miss Violet worked frantically to revive him. She was very worried.

"Here." Red had gone for water which he splashed on the Kid's face. The Kid groaned and opened his eyes.

"¡Cabrón Caballo!" he cursed.

The rest of us were either putting on the silly robes and towels to make us look like shepherds, or wandering around the stage. Someone tipped the Christ child over and it lost its head.

"There ain't no such thing as virgin birth," Florence said looking down at the decapitated doll. He looked like a madman, with his long legs sticking out beneath the short robe and his head wound in a turban.

"You're all a bunch of sissies!" Bones shouted from above. Horse aimed the two-by-four again but Miss Violet stopped him in time.

"Go put the head on the doll," she said.

"I gotta go to the bathroom," Abel said. He held the front of his pants.

Miss Violet nodded her head slowly, closed her eyes and said, "no."

"You could be sued for not letting him go," Lloyd said in his girlish voice. He was chewing on a Tootsie Roll. Chocolate dripped down the sides of his mouth and made him look evil.

"I could also be tried for murder!" Miss Violet reached for Lloyd, but he ducked and disappeared behind one of the cardboard cows by the manger.

"Come on you guys, let's cooperate!" Red shouted. He had been busy trying to get everyone to stand in their places. We had decided to make everyone stand in one place during the play. It would be easier that way. Only the kings would step forth to the manger and offer their gifts.

"Places! Places!" Miss Violet shouted. "Joseph?" she called and I stepped forward. "Mary? Who is Mary?"

"Horse!" Red answered.

"No! No! No!" Horse cried. We chased him down on the stage and knocked over a lot of the props, but we finally got the beautiful blue robe on him.

"Horse is a virgin!" Bones called.

" ¡Aghhhhh! ¡Cabrón!" Horse started up the rope but we pulled him down.

"Horse! Horse!" Miss Violet tried to subdue him, "it's only for a little while. And no one will know. Here." She put a heavy veil on his head and tied it around his face so that it covered all except his eyes.

" ¡Naggggggh!" Horse screamed. It was awful to hear him cry, like he was in pain.

"I'll give you an A," Miss Violet said in exasperation. That made Horse think. He had never gotten an A in anything in his life.

"An A," he muttered, his large horse jaws working as he weighed the disgrace of his role for the grade. "Okay," he said finally, "okay. But remember, you said an A!"

"I'll be your witness," Lloyd said from behind the cow.

"Horse is a virgin!" Bones sang, and Horse quit the job and we had to persuade him all over again.

"Bones is just jealous," Red convinced him.

"Come down!" Miss Violet yelled at Bones.

"Gimme an A," Bones growled.

"All right," she agreed.

He thought awhile then yelled, "no, gimme two A's!"

"Go to—" She stopped herself and said, "stay up there. But if you fall and break your neck it's not my fault!"

"You could be sued by his family for saying that," Lloyd said. He wiped his mouth and the chocolate spread all over his face.

"I got to pee—" Abel groaned.

"Horse, kneel here." Horse was to kneel by the manger and I stood at his side, with one hand on his shoulder. When I put my arm around his shoulder Horse's lips sputtered and I thought he would bolt. His big horse-eyes looked up at me nervously. One of the cardboard donkeys kept tipping over and hitting Horse, this only served to make him more nervous. Some of the kids were stationed behind the cardboard animals to keep them up, and they giggled and kept looking around the edges at each other. They started a spit-wad game and that really made Miss Violet angry.

"Please behave!" she shouted, "pleeeeeeee-z!" The Vitamin Kid had recovered and was running around the stage. She collared him and made him stand in one spot. "Kings here," she said. I guess someone had put the robe on the Kid when he was knocked out, because otherwise no one could have held him long enough to slip the robe on.

"Does everybody have copies of the play?" Red shouted. "If you have to look at the lines, keep the script hidden so the audience doesn't see—"

"I can seeeeee—" It was Bones. He leaned to look down at Florence's copy of the play and almost fell off the rafter. We all gasped, but he recovered. Then he bragged, "Tarzuuuuuuun, king of the jungle!" And he started calling elephants like Tarzan does in the movie, "Aghhh-uhhhh-uhhhh-uhhhhhhhhhh—"

" ¡Cabrón!" " ¡Chingada!" Everyone was laughing.

"Bones," Miss Violet pleaded. I thought she was going to cry. "Please come down."

"I ain't no sissy!" he snarled.

"You know, I'm going to have to report you to the principal—"

Bones laughed. He had been spanked so many times by the principal that it didn't mean anything anymore. They had become almost like friends, or like enemies that respected each other. Now when Bones was sent in for misbehaving he said the principal just made him sit. Then, Bones said, the principal very slowly lit a cigarette and smoked it, blowing rings of smoke in

Bones' face all the while. Bones liked it. I guess they both got a satisfaction out of it. When the cigarette was gone and its light crushed in the ashtray Bones was excused. Then Bones went back to the room and told the teacher he had really gotten it this time and he promised to be a good boy and not break any rules. But five minutes later he broke a rule, and of course he couldn't help it because they said his brother who worked in the meat market had brought Bones up on raw meat.

"I ain't got page five," Abel cried. His face was red and he looked sick.

"You don't need page five, your lines are on page two," Red told him. He was very good about helping Miss Violet; I only wished I could help more. But the kids wouldn't listen to me because I wasn't big like Red, and besides there I was stuck with my arm around Horse.

"Florence by the light—" Tall angelic Florence moved under the lightbulb that was the star of the east. When the rest of the lights were turned off the lightbulb behind Florence would be the only light. "Watch your head—"

"Everybody ready?" The three wise men were ready, Samuel, Florence, and the Kid. Horse and I were ready. The fellows holding up the cardboard animals were ready, and Red was ready.

"Here they come," Miss Violet whispered. She stepped into the wings.

I glanced up and saw the screaming horde of first graders rushing down the aisle to sit in the front rows. The fourth and fifth graders sat behind them. Their teachers looked at the stage, shook their heads and left, closing the doors behind them. The audience was all ours.

"I got to pee," Abel whispered.

"Shhhhhh," Miss Violet coaxed, "everybody quiet." She hit the light switch and the auditorium darkened. Only the star of the east shone on stage. Miss Violet whispered for Red to begin. He stepped to the center of the stage and began his narration.

"The First Christmas!" he announced loudly. He was a good reader.

"Hey, it's Red!" someone in the audience shouted, and everybody giggled. I'm sure Red blushed, but he went on; he wasn't ashamed of stuff like that.

"I got to—" Abel moaned.

Lloyd began to unwrap another Tootsie Roll and the cow he

was holding teetered. "The cow's moving," someone in the first row whispered. Horse glanced nervously behind me. I was afraid he would run. He was trembling.

"—And they were led by the star of the east—" and here Red pointed to the light bulb. The kids went wild with laughter. "—So they journeyed that cold night until they came to the town of Bethlehem—"

"Abel peed!" Bones called from above. We turned and saw the light of the east reflecting off a golden pool at Abel's feet. Abel looked relieved.

" ¡Ah la veca!" " ¡Puto!"

"How nasty," Lloyd scoffed. He turned and spit a mouthful of chewed-up Tootsie Roll. It landed on Maxie, who was holding up a cardboard donkey behind us.

Maxie got up cleaning himself. The donkey toppled over. " ¡Jodido!" He cursed Lloyd and shoved him. Lloyd fell over his cow.

"You could be sued for that," he threatened from the floor.

"Boys! Boys!" Miss Violet called excitedly from the dark.

I felt Horse's head tossing at the excitement. I clamped my arm down to hold him, and he bit my hand.

" ¡Ay!"

"And there in a manger, they found the babe—" Red turned and nodded for me to speak.

"I am Joseph!" I said as loud as I could, trying to ignore the sting of the horse bite, "and this is the baby's mother—"

"Damn you!" Horse cursed when I said that. He jumped up and let me have a hard fist in the face.

"It's Horse!" the audience squealed. He had dropped his veil, and he stood there trembling, like a trapped animal.

"Horse the virgin!" Bones called.

"Boys, Bowoooo-oizz!" Miss Violet pleaded.

"—AndthethreekingsbroughtgiftstotheChristchild—" Red was reading very fast to try to get through the play, because everything was really falling apart on stage.

The audience wasn't helping either, because they kept shouting, "Is that you, Horse?" or "Is that you, Tony?"

The Kid stepped up with the first gift. "I bring, I bring—" He looked at his script but he couldn't read.

"Incense," I whispered.

"¿Qué?"

"Incense," I repeated. Miss Violet had rearranged Horse's

robe and pushed him back to kneel by me. My eyes were watering from his blow.

"In-sense," the Kid said and he threw the crayon box we were using for incense right into the manger and busted the doll's head again. The round head just rolled out into the center of the stage near where Red stood and he looked down at it with a puzzled expression on his face.

Then the Kid stepped back and slipped on Abel's pee. He tried to get up and run, but that only made it worse. He kept slipping and getting up, and slipping and getting up, and all the while the audience had gone wild with laughter and hysteria.

"Andthesecondwisemanbroughtmyrrh!" Red shouted above the din.

"Meerrrr, merrrrda, ¡mierda!" Bones cried like a monkey.

"I bring myra," Samuel said.

"Myra!" someone in the audience shouted, and all the fifth graders turned to look at a girl named Myra. All of the boys said she sat on her wall at home after school and showed her panties to those that wanted to see.

"Hey, Horse!"

"¡Chingada!" the Horse said, working his teeth nervously. He stood up and I pushed and he knelt again.

The Kid was holding on to Abel, trying to regain his footing, and Abel just stood very straight and said, "I had to."

"And the third wise man brought gold!" Red shouted triumphantly. We were nearing the end.

Florence stepped forward, bowed low and handed an empty cigar box to Horse. "For the virgin," he grinned.

"¡Cabrón!" The Horse jumped up and shoved Florence across the stage, and at the same time a blood-curdling scream filled the air and Bones came sailing through the air and landed on Horse.

"For the verrrrrr-gin!" Bones cried.

Florence must have hit the light bulb as he went back because there was a pop and darkness as the light of the east went out.

"—And that's how it was on the first Christmas!" I heard brave Red call out above the confusion and free-for-all on stage and the howling of the audience. And the bell rang and everybody ran out shouting, "Merry Christmas!" "Merry Christmas!" "¡Chingada!"

In a very few moments the auditorium was quiet. Only Red

and I and Miss Violet remained on the stage. My ears were ringing, like when I stood under the railroad bridge while a train went by overhead. For the first time since we came in it was quiet in the auditorium. Overhead the wind began to blow. The blizzard had not died out.

"What a play," Miss Violet laughed, "my Lord what a play!" She sat on a crate in the middle of the jumbled mess and laughed. Then she looked up at the empty beam and called, "Bones, come down!" Her voice echoed in the lonely auditorium. Red and I stood quietly by her.

"Shall we start putting the things away?" Red finally asked. Miss Violet looked up at us and nodded and smiled. We straightened up the stage as best we could. While we worked we felt the wind of the blizzard increase, and overhead the skylight of the auditorium grew dark with snow.

"I think that's about all we can do," Miss Violet said. "The storm seems to be getting worse—"

We put on our jackets, closed the auditorium door and walked down the big, empty hall. The janitor must have turned off the furnace, because there was no noise.

"This place is like a tomb," Miss Violet shivered.

It was like a tomb; without the kids the schoolhouse was a giant, quiet tomb with the moaning wind crying around its edges. It was strange how everything had been so full of life and funny and in a way sad, and now everything was quiet. Our footsteps echoed in the hall.

I didn't know how bad it was snowing until we reached the door. We looked out and saw a gray sheet of snow. It was falling so thick we could hardly see the street at the far end of the schoolground.

"I've never seen snow like this," Red remarked, "it looks dark—"

It was true, the snow looked dark.

"Will you be able to get home all right, Tony?" Miss Violet asked. She was putting on her gloves.

"Yes," I replied. "You?"

She smiled. "Red will walk with me," she said. Red lived down by the Methodist church and Miss Violet lived just beyond, so they could walk together. Miss Violet was not married and I knew she lived with her mother in a house that had a high brick wall around it.

"Merry Christmas, Tony." She bent down and kissed my cheek. "Take care of yourself—"

"See you, Tony," Red called. I saw them lean and walk into the darkness of the storm.

"Merry Christmas!" I called after them, and in just seconds the two figures disappeared. The snow was so thick that it blurred my sight. I zipped my jacket and pulled it tight around me. I did not want to leave the alcove of the doorway. I did not want to struggle into the storm. I thought of home and my mother and Ultima, and I longed to be there in the warmth. It was not that I was afraid of the storm, I had seen the winter storms of the llano and I knew that if I was careful I would arrive home safely, I guess it was just the darkness of it that made me hesitate. I don't know how long I stood there thinking.

Finally a cold shiver shook me from my thoughts. I leaned into the cold wind and ran towards the street. Once on Main I made my way along the protective sides of the buildings. All of the stores were brightly lighted, but there were few people in the streets. When people did come into view it seemed they were upon me suddenly, then they stumbled on and were lost in the wind-swept snow. Cars moved slowly up and down the street. It was hard to believe that it was only three in the afternoon; it seemed rather like the midnight of a long, dark night.

I turned at Allen's Market and the blast of wind struck me in the face. There was no protection here. I thought of going into the store but I remembered that Andrew hadn't come to work. He was probably home, sleeping safe and warm.

I buried my head in my jacket and edged my way down the sides of the buildings. I was moving carefully, so as not to slip on the ice, when I passed the doors of the Longhorn Saloon. Suddenly the door of the bar crashed open and two giant figures came hurtling out. They bumped against me as they tumbled into the street, and sent me reeling against the wall. From there I watched the most savage fight I had ever seen.

"¡Te voy a matar, cabrón!" one of the men screamed, and I recognized the evil voice of Tenorio. My blood ran cold.

They tumbled into the snow like two drunken bears, kicking and striking at each other, and their cries and curses filled the air.

"¡Jodido!" the heavier man grunted. It was Narciso!

When I recognized Tenorio my first impulse was to run, but now I could not move. I remained frozen against the wall, watching the fearful scene.

"¡Hijo de tu chingada—!"

"¡Pinche—!"

Blood from their battered faces stained the snow. They dropped to their knees clawing for each other's throats. It was only the bartender and the two men who followed him into the street that prevented them from killing each other.

"¡Basta! ¡Basta!" the bartender shouted. He grabbed Narciso and tried to pull him off Tenorio. One of the men helped him while the third one got in front of Tenorio and pushed him back.

"¡Por la madre de Dios!" they pleaded.

"I am going to kill that bastard!" Tenorio screamed.

"You do not have the huevos!" Narciso shouted back, "you are only good for raising putas—"

"¡Ay maldecido!" Tenorio grunted and hurled himself at Narciso. The two came together again, like two rams locking horns, and the bartender and the other two men had to pull with all their strength to pry them loose.

"¡Cabrón! Cuckold of the devil himself, who slept in your bed and left your wife fat with brujas for daughters!" Narciso taunted, and even as the men struggled to separate them his huge arms flew out and landed with dull, sick thuds on Tenorio's face and body.

"No more! No more!" the bartender cried as the three men struggled and grunted to hold the two apart. Finally Tenorio pulled away. His face was dripping with sweat and blood. He had had enough. I thought I would vomit and I wanted to run away, but the frightful scene held me spellbound.

"¡Borracho! ¡Puto!" Tenorio called from his safer distance. When he backed away I thought he would see me leaning against the wall, but the snow was thick and his attention was focused on Narciso.

"Old woman with a hot tail for gossip!" Narciso retorted. Both men stood trembling with rage, but they would not clash again. I think they both realized that a second encounter would mean death to one of them. The three men did not have to hold them anymore.

"It is not gossip that another of my daughters is sick!"

Tenorio shouted, "and she too will die, like the first one! And it is because of the old witch Ultima from Las Pasturas—"

It isn't true I wanted to shout, but my voice stifled in my throat. The wind snapped around us and flung our words away.

"It was your daughters who started the evil!" Narciso retorted, "and if you seek to do evil to la Grande I will cut your heart out!"

"We shall see!" Tenorio sneered and backed away with a parting threatening gesture, "I shall find a way to get to the bruja, and if you get in my way I will kill you!" He stumbled across the wind-swept street to his truck.

"¡Ay que diablo!" Narciso cursed, "he is up to no good!" The other men shrugged and shivered in the cold.

"Ah! Only words. Forget this bad thing before it gets you in trouble with the sheriff. Come and have a drink—" They were relieved the fight was over, and wet and shivering they moved back into the bar.

"That devil is up to evil, I must warn la Grande!" Narciso muttered.

"It is nothing!" the bartender called from the door. "Come in before you freeze out there! I'll buy you a drink!"

Narciso waved them off and the door closed. He stood and watched Tenorio's truck pull away and disappear in the blinding snow. "I must warn la Grande," Narciso repeated, "But in this storm I cannot go to Márez!"

I was trembling from fright but now the nausea left me. I was covered with snow and wet, but my face and forehead felt hot. Like Narciso, I was now concerned with Ultima's safety. I thought that no man in his right mind would take on Narciso's brute strength, but Tenorio had and so he must be desperate because of what was happening to his daughter. I was about to approach Narciso to tell him I was going home and would warn Ultima, but he stumbled off into the snow and I heard him mumble, "I will go to Andrew!"

I thought Andrew was at home but Narciso set off down the street, in the direction of the river. If Andrew was in town, he would be at Allen's store or at the Eight Ball shooting pool. Concerned for Ultima's safety and feverish with the cold, I struggled to keep up with him because in the thick snow a person quickly disappeared from sight. I followed the stumbling figure ahead of me, and between the blasts of wind I could hear him talk to himself about Tenorio's threat and how he would warn Andrew.

He turned on the church road and went towards the bridge and I believed that his intentions were to go to my father's house anyway, but when he came to Rosie's house he paused at the snow-laden gate of the picket fence.

A single red light bulb shone at the porch door. It seemed like a beacon of warmth inviting weary travelers in from the storm. The shades of the windows were drawn but light shone through them, and from somewhere in the house a faint melody seeped out and was lost in the wind.

"Cabronas putas—" Narciso mumbled and walked up the path. The snow quickly covered his footprints.

I did not know why he would pause here while delivering such an important message. I did not know what to do. I had to get home before the storm got any worse, but something held me at the gate of the evil women. Narciso was already pounding at the door and shouting to be let in. Without thinking, I ran up the walk and around the side of the porch. I peered over the porch wall and through the screen.

The door opened and a crack of light illuminated Narciso's face. His face was puffed and bloody from the fight, and the wet snow made the blood run in trickles down his face. He would have frightened anyone, and he did. The woman who opened the door screamed.

"Narciso! What has happened!" she cried.

"Let me in!" Narciso roared and pushed at the door, but it was held by a chain inside and would not budge.

"You are drunk! Or mad! Or both!" the woman shouted. "You know I allow only gentlemen to visit my girls—"

Her face was painted red, and when she smiled at Narciso her teeth were shiny white. Her sweet perfume wafted through the open door, and mixed with the music from within. I could hear laughter inside. Something told me to flee the house of the naked women, and another thought whispered for me to stay and know the awful truth. I felt paralyzed.

"I did not come for pleasure, whore!" Narciso roared, "I have to see Márez! Is he here?"

My ears seemed to explode with a ringing noise. I felt as if I had stood for an hour with the cold wind drumming at exposed nerves. I felt free, as if the wind had picked me up and carried me away. I felt very small and lonely. And in reality the realization of the truth discovered swept over me in a few seconds.

"Which Márez?" I heard the woman cry out, and her laughter was echoed by a burst of laughter from within.

"Don't play games with me, whore!" Narciso shouted, "call Márez!" He reached through the opening and would have grabbed her if she had not jumped back.

"Hokay! Hokay!" I heard her shout. "Andrés! Androoo-ooo!"

I did not want to accept the knowledge of her words, but I did. I think I knew now that I had followed Narciso and that I stood with the wind whipping at my back because I had expected to hear my brother's name called. For a while I had even dreaded that the Márez at the house of the sinful women might be my father, because I remembered the way he and Serrano had whispered jokes about the women here when the bull was humped over the cow.

"Androooooooooo . . ." The wind seemed to taunt me with the name. My brother.

I felt very feverish now. I felt weak and useless. I remembered the day my brothers left for the big city, how they shouted about coming here before they left. And Andrew always lingering here, not telling my mother who his girl was, all seemed to fit. And I remembered my dream, Andrew had said that he would not enter the house of the naked women until I had lost my innocence.

Had I already lost my innocence? How? I had seen Lupito murdered . . . I had seen Ultima's cure . . . I had seen the men come to hang her . . . I had seen the awful fight just now . . . I had seen and reveled in the beauty of the golden carp!

Oh God! my soul groaned and I thought that it would burst and I would die huddled against the evil house. How had I sinned?

"¿Quién? Who? Ah, Narciso, you!" It was Andrew. He threw open the door. "Come in, come in," he motioned. One arm was around a young girl. She was dressed in a flowing robe, a robe so loose it exposed her pink shoulders and the soft cleft of curving breasts.

I did not want to see anymore. I pressed my forehead against the cold wood of the porch wall and closed my eyes. I wanted the cold to draw all the heat out of my tired, wet body and make me well again. The day had been so long, it seemed to stretch back to eternity. I only wanted to be home, where it was safe and warm. I wanted to hate Andrew for being with the bad women, but I could not. I only felt tired, and older.

"No! No!" Narciso resisted the pull. "There is trouble!"

"Where? You're hurt—"

"No matter—not important!" Narciso nodded, "You must get home and warn your parents!"

"What?" Andrew asked in surprise.

"Tell him to go away and close the door," the girl giggled.

"Tenorio! Tenorio, that cursed dog! He is making trouble for la Grande! He has made threats!"

"Oh," Andrew laughed, "is that all. You had me worried for a moment, amigo—"

"Is that all!" Narciso cried, "he has made threats! Even now he might be up to no good! You must get home, I cannot, I am too old, I cannot get there in this storm—"

"Shut the door! It's cold!" the girl whimpered.

"Where is Tenorio?" Andrew asked. I prayed that he would listen to Narciso. I wanted him to leave this evil place and help Ultima. I knew that Narciso was exhausted, and the storm was too much for him. I even doubted that I could get home. My body was numbed and feverish, and the way home was long and hard.

"He drove off in his truck! Just now we fought at the—"

"At the saloon," Andrew finished. "You two have been drinking and quarreling. Now you make a big story out of it—"

"¡Ay Dios! For the sake of your mother please come!" Narciso implored.

"But where?" Andrew answered. "If there is trouble, my father is home. He can take care of things, and Tenorio would not dare to face him again, you know that. Besides, Tenorio has probably crawled into a warm bed by now, to sleep off his drunk!"

The girl giggled. "Come in, Andrew," she pleaded.

"If you won't go, get the sheriff to go!" Narciso cried in exasperation. But it was no use, Andrew simply did not see the urgency of the situation.

"To the sheriff!" he said in disbelief, "and make a fool out of myself!"

"He would throw you both in the drunk tank," the young girl scoffed, "then I would be alone all night, and—" Her voice was sweet with allurement.

Andrew laughed. "That's true, Narciso. But come in. I'll get Rosie to make an exception—"

"¡Ay, pendejo!" Narciso pulled away, "the diablas putas have turned your mind! You do not think with your brains, but with your balls—I tell you, Andrés, you will be lost, like your brothers—" He stumbled away from the door.

"Close the door, Andrew," the girl begged, "only fools and drunks would be out in that storm—"

" ¡Narciso!"

The door banged shut. Narciso stood in the dark. "Fools and drunks and the devil," he mumbled. "So the young buck will sleep with his whore while that devil Tenorio is out plotting evil on his family—there is no one else that will cross the bridge and climb the hill—then I will go. Am I so old that a storm of the llano can frighten me? I will go warn Márez myself, just as I did before—"

I looked over the edge of the porch and saw him fumbling in his pocket. He retrieved a bottle and gurgled down the last draft of sweet wine. He tossed the bottle aside, shrugged his shoulders and walked into the blinding snowstorm. "The llano bred and sustained me," he murmured, "it can bury me—"

I lifted myself up from where I had crouched and followed him. My clothes were wet and ice was beginning to form on the outside as the cold increased. I did not know what time it was nor did I care. I followed Narciso mechanically, weak and disillusioned I tramped after him into the dark twilight of the storm.

I clung to him like his guardian shadow, staying just far enough behind so that he would not see me. I wanted no one to see me, and the storm swirled its eddies of snow around me and obscured me from the world. I had seen evil, and so I carried the evil within me, and the holy sacraments of confession and the holy eucharist were far away. I had somehow lost my innocence and let sin enter into my soul, and the knowledge of God, the saving grace, was far away.

The sins of the town would be washed in the waters of the golden carp . . .

The two lightposts of the bridge were a welcome sight. They signaled the dividing line between the turbulence of the town and its sins and the quiet peace of the hills of the llano. I felt somewhat relieved as we crossed the storm-swept bridge. Beyond was home and safety, the warm arms of my mother, the curing power of Ultima, and the strength of my father. He would not allow Tenorio to intrude upon our quiet hills.

But could he stop the intrusion? The townspeople had killed Lupito at the bridge and desecrated the river. Then Tenorio and his men had come upon the hill with hate in their hearts. My father had tried to keep his land holy and pure, but perhaps it was impossible. Perhaps the llano was like me, as I grew the innocence was gone, and so too the land changed. The people would come to commit murder on it.

My leaden feet turned at the end of the bridge and I felt the pebbles of the goat path beneath the drift of snow. I was very tired, and lightheaded. I was not able to control my thoughts, I walked as if in a dream. But the closer we got to home the more assured I was of Ultima's safety. I did not worry about Narciso getting ahead of me now. I was concerned only with struggling up the slope of the hill. Perhaps if I had been closer to Narciso what happened would not have happened, or perhaps we would both be dead.

I heard a pistol shot just ahead of me. I paused and listened for the report that always follows a shot, but the screaming wind muffled it. Still I was positive it had been a shot and I bolted forward. It was beneath the big juniper that I caught sight of the two figures. As before, I was almost upon them before I knew what was happening. They were locked together in a death-grip, rocking back and forth in their death-dance. They cursed and pounded at each other, and this time there was no one to stop them.

I knew now what Tenorio had done, and I hated myself for not having guessed it, and I hated Andrew for not listening to Narciso. The devil Tenorio had sneaked around while we lingered at Rosie's house, and had waited to ambush Narciso under the juniper tree. I looked for help, but there was none. Their battle would be to the end this time, with only me to witness.

"Ay diablo, you have shot me in cowardly fashion!" Narciso cried in pain and rage.

"You are a dead man, cabrón!" Tenorio shouted back.

They clutched at each other and spun around and around, like two huge animals. Blood was already blackening the snow as the wind buckled the two to the ground.

Under the protection of the juniper they rolled and grunted and cursed. I stood frozen, watching the deadly scene, unable to do anything. Then I heard the second shot. This time it was not muffled by the wind but by the body against which it had been fired. I held my breath as the living man untangled himself from the dead one and stumbled to his feet. It was Tenorio.

They were locked together in a death-grip . . .

"May your soul be damned and go to hell!" Tenorio cursed. His body heaved as he gasped and grunted for breath. Then to add to his curse he spit on the body of Narciso. I heard a low moan as Tenorio aimed his pistol at the head of Narciso. I screamed with fear and Tenorio spun around and saw me. He aimed the pistol at me and I heard the click of the firing pin. But there was no shot.

"You bastard of the witch!" he snarled. He stuffed the pistol into his pocket, turned and fled towards the highway.

For some time I did not move. I could not believe I was alive, I could not believe I was not dreaming a frightful nightmare. Then a moan from the dying man called me and I walked to Narciso and knelt at his side.

It was peaceful under the juniper tree. The snow continued to fall dense and heavy, but the wind was still. The tree's huge, dark branches offered protection, like a confessional. I looked down at the bloodied face of Narciso, and I almost felt relieved of the terrible tension my fevered body had carried for so many hours. He seemed asleep. Snow covered the huge, brown, mustached face. I brushed some of the snow away and his eyelids fluttered.

"Narciso," I heard myself say faintly.

"Hijo—" he murmured.

I slipped my hand under his head and whispered, "are you dead?"

He smiled faintly, his eyelids fluttered open and I saw a glaze on his eyes that I had never seen before. Blood trickled from the corners of his mouth, and when his huge hand moved from his chest I saw that he had been clutching the wound from the bullet. A warm, pulsating stream of blood wet his jacket and the snow. He made the sign of the cross, leaving dabs of blood where he touched his forehead, his chest, and the sides.

"Muchacho," his hoarse voice whispered, "I need confession—I am dying—"

I shook my head in desperation. There would be no time to go for the priest. I couldn't, I couldn't make it back across the bridge, back to town, to the church. My cheeks did not feel the warm, salty tears that began flowing down and splattering on his bloodied face.

"I am not a priest," I said. I felt his body jerk and stiffen. He was dying.

"Ultima—" His voice was very faint, dying.

"There is not time," I whispered.

"Then pray for me," he said weakly and closed his eyes, "you are pure of heart—"

I knew what I had to pray. I had to pray an Act of Contrition for his departing soul. Like I prayed for Lupito. But I had not held Lupito while his body went cold. I had not bloodied my hands with his life's blood. I looked at the wound on the chest and saw the blood stop flowing; rage and protest filled me. I wanted to cry out into the storm that it was not fair that Narciso die for doing good, that it was not fair for a mere boy to be at the dying of a man.

"Confess me—"

I placed my ear to his mouth and heard his mumbled confession. I felt the tears running now, flooding my eyes and blinding me, flowing into the corners of my mouth, and I felt great sobs choking at my throat, trying to get loose.

"Thank you, father, I will sin no more—"

I prayed, "Oh my God, I am sorry for all of my sins, not because I dread the fires of Hell, but because they displease you, Lord, Who art all good, and deserving of all my love—and with Thy help, I will sin no more—"

Then I made the sign of the cross over him.

"It is good to die on a hill of the llano, beneath the juniper—" were his last words. I felt his last intake of air, and the moan as he breathed for the last time. I slipped my hand from under his head, then the sobs came. I knelt by his side for a long time, crying, thinking of all that had happened.

And when the crying had cleansed my soul of the great weight of pity, I got up and ran home. I felt very weak and sick by the time I burst into my mother's kitchen.

"¡Antonio!" my mother cried. I rushed into her warm arms and was safe. "Ay, Jesús, María y José—"

"Where have you been?" I heard my father ask from his chair.

"School's been out a long time—" It was Deborah teasing.

I think I started laughing, or crying, because my mother looked at me strangely and felt my forehead. "Your clothes are wet, and you have a fever!"

Then I felt Ultima's hand on mine. "¡Sangre!" she whispered. It was the blood of Narciso on my hands. The room and the faces staring at me began to swim, as if I was the center of a dark, rushing whirlpool.

" ¡Dios mío!" my mother cried. "Are you hurt, Tony?"

"I knew those were pistol shots I heard!" my father leaped from his chair and grabbed me by the collar of my jacket. "Are you hurt? What has happened?"

"Narciso!" I blurted out.

"By the juniper—" I thought I heard Ultima say. She knit her brow and seemed to be testing the air for any trace of danger left to us.

"He is dead!" I cried.

"But where?" My father said in disbelief. My mother's eyes fluttered and she stumbled back. Ultima picked me up.

"On the goat path—"

"But how? Did you see it?" He was already reaching for his jacket.

"The boy can speak no more. He must rest," Ultima said.

"Sí," my mother cried anxiously. Together they carried me to her room.

"I will go and see," my father said. I heard the door bang.

"More blankets," Ultima told my mother and she ran to obey. They had taken off my wet, frozen clothes and stuffed me under thick, warm blankets.

"He was coming to warn you," I whispered to Ultima, "Tenorio threatened to kill you, there was a terrible fight, he was coming to warn you—"

"He was a good man," her sad eyes filled with sympathy, "but you must not talk now, my son, you must rest—"

My mother brought the blankets. Ultima rubbed my body with an ointment of Vicks and many of her herbs, then she gave me something cool to drink. She begged me to be still, but the fever compelled me to repeat my awful tale over and over.

"Beneath our juniper, on the goat path, he shot Narciso! I saw all, I gave confession—"

"My son!" my mother cried. I could see in their eyes that they were very worried, and I tried to tell them that I was not sick, that I simply had to tell my story to purge the fever. Over and over I shouted out the scene of the murder. Then the cold spells came and I shivered with a cold that could not be thawed by the warmth of the blankets. Late into the afternoon I alternated between the burning fever and the shivering cold.

Soon I lost track of time. Sometime during the illness I saw the face of the doctor from town, and later I saw Andrew. And always Ultima was near me, caring for every turn I made in the progress of that hideous journey. It was a long night during which the nightmares, like a herd of wild horses, trampled through my fevered mind.

Strange scenes swirled in my ocean of pesadilla, and each one seemed to drown me with its awful power.

I saw Andrew and the young girl from Rosie's. They held each other and danced while Narciso pounded at the cold door. She was naked, and her long, flowing hair enveloped Andrew and kept him from helping Narciso. She pulled Andrew away, and he followed her into the frightful fires of hell.

Androooooooo! I cried. I struggled desperately to help him, but I could not move beneath the heavy blankets.

God forgive him! I screamed. And from the dancing flames there issued a thunderous voice.

I am not a God of forgiveness! the Voice roared.

Hear me! I begged.

I hear no one who has not communed with me! God answered. Your brother has sinned with the whores, and so I condemn him to hell for eternity!

No! I pleaded, hear me and I shall be your priest!

I can have no priest who has golden idols before him, God answered, and the flames roared and consumed everything.

In the cracking, frolicking flames I saw the face of Narciso. His face was bloody, and his eyes dark with death.

Forgive Narciso! I cried to God.

I will, the terrible Voice responded, if you also ask me to forgive Tenorio.

But Tenorio murdered Narciso! Tenorio did evil!

A loud peal of laughter boomed and rang out in the valley of flames. It rolled in clouds of dark smoke like the thunder of the summer thunderstorms.

I will forgive Tenorio, a soft voice called. I turned and saw the forgiving Virgin.

No! No! I cried, it is Narciso that you must forgive! Intercede for him so that he may gain the joys of heaven.

Antonio, she smiled, I forgive all.

You cannot! I persisted in my delirium, you must punish Tenorio for killing Narciso!

And again the laughter rang from the flames. You foolish boy, God roared, don't you see you are caught in your own trap! You would have a God who forgives all, but when it comes to your personal whims you seek punishment for your vengeance. You would have my mother rule my heavens, you would send all sinners to her for forgiveness, but you would also have her taint her hands with the blood of vengeance—

Vengeance is Mine! He shouted, not even your golden carp would give up that power as a god!

Oh, I cried, forgive me Lord! I have sinned, I have sinned exceedingly in thought, word, and deed. My thoughts have trapped me and made me flee from You!

Then the flames parted and I saw the blood of Narciso flow into the river and mix with the blood of Lupito. Many people were drawn by the sweet smell of blood. There was much excitement in the town as the news spread that the blood on the hill was sweet and a curative for all sins.

The mob gathered and chanted, taste but one drop of the blood of la curandera and the key to heaven is assured.

We must have the blood of Ultima! they cried, and they formed a long caravan to cross the bridge and come unto the hill. Like Tenorio and the men who killed Lupito they trampled the once pure pebbles of the goat path.

At the head of the caravan were three men. They were three tortured spirits led by three women who drove them with whips.

Antonio-ooooooo, they called, Antonio-foroooooooos. Help us. We are your brothers who have lost the way—

Their voices cried in the gathering wind.

Oh, help us, our sweet brother, help us. We followed neither the laws of God or of your pagan god, and we paid no heed to the magic of your Ultima. We have sinned in every way. Bless us, brother, bless us and forgive us.

My heart was wrenched at the sight of their flagellation, but I was helpless. I am not a priest, I cried, I too have sinned! I have doubted the Lord!

But you have the blood of the Luna priest, they persisted, but touch our foreheads and we shall be saved!

I held my bloodied hands out to touch them and felt the cloven hooves of hairy animals. I looked up and saw the three Trementina sisters dancing around me.

Hie! Hie! They cried and danced, through your body went the spell that cured Lucas, and your name lent strength to the curse that took one of us from the service of our Master. We will have our vengeance on you, their voices crackled.

They cut my black hair with rusty scissors and mixed the

hair with the blood of bats. This they poured, together with the insides of a toad, into a bowl. They knew the toad was the animal opposed to me in life, and that its touch or even its sight made me sick. They brewed this mixture over their evil fire, and when it was done they drank it.

I saw my body withering away. My mother came and touched my forehead then began her mourning wail. Ultima sat by me, powerless in the face of death. I saw the priest from town come, and he rubbed the holy oil at my feet and prayed. A long, dark night came upon me in which I sought the face of God, but I could not find Him. Even the Virgin and my Saint Anthony would not look at my face. I had died without having taken the Eucharist, and I was cursed. In front of the dark doors of Purgatory my bleached bones were laid to rest.

And the Trementina sisters led the caravan over the path and onto our hill. Before the maddened crowd the she-goats and the he-goats ran in fright. Florence, Red, Ernie, Bones, Horse, and all the rest also tried to flee, but they were captured and put in chains. Even the girls, Rita and Agnes and Lydia and Ida and June, were caught and put in heavy chains of iron. Under the weight of the chains their young faces wrinkled and grew old.

The wicked people burned our castle on the hill. My father and mother and my sisters perished in the flames. They killed the owl and made Ultima powerless, then they beheaded her and drank her blood. When they were bathed in blood they tied her to a post, drove a stake through her heart, and burned her. They went to the river and caught the carp that swam there, and brought the fish back and cooked it in the fires of Ultima's ashes. And they ate the flesh of the carp.

Then there was a thundering of the earth, and a great rift opened. The church building crumbled, and the school collapsed into dust, then the whole town disappeared into the chasm. A great cry went up from the people as they saw crashing, tumultuous waters fill the dark hole. The people were afraid.

Do not fear! Do not fear! the Trementinas danced and sang, we are on the holy hill and we are saved. Then the people laughed and continued their feasting on the meat of the carp.

The wind blew dusty now, and the sun turned blood red. The people looked upon each other and they saw their skin rot and fall off. Shrieks of pain and agony filled the air, and the whole countryside cried in mourning as the walking-dead buried their sleeping-dead. A putrid, rotting smell was everywhere. There was disease and filth throughout.

In the end no one was left, and the she-goats and the he-goats returned from the hills whence they had fled, and they looked in innocence at the death camp of the people. The wind ceased its lapping of stagnant water against the shores of the lake, and there was quiet. The farmers from El Puerto, my uncles, came and stirred the ashes, and finding the ashes of my family and Ultima they gathered them and returned to El Puerto to bury them in the holy ground of their fields.

Evening settled over the land and the waters. The stars came out and glittered in the dark sky. In the lake the golden carp appeared. His beautiful body glittered in the moonlight. He had been witness to everything that happened, and he decided that everyone should survive, but in new form. He opened his huge mouth and swallowed everything, everything there was, good and evil. Then he swam into the blue velvet of the night, glittering as he rose towards the stars. The moon smiled on him and guided him, and his golden body burned with such beautiful brilliance that he became a new sun in the heavens. A new sun to shine its good light upon a new earth.

Quince

After the fever broke I was in bed for many days. The doctor told my mother I had had pneumonia and that I was to get as much rest as possible. As I regained my strength I learned what had happened. My father had found the body of Narciso, frozen stiff under the juniper tree. My father went to the sheriff and accused Tenorio, but he had only the word of a small, sick boy to back his accusation. The coroner's jury that gathered under the juniper tree found the cause of death to be accidental or self-inflicted, then they hurried away from the cold to the warmth of their homes. Because Narciso was the town drunk, nobody cared much. My father protested, but there was little he could do, and so Narciso was buried and the town said he had died during one of his drunks.

He was a big and wild man; he drank and cursed like most men do, but he was a good man. He died trying to help an old friend. He had the magic of growth in his hands and he passed it into the earth. Now his house was deserted and his garden withered away, and few people remembered anything good about Narciso.

While I was still in bed, recovering, Andrew stopped by to talk to me. I guess he figured that if he had listened to Narciso that he would still be alive, because the first thing he said was, "I'm sorry about Narciso—"

"Yes," I nodded. I did not tell him that I had seen him at Rosie's house. I had not told anyone, and I never would.

"I'm sorry you saw the murder—" he stammered.

"Why?" I asked. I did not feel comfortable talking to him. I looked at Ultima, who had not left my side since that dreadful night, and I guess she understood because she stood up from where she sat crocheting. Andrew understood that it was a signal to leave.

"I don't know," he said, "you're only a kid—I'm just sorry."

"He must rest," Ultima said kindly.

"Yes," Andrew agreed, "I just wanted to see how he was. How do you feel, Tony?" He was nervous.

"Fine," I answered.

"Good, good," he muttered. "Well, I'll let you rest. I wish there was something I could do—I'm sorry, that's all." He turned and left. After that he brought me candy and fruit from the store, but he gave it to my mother to deliver to me, he never came into the room. He would only wave from the door as he went off to work in the mornings.

Later I asked Ultima, "Did I talk about Andrew when I was in the fever?"

"Your blood is tied to the blood of your brothers," she answered, "and you spoke your dreams and love for them, but you did not reveal Andrew's secret—"

I was glad Ultima understood, and I was glad I had not talked about what I had seen at Rosie's. Like other unpleasant things, I began to blot it from my memory.

So Christmas came and went. We had a small tree and we got clothes for presents, but the most important thing was going to visit the Nativity scene at the church and going to la misa de gallo, midnight mass. I did not go, of course, but when everyone returned I was up and waiting for them and we ate posole. For dessert we ate bizcochitos and hot coffee flavored with sugar and cinnamon. When I could get up I sat with Ultima in her room while she did her embroidery work. She told me stories about the old people of Las Pasturas. She told me about Narciso when he was a young man, a fine vaquero, and very respected. He had married a lovely young girl but before they could raise a family she had died. The diptheria epidemic that had destroyed so many things in Las Pasturas had claimed her.

After that Narciso turned to drink and lost everything, but he remained forever grateful to Ultima who worked so hard to try to save his young wife. The old people, Ultima said, always helped each other; through good or bad they stuck together, and the friendships that were formed in that desolate llano were bonds for life.

Part of the time I had to spend with my mother, reciting my catechism. I already knew most of my prayers by memory. So I would sit with her in the kitchen while she cooked or ironed and she would ask me to recite such and such a prayer and I would. That made her very happy.

"In the spring I will make arrangements for you to start catechism with the padre at the church, and then on Easter Sunday you will make your first holy communion. Just think, Antonio, for the first time you will hold God in your mouth, in your body, in your soul—you will speak to Him, and He will answer—" she said to me. And she smiled, and there were tears in her eyes.

"Then I will have the knowledge of God?" I asked.

"Yes," she sighed. "I hope you will use your knowledge to carry out God's will. You are a very bright boy, you understand so much, you can be a great leader, a priest— I do not want you to waste your life in dreams, like your father. You must make something of yourself, you must serve the people. The people need good leaders, and the greatest leader is a priest—"

"Yes," I agreed.

"And then in the summer," she continued, "you will go and stay with your uncles at El Puerto. You will learn their ways, old secret ways in farming, they will teach you. It will be good for you to be out in the sun, working. You have been sick, and you have seen things I would not have wanted you to see, you are just a boy—but that is in the past. Now you have your communion and the summer to look forward to—"

"Yes," I agreed.

"Now read the prayers to me in English." She liked to hear me read the catechism in English, although she could not understand all I read, and I myself could not yet read with complete comprehension. Many of the old people did not accept the new language and refused to let their children speak it, but my mother believed that if I was to be successful as a priest I should know both languages, and so she encouraged me in both.

"Ah, such intelligence," she beamed when I finished stutter-

ing through the Hail Mary in English, "a true man of learning!"
And she kissed my head and gave me some empanaditas she had
saved from Christmas day.

One thing that helped to break the monotony of being
locked in by the storm was the arrival of León and Eugene.
They had not come for Christmas and my mother was sad and
worried. The only news she had about them was from people
who happened to run into them at Las Vegas. León and Eugene
never bothered writing.

It was early one morning when we were seated at breakfast
that my mother heard a car and looked out the frosty window.
"¡Jesús, María, y José!" she exclaimed, "¡el policía!"

We ran and crowded at the window and watched the state
police car coming up the goat path. The car came slowly because of the deep snow. When it came to a stop León and
Eugene stepped out.

"¡Mis hijos!" my mother cried. She threw open the door
and they came in, grinning shyly as she gathered them in her
arms.

"Hi, jefa," they smiled.

"León, Eugenio," my father embraced them.

"Jefe," they nodded and took his hand.

"Ave María Purísima," my mother cried and made the sign
of the cross.

"Hey, León, Gene," Andrew shook hands with them while
Deborah and Theresa shouted greetings and tugged at them. We
all surrounded them with our embraces.

"But why did the state police bring you?" my mother asked
anxiously.

"Was it Vigil?" Andrew asked, and León nodded.

"Was there any trouble?" my father asked. He was at the
window, waving at the departing state cop.

"No, no trouble—"

"Greet your Grande," my mother smiled, "and don't call her
a jefa—" We all laughed.

"¿Cómo está, Grande?" they said politely and hugged Ultima.

"Bien, bien, gracias a Dios," Ultima smiled, and knowing
they would be hungry she turned to the stove to make them
breakfast.

"But you haven't told us why the state cop brought you,"
Andrew repeated.

"Tell them, Gene," León smiled.

"I knew you would return," my father murmured, "I knew you would come back!" And he hugged them and led them to the table. He took out the bottle of whiskey while they removed their soiled, wrinkled jackets. They looked older than I remembered them.

"Tell us what?" my mother bustled around them.

"Feed them first, María," Ultima said wisely, she was already setting down plates. León and Gene ate everything set before them like starved animals

"Heard about Narciso—" León said through a mouthful, "too bad—"

"How's Tony?" Gene asked.

"Fine," my mother answered for me, "but you still haven't told us why Vigil brought you. Deborah, take Theresa upstairs and play—" Deborah and Theresa only moved to a corner of the kitchen and stayed to listen.

"Tell 'em, Gene," León said.

"Hell, you tell 'em!" Gene snarled. "It's your fault this happened! You're the one who wanted to come home—" He drank the shot of whiskey my father had poured for him and went off by the stove to brood.

"¡Eugenio! Do not speak that way in front of Grande!" My mother was stern now. Not even the joy of having her sons back could break this rule of respect for the elders.

"What happened?" Andrew pleaded.

"I apologize to Grande," Gene pouted.

"Gene, it's nobody's fault," León said in his slow way, "and what's done is done—"

"But what?" my father implored.

"We wrecked the car—"

"You had a car!" Andrew exclaimed approvingly.

"Had is right!" Gene cut in.

"Yeah, we saved our money, bought a really nice Chevy— last night, on the spur of the moment we decided to take off—"

"You decided!" Gene corrected him.

"Wrecked it, where?" "How?" "Shhhhh! Let him go on!"

"Just this side of Antón Chico," León said unperturbed, "we hit a slick spot, solid ice, and we went down the ditch—"

"But the road was closed last night," my father said, "that stretch of road has been closed every night for a week—"

"But would he listen to that!" Gene exploded.

"I wanted to come home," León said patiently, he understood his brother's mood.

"¡Ay mi hijito!" My mother went to him and hugged him and León just sat there, smiling, his blue eyes watering. "As long as you are safe, who cares about a car. He wanted to come home to see his mother!" she beamed.

"But the car's not too badly damaged?" Andrew asked.

"Burned!" Gene shouted.

"Burned?" Andrew gasped. There was silence.

"We waited a long time in the cold," León was barely audible, "there was no traffic. We burned the blankets, then the seats, the gas, the tires—sometime this morning we fell asleep, huddled against the car, and all of a sudden everything was on fire, burning."

"That's when Vigil found you," my father said.

León nodded. "At least we hadn't frozen to death—"

"Thank God you are home safe," my mother said. She crossed her forehead. "I must give thanks to the Virgin—" She went to the sala to pray before her altar.

"We shouldn't have come," Eugene groaned.

León and Eugene spent the rest of the morning in Andrew's room. I could hear them laughing. They were talking about the great times they had in Vegas. In the afternoon they dressed and went to town, to play pool they said. My father drank the rest of the day so that by suppertime he was quite drunk. But he did not rant and rave; he was quiet and brooding, and we knew that was the worst kind of drunk. He had been happy to see his boys, but the happiness had been short-lived. He too had heard them planning new adventures together, and he knew that come spring when his yearning to move west filled him that there would be no one to go with him.

In the morning my father's disquietude was proven. We were eating a late breakfast when my father came in from feeding the animals. He stamped his feet and went to the stove to drink a cup of coffee. He stared at my brothers while he drank, and his gaze made them uneasy.

"It is colder than hell outside," he said.

"Gabriel! The children—" my mother reprimanded him. "And take off your jacket, it is wet—" The melting snow was dropping on the hot stove. The little water droplets did a crazy, sizzling dance on the hot iron then disappeared.

"I have to go out again," my father answered without taking his eyes off my brothers, "the wind has cut the tie-wire of the windmill. If I don't tie it down the wind will tear down the crazy thing before noon—"

"Ay, if it's not one thing, it's another," my mother moaned.

I went to the window and through a small, round hole in the frosted windowpane I could see the whirling blades of the windmill. The cold wind spun them so fast that the whole housing shook and seemed ready to come crashing down. If the windmill broke it would mean many days without water because the cistern was already dry of summer water, and melting snow would be a hard job. Melting snow meant frozen hands and feet, and the worst part was that it seemed a ton of melted snow only produced a quart of water.

"How was town last night, boys?" my father asked.

They glanced up at him nervously, and Andrew said, "Quiet. The men at the Eight Ball asked for you, send their regards— they were glad to see León and Gene though."

"Ay," my father nodded and sipped his coffee, "glad to see the wandering Márez brothers, huh." His voice was bitter. I guess he knew they would be leaving again, and he couldn't accept it.

"We've been working, father," Gene said.

"Uh-huh," my father nodded. "I was just thinking, we used to work together. Hey!" he smiled, "it wasn't so long ago we built this house, huh. Well you boys did most of it, and I'm proud of it. I would get off work on the highway in the afternoon, and far down the goat path, near the juniper where Narciso died, I could hear the hammering, and no matter how tired I was I would hurry, come and help you. It was a wonderful time, huh, a man working, planning with his sons—"

"Yeah," Andrew said, "sure."

"Yeah," León agreed and nodded.

"Gabriel—" my mother's voice pleaded.

"Ah," he smiled, "just remembering old times, no harm in that is there. And remember the summer I took you to work with me on the highway? I wanted you by my side, I was proud of you—" he laughed and slapped his thigh. "You were so small those air hammers just tossed the three of you around like rag dolls—" Tears streamed from his eyes.

"Yeah, those were great times," León said vigorously. His blue, melancholy eyes lit up. Even Gene nodded his head in agreement.

He looked for the last time at his sons, but they avoided his gaze. Then he went out.

"We remember, father," Andrew smiled. Then they were quiet for a long time as they looked at each other, the sons seeing the father suddenly old, and the father knowing his sons were men and going away.

"Well," he cleared his throat and blew his nose, "I guess those days are gone forever, in the past—" He laid down his cup. "I'll go fix that windmill now," he said.

"But the wind, Gabriel," my mother said with some anxiety.

"It has to be done," he shrugged. The wind was blowing hard and the ladder up to the platform that held the housing would be thick with ice. He looked for the last time at his sons, but they avoided his gaze. Then he went out.

"He should have waited for the wind to die down," Andrew said uneasily.

"Or until it froze over and stopped itself," León added lamely.

"Or until the damned thing broke off," Gene whispered, "there's no sense in risking your neck for a hick-town windmill—"

I went to the window and watched my father work his way up the treacherous ladder. It was slow and dangerous work. He worked his way onto the small platform and avoiding the cranking, spinning blades he grabbed the loose wire. Carefully he pulled it down, tied the loose ends and put the brake on the turning blades. When he came back into the kitchen his hands and face were frozen white and he was dripping with the sweat of exhaustion, but there was a look of satisfaction on his face.

Next day León and Eugene left. This time they took Andrew with them. He quit his job at Allen's Market and dropped his plans for finishing high school and went to Santa Fe with them. My father was not there when they left; the roads were opening up and all the highway crews were working. My mother cried when she kissed her sons goodbye, but she was resigned. I waved goodbye to them with some misgivings. I wondered if I would ever really know my brothers, or would they remain but phantoms of my dreams. And I wondered if the death of Narciso had anything to do with Andrew's decision to go.

Dieciséis

After Christmas I returned to school. I missed walking with
Andrew in the mornings. At first the kids wanted to know
about the murder of Narciso, but I told them nothing and
soon the news was old and they went on to something else. My
life had changed, I thought; I seemed older, and yet the lives of
my schoolmates seemed unchanged. The Kid still raced at the
bridge, Samuel nodded and walked on, Horse and Bones kicked
at each other, and the yellow buses still came in with their loads
of solemn farm kids. And catechism loomed in the future for all
of us.

I talked only once to Cico. He said, "We have lost a friend.
We shall wait until summer to take the news to the golden carp.
He will tell us what to do—" After that I didn't see him much.

I kept, as much as possible, to myself. I even lost touch with
Jasón, which was too bad because I learned later that he would
have understood. Of course, the dreams that I had during my
illness continued to preoccupy me. I could not understand why
Narciso, who did good in trying to help Ultima, had lost his
life; and why Tenorio, who was evil and had taken a life, was
free and unpunished. It didn't seem fair. I thought a great deal
about God and why he let such things happen. When the

weather was warmer I sometimes paused beneath the juniper tree and looked at the stained ground. Then my mind wandered and my thoughts became a living part of me.

Perhaps, I thought, God had not seen the murder take place, and that is why He had not punished Tenorio. Perhaps God was too busy in heaven to worry or care about us.

Sometimes, after school let out in the afternoon, I went alone to church and kneeled and prayed very hard. I asked God to answer my questions, but the only sound was always the whistling of the wind filling the empty space. I turned more and more to praying before the altar of the Virgin, because when I talked to Her I felt as if she listened, like my mother listened. I would look very hard at the red altar candles burning before her feet then I would bow my head and close my eyes and imagine that I saw Her turn to God and tell Him exactly what I had asked.

And the Lord would shake His head and answer, the boy is not yet ready to understand.

Perhaps when I make my communion I will understand, I thought. But to some the answers to their questions had come so soon. My mother had told me the story of the Mexican boy, Diego, who had seen la Virgen de Guadalupe in Mexico. She had appeared to him and spoken to him, and She had given him a sign. She had made the roses grow in a barren, rocky hill, a hill much like ours. And so I dreamed that I too would meet the Virgin. I expected to see her around every corner I turned.

It was during one of these moods of thought that I met Tenorio one afternoon on my way home from school. The blowing wind was full of choking dust and so I walked up the path with my head tucked down. I did not see Tenorio until he shouted into the howling wind. He was standing under the juniper tree at the exact spot where he had murdered Narciso. I was so startled and frightened that I jumped like a wounded rabbit, but he made no move to catch me. He wore a long, black coat and as was his custom, his wide-brimmed hat pulled low. His blind eye was a dark blue pit and the other glared yellow in the dust. He laughed and howled as he looked down at me and I thought he was drunk.

"¡Maldito!" he cursed me, "¡desgraciado!"

"¡Jesús, María y José!" I found the courage to shout back, and I crossed my thumb over my first finger and held it up to ward off his evil, for I truly thought he was the reincarnation of the devil.

"¡Cabroncito! Do you think you can scare me with that? Do you think I am a witch like your grandmother? ¡Bruja! May coyotes disturb her grave—the grave I will send her to," he added. His vicious face twisted with hate. I felt my legs tremble. He took a step towards me and stopped. "My daughter is dying," he moaned, and the wind snapped at his pitiful, animal cry. "My second daughter is dying, and it is because of the witch Ultima. She put the curse on my first daughter, and now she murders the second—but I will find a way," he threatened me with his closed fist, "I will find a way to get to her and destroy her!"

Not even when he killed Narciso had I seen so much hate in Tenorio's evil face. I seemed too small to stand in the way of a man bent upon destruction with such fury, but I remembered that my father had stood up to him, and Narciso had stood up to him, and even Ultima had stood against his evil; and although I was trembling with fright I answered him, "No! I will not let you!"

He took another step towards me then paused. His evil eye grew narrow as he grinned. He glanced suspiciously into the whirling dust around us then said, "I killed the entremetido Narciso! Right here!" He pointed to the ground at his feet. "And the sheriff did not touch me. I will find a way to kill the witch—"

"You are a murderer!" I shouted with defiance. "My father will stop you if you try to harm Ultima, and the owl will scratch out your other eye—"

He crouched as if to pounce on me, but he remained motionless, thinking. I braced to ward off his blow, but it did not come. Instead he straightened up and smiled, as if a thought had crossed his mind, and he said, "ay cabroncito, your curse is that you know too much!" And he turned and disappeared in the swirling dust. His evil laughter trailed after him, until the wind drowned it.

I hurried home, and when I could get Ultima alone I told her what had happened.

"Did he harm you in any way?" she asked when I was through relating the encounter.

"No," I assured her.

"Did he touch you, even in the slightest manner?"

"No," I replied.

"He didn't leave anything by the tree, anything you might have touched, or picked up?" she asked.

"Nothing," I answered, "but he threatened you. He said he was seeking a way to kill you like he did Narciso—"

"Ay," she smiled and put her arms around me, "do not worry about Tenorio's threats, he has no manly strength to carry them out. He murdered Narciso because he ambushed him in cold blood, but he will not find me so easy to ambush— He is like an old wolf who drags around the ground where he has made his kill, his conscience will not let him rest. He returned to the tree where he committed his mortal sin to find some absolution for his crime. But where there is no acknowledgement of guilt and penance done for the wrong, there can be no forgiveness—"

I understood what she said and so I went away somewhat comforted in the knowledge that at least Ultima did not fear Tenorio's plotting. But often at night I awoke from nightmares in which I saw Tenorio shooting Ultima as he had shot Narciso. Then I felt relief only after I crept down the stairs and went to her door to listen, to see if she was safe. She seemed never to sleep because if I listened long enough I could hear a swishing sound and then a humming as she worked with her herbs. I had been close to Ultima since she came to stay with us, but I was never closer or more appreciative of her good than those weeks when I was sick and she cared for me.

Diecisiete

Aleluya! Aleluya! Aleluya!

The Holy Mother Church took us under her wings and instructed us in Her ways. By the end of March we were well on our way with our catechism lessons. There was no more exciting experience than to be on the road to communion with God! School work grew monotonous beside it. Every afternoon when the school bell rang we ran across the schoolgrounds and over dusty streets and alleys to the church. There father Byrnes waited for us, waited to instruct us in the mysteries of God.

The spring dust storms of the llano continued and I heard many grown-ups blame the harsh winter and the sandstorms of spring on the new bomb that had been made to end the war. "The atomic bomb," they whispered, "a ball of white heat beyond the imagination, beyond hell—" And they pointed south, beyond the green valley of El Puerto. "Man was not made to know so much," the old ladies cried in hushed, hoarse voices, "they compete with God, they disturb the seasons, they seek to know more than God Himself. In the end, that knowledge they seek will destroy us all—" And with bent backs they pulled black shawls around their humped shoulders and walked into the howling winds.

"What does God know?" the priest asked.

"God knows everything," Agnes answered.

I sat on the hard, wooden pew and shivered. God knows everything. Man tries to know and his knowledge will kill us all. I want to know. I want to know the mysteries of God. I want to take God into my body and have Him answer my questions. Why was Narciso killed? Why does evil go unpunished? Why does He allow evil to exist? I wondered if the knowledge I sought would destroy me. But it couldn't, it was God's knowledge—

Did we ask too much when we asked to share His knowledge?

"Papá," I asked, "the people say *the bomb* causes the winds to blow—" We were hauling the piles of manure we had cleaned out of the animal pens during the winter and dumping it on the garden plot. My father laughed.

"That is nonsense," he said.

"But why are the storms so strong, and full of dust?" I asked.

"It is the way of the llano," he said, "and the wind is the voice of the llano. It speaks to us, it tells us something is not right." He straightened from his labor and looked across the rolling hills. He listened, and I listened, and I could almost hear the wind speak to me.

"The wind says the llano gave us good weather, it gave us mild winters and rain in the summer to make the grass grow tall. The vaqueros rode out and saw their flocks multiply; the herds of sheep and cattle grew. Everyone was happy, ah," he whispered, "the llano can be the most beautiful place in the world— but it can also be the cruelest. It changes, like a woman changes. The rich rancheros sucked the earth dry with their deep wells, and so the heavy snows had to come to replenish the water in the earth. The greedy men overgrazed their ranches, and so now the wind picks up the barren soil and throws it in their faces. You have used me too much, the wind says for the earth, you have sucked me dry and stripped me bare—"

He paused and looked down at me. I guess for a while he had forgotten he was talking to me, and he was repeating to himself the message in the wind. He smiled and said, "a wise man listens to the voice of the earth, Antonio. He listens because the weather the winds bring will be his salvation or his destruction. Like a young tree bends with the wind, so a man must bow to the earth— It is only when man grows old and refuses to admit his earth-tie and dependence on mother nature that the powers of mother nature will turn upon him and destroy him, like the strong wind cracks an old, dry tree. It is not manly to blame our mistakes on the bomb, or any other thing. It is we who misuse the earth and must pay for our sins—"

"But what is *sin?*" Florence asked me.

"It is not doing the will of God—" I ducked my head and gritted my teeth on the fine sand the wind carried.

"Is it a sin to do this?" He threw a finger.

"Yes," I answered.

"Why?"

"It's a bad sign—"

"But nothing happens when I throw it." He did it again.

"You will be punished—"

"When?"

"When you die," I said.

"What if I go to confession?"

"Then your sins are forgiven, your soul is clean and you are saved—"

"You mean I can go out and sin, do bad things, throw fingers, say bad words, look through the peep-hole into the girls bathroom, do a million bad things and then when I'm about to die I just go to confession and make communion, and I go to heaven?"

"Yes," I said, "if you're sorry you sinned—"

"Ohhhhh," he laughed, "I'll be sorry! Chingada I will! I can be the worst cabrón in the world, and when I'm ninety-nine I can be sorry for being such a culo, and I go to heaven— You know, it doesn't seem fair—"

No, it didn't seem fair, but it could happen. This was another question for which I wanted an answer to. I was thinking about how it could be answered when I heard a blasting goat cry behind me.

"WHAGGGGGGGGGGGHH. . . . ."

I ducked, but too late. Horse's strong arms went around my neck and his momentum made us slide ten feet. Half of my face scraped along the thorn covered ground and came up covered with little bull-headed diablitos.

"Hey, Tony, you missed the fight!" Horse smiled into my face. He still held me in a tight embrace. His horse-eyes were wild with excitement and his big, yellow teeth chomped on something that smelled like spoiled eggs. I wanted to curse him, but I glanced up and saw Florence standing, waiting for my response.

"That was a real good tackle, Horse," I said as calmly as possible, "real good. Now let me up." I stood up and began pulling thorns out of my bloody cheek.

"What fight?" Florence asked. He dusted my jacket.

"Roque and Willie, down in the bathroom!" Lloyd came puffing along with the rest of the gang.

"¡Chingada! You know how Roque's always teasing Willie—"

"Yeah," we nodded.

"Willie's your friend ain't he?" Ernie asked.

"Yes," I answered. Big Willie was one of the farm boys from Delia. He and George were always together, they never messed around with anyone. Willie was big but Roque picked on him because Willie never defended himself. He was timid, and Roque was a bully.

"Roque's always singing: Willie Willie two-by-four, can't get into the bathroom door so he does it on the floor—" Bones panted.

"And he always pushes you when you're peeing and makes you wet your pants," Lloyd closed his eyes in disgust. He took out a Hershey bar.

"Halfers!" Bones growled. Lloyd threw a piece of chocolate on the ground and while Bones retrieved it he stuck the rest in his mouth.

"¡Chingada!"

"That wasn't halfers!" Bones growled, chewing on chocolate and sand.

"I had my fingers crossed," Lloyd said haughtily. Then he stuck out his tongue and the chocolate mess in his mouth dripped.

"Ughhhhhhh!" Bones went wild, leaped on Lloyd and began strangling him. Then Horse got excited again and jumped on Bones.

"You could be sued for that—" Lloyd threatened as he pulled himself free from the pile. We continued walking and left Bones and Horse behind, slugging and kicking at each other.

"So why the fight?" Florence asked impatiently.

"Well, after school," Lloyd said, "Roque went in and pushed Willie, but Willie must have been waiting, because he stepped aside and Roque almost fell in the bowl, anyway Willie continued peeing, and he peed all over Roque's shoes—"

"It was funny as hell," Ernie said, "seeing Roque standing there, and Willie peeing on his shoes—"

Horse and Bones caught up to us.

"And then old Roque slugs Willie—" Lloyd laughed.

"But Willie just stands there," Ernie added.

"And then Willie busts Roque!" Horse cried out.

"And there's blood all over the place!" Bones panted, and the thought of blood got them going all over again. Horse whinnied and reared up and Bones was on him like a mad dog.

"Roque was bleeding like a pig, and crying, and his shoes all wet—"

"Man, don't mess with Willie," Ernie cautioned. "Hey, he's your friend, ain't he Tony?" he repeated.

"Yeah," I answered. I knew Ernie always weighed friendships. If Willie had lost the fight Ernie would be bothering me about it, but as it was I had somehow gained respect because I was the friend of a farm boy who made Roque's nose bloody.

"Hey! How come those guys don't have to go to catechism?" Abel asked.

"They'd miss the bus, stupid," Florence said.

"Protestants don't have to go either," Ernie nodded.

"They go to hell!" Bones cried out.

"No they don't," Florence defended the Protestants, "Red's a Protestant, do you think he'll go to hell?"

"You'll go to hell too, Florence!" Horse shouted, "you don't believe in God!"

"So what," Florence shrugged, "if you don't believe in God then there is no hell to go to—"

"But why do you go to catechism?" I asked him.

He shrugged. "I wanna be with you guys. I just don't want to feel left out," he said softly.

"Come on! Let's go tease the girls!" Bones shouted. He had caught scent of the girls who were just up ahead. The others rallied to his cry and they went off howling like a pack of wild dogs.

"But what if you're left out of heaven in the end?" I asked Florence. We had both hung back.

"Then that would be hell," he nodded. "I think if there is a hell it's just a place where you're left all alone, with nobody around you. Man, when you're alone you don't have to burn,

just being by yourself for all of time would be the worst punishment the Old Man could give you—"

"The Old Man?" I asked, my question intermingled with a
feeling of sadness for Florence.

"God," he answered.

"I thought you didn't believe—"

"I don't."

"Why?" I asked.

"I don't know," he kicked at a rock. "My mother died when
I was three, my old man drank himself to death, and," he
paused and looked towards the church which already loomed
ahead of us. His inquiring, angelic face smiled. "And my sisters
are whores, working at Rosie's place—"

The wind swirled around us and made a strange noise, like
the sound of doves crying at the river. I wondered if Andrew
had known one of Florence's sisters when he went to Rosie's.
That and the pity I had for him made me feel close to Florence.

"So I ask myself," he continued, "how can God let this
happen to a kid. I never asked to be born. But he gives me birth,
a soul, and puts me here to punish me. Why? What did I ever do
to Him to deserve this, huh?"

For a moment I couldn't answer. The questions Florence
had posed were the same questions I wanted answered. Why was
the murder of Narciso allowed? Why was evil allowed?

"Maybe it's like the priest said," I finally stammered, "maybe God puts obstacles in front of us so that we will have to
overcome them. And if we overcome all the hard and bad
things, then we will be good Catholics, and earn the right to be
with Him in heaven—"

Florence shook his head. "I thought about that," he said,
"but the way I figured it, if God is really as smart as the priest
says, then he wouldn't have needed any of that testing us to see
if we're good Catholics. Look, how do you test a three-year-old
kid who doesn't know anything. God is supposed to know
everything, all right, then why didn't he make this earth without bad or evil things in it? Why didn't he make us so that we
would always be kind to each other? He could of made it so
that it was always summer, and there's always apples in the
trees, and the water at the Blue Lake is always clean and warm
for swimming—instead He made it so that some of us get polio
when we go swimming and we're crippled for life! Is that
right?"

"I don't know," I shook my head, and I didn't. "Once everything was all right; in the Garden of Eden there was no sin and man was happy, but we sinned—"

"Bullshit we sinned," Florence disagreed, "old Eve sinned! But why should we have to suffer because she broke the rules, huh?"

"But it wasn't just breaking the rules," I countered, I guess because I was still trying to hold on to God. I didn't want to give Him up like Florence had. I did not think that I could live without God.

"What was it?" he asked.

"They wanted to be like Him! Don't you remember the priest saying the apple contained the knowledge that would make them know more things, like God they would know about good and about evil. He punished them because they wanted knowledge—"

Florence smiled. "That still doesn't seem right, does it? Why should knowledge hurt anyone? We go to school to learn, we even go to catechism to learn—"

"Yes," I answered. There seemed to be so many pitfalls in the questions we asked. I wanted answers to the questions, but would the knowledge of the answers make me share in the original sin of Adam and Eve?

"And if we didn't have any knowledge?" I asked.

"Then we would be like the dumb animals of the fields," Florence replied.

Animals, I thought. Were the fish of the golden carp happier than we were? Was the golden carp a better God?

"—last year Maxie got polio," Florence was going on, "and my cousin got dragged by that damned horse and got his skull busted. They found him two weeks later, along the river, half eaten away by the crows and buzzards. And his mom went crazy. Is that right?"

"No," I answered, "it's not right—"

We came out of the dusty alley and onto the wind-swept barren grounds that surrounded the church. The massive brown structure rose into the dusty sky and held the cross of Christ for all to see. I had listened to Florence's heresy, but the God of the church had not hurled his thunder at me. I wanted to call out that I was not afraid.

"My father says the weather comes in cycles," I said instead, "there are years of good weather, and there are years of bad weather—"

"I don't understand?" Florence said.

Perhaps I didn't either, but my mind was seeking answers to Florence's questions. "Maybe God comes in cycles, like the weather," I answered. "Maybe there are times when God is with us, and times when he is not. Maybe it is like that now. God is hidden. He will be gone for many years, maybe centuries—" I talked rapidly, excited about the possibilities my mind seemed to be reaching.

"But we cannot change the weather," Florence said, "and we cannot ask God to return—"

"No," I nodded, "but what if there were different gods to rule in his absence?" Florence could not have been more surprised by what I said than I. I grabbed him by the collar and shouted, "What if the Virgin Mary or the Golden Carp ruled instead of—!"

In that moment of blasphemy the wind swirled around me and drowned my words, and the heavens trembled with thunder. I gasped and looked up at the bell tower.

"DAH-NNNNNGGGGGgggggg . . ." The first clap of bell-thunder split the air. I turned and cringed at its sound. I crossed my forehead, and cried "Forgive me, Lord!" Then the second loud ring sounded.

"Come on, Tony," Florence pulled me, "we'll be late—"

We ran up the steps past Horse and Bones who were swinging like monkeys on the bell ropes. We hurried to get in line but Father Byrnes had seen us. He grabbed Florence and pulled him out of line, and he whispered to me, "I would not have expected you to be late, Tony. I will excuse you this time, but take care of your company, for the Devil has many ways to mislead."

I glanced back at Florence but he nodded that I go on. The line moved past the water fonts where we wet our fingers and genuflected as we made the sign of the cross. The water was icy. The church was cold and musty. We marched down the aisle to the front pews. The girls' line filed into the right pew and the boys' went to the left.

"Enough," the father's voice echoed in the lonely church, and the bells that called us were silent. Horse and Bones came running to join us. Then the father came. I took a chance and glanced back. Florence's punishment for being late was to stand in the middle of the aisle with his arms outspread. He stood very straight and quiet, almost smiling. The afternoon sun poured in through one of the stained glass windows that lined the walls and the golden hue made Florence look like an angel. I felt sorry for him, and I felt bad that he had been punished while I had been excused.

"Let us pray," Father Byrnes said and knelt. We followed suit, kneeling on the rough, splintery knee boards of the pew. Only Florence remained standing, holding the weight of his arms which would become numb like lead before catechism was over.

"Padre nuestro que estás en los cielos—" I prayed to myself, sharing my prayers with no one. Everyone else prayed in English.

Down the row I heard Bones faking it. "Buzz, buzz, buzz," his mouth moved to the words, but he didn't know them. His head was bowed, his eyes closed, and he looked so devout that no one could doubt his sincerity.

Then the priest quizzed us on some lessons we had already been through.

"Who made you?" he asked.

"God made me," we answered in unison.

"Why did God make you?" he asked, and I saw him look down the aisle at Florence.

"God made us to love, honor, serve and obey Him."

"Where is God?"

"God is everywhere."

"At Rosie's," Bones whispered and rolled his eyes.

Father Byrnes didn't hear him. "How many persons are there in one God?" he continued.

"Three. The Father, the Son, and the Holy Ghost."

"They have to squeeze in tight," Horse grinned with his ugly horse teeth, and he took the white stuff he had been picking from them and wiped it on his pants.

"The ghost," Bones said secretly, "the holy ghoooooo-st."

Father Byrnes went on to discuss the difference between mortal and venial sins. His explanation was very simple, and in a way frightful. Venial sins were small sins, like saying bad words or not going to the Stations of the Cross during Lent. If you died with a venial sin on your soul you could not enter heaven until the sin was absolved by prayers or rosaries or masses from your family on earth. But if you died with a mortal sin on your soul you could never enter heaven. Never. It was frightening to think of missing mass on Sunday, then dying, and for that one mortal sin to go to hell forever.

"If you die with a venial sin on your soul, where do you go?" he asked.

"To Purgatory," Rita answered. The girls always knew the exact answers. I knew most of the answers but I never raised my hand, because I often wanted to ask questions and I knew it would displease father if I did. Really, the only one who ever asked any questions was Florence, and today he was doing penance.

"That's right, Rita," he smiled. "And what is Purgatory?"

"Purga," Abel whispered. The boys giggled.

"I know! I know!" Agnes waved enthusiastically and father smiled. "It's a place where souls are cleaned so they can go to heaven!"

"And if you die with a mortal sin on your soul?" he asked, and his voice was cold. The church seemed to shudder from a blast of wind outside, and when it settled a side door opened and an old lady dressed in black hobbled up the side aisle to the altar of the Virgin. She lighted one of the candles in a red glass and then she knelt to pray.

"Hell!" Ida gasped, sucking in her breath.

The father nodded. "And is there any escape from hell?" he raised his finger. We nodded no in silence. "No!" he shouted and slapped his hands so we all jumped in our seats. "There is no hope in hell! Hell is the place of eternal damnation! The fires of hell burn forever and ever—"

"Forever and ever," Agnes said thoughtfully.

"For eternity!" Father Byrnes said emphatically. He reached under his frock and pulled out a tattered, well-worn copy of the catechism book. He hardly ever used it because he knew it by heart, but now he fumbled through and pointed. "Look there on page seventeen. Eternity. What does the word eternity mean?"

We turned to page seventeen. "Forever," Agnes said.

"Without end," Rita shuddered.

"About twenty years," Bones growled. He hadn't raised his hand and he made everyone laugh so he had to go up to Father Byrnes and hold out his hands, palms up. Father Byrnes took the flat board he kept for such occasions and laid into Bones. One swat of the board was enough to blister the palms, but Bones didn't seem to feel it. He nodded happily and said "thank you father," then came back to sit down. I saw the old woman at the Virgin's altar turn and nod approvingly when she saw Father Byrnes strike Bones.

"Now I'm going to tell you a story that will teach you how long eternity lasts. Now, keep in mind, this is how long your soul will be burning in hell if you die with the black spots of mortal sins on it. First, try to imagine our whole country is a mountain of sand. A mountain of sand so high that it reaches to the clouds, and so wide that it stretches from one ocean to the other—"

"Gee whiz!" Abel's eyes opened wide. Horse, sensing something he could not understand, began to get nervous. Bones rolled his eyes. We all waited patiently for father's story to develop, because we knew he had a way of telling stories that very clearly illustrated the point he wanted to make. I thought of Florence holding his arms outstretched for eternity.

"Now, suppose across the ocean there is a flat country. The ocean is very wide and it takes weeks to cross it, right. But you want to move this huge mountain of sand from here to there—"

"Get a boat!" Horse nodded nervously.

"No, no, Horse," Father Byrnes groaned, "keep quiet! Listen! Now girls," he turned to them, "how long do you think it would take to move this mountain of sand, all the way across the ocean, until you have the mountain over there and an empty place here?" Several hands went up, but he only smiled and relished his question. "Ah, ah, ah," he grinned, "before you answer, let me tell you how you have to move that enormous mountain of sand. And it's not with a boat like Horse says—" Everyone laughed. "A little bird, a sparrow, is going to move that mountain for you. And the sparrow can only hold one little grain of sand in its beak. It has to pick up only one grain of sand, fly all the way across the wide ocean, put down the grain of sand, then fly all the way back for another grain of sand. It takes the little bird weeks just to fly across the ocean, and each time it carries only one grain of sand—"

"It would never finish," June shook her head sadly. "Just in a bucket of sand there must be a million grains, and to move that would take thousands of years. But to move the whole mountain of sand—" She ended her sentence in despair. Horse whinnied and began to bolt in his pew, and Bones had latched his teeth to the back of the pew and was viciously tearing at it, his eyes rolling wildly all the time and the white froth came foaming from his mouth. Even Abel and Lloyd, and the girls, seemed nervous with the impending conclusion of the story.

"Is that how long eternity is?" Agnes asked bravely, "Is that how long the souls have to burn?"

"No," Father Byrnes said softly and we looked to him for help, but instead he finished by saying, "when the little bird has moved that mountain of sand across the ocean, that is only the first day of eternity!"

We gasped and fell back in our seats, shuddering at the thought of spending eternity in hell. The story made a great impression on us. Nobody moved. The wind whistled around the church, and as the sun sank in the west one penetrating ray of light gathered the colors of the stained glass window and softly laid them, like flowers, around the Virgin's altar. The old woman who had been praying there was gone. In the dark aisle of the church Florence stood, his numbed arms outstretched, unafraid of eternity.

Dieciocho

Ash Wednesday. There is no other day like Ash Wednesday. The proud and the meek, the arrogant and the humble are all made equal on Ash Wednesday. The healthy and the sick, the assured and the sick in spirit, all make their way to church in the gray morning or in the dusty afternoon. They line up silently, eyes downcast, bony fingers counting the beads of the rosary, lips mumbling prayers. All are repentant, all are preparing themselves for the shock of the laying of the ashes on the forehead and the priest's agonizing words, "Thou art dust, and to dust thou shalt return."

The annointment is done, and the priest moves on, only the dull feeling of helplessness remains. The body is not important. It is made of dust; it is made of ashes. It is food for the worms. The winds and the waters dissolve it and scatter it to the four corners of the earth. In the end, what we care most for lasts only a brief lifetime, then there is eternity. Time forever. Millions of worlds are born, evolve, and pass away into nebulous, unmeasured skies; and there is still eternity. Time always. The body becomes dust and trees and exploding fire, it becomes gaseous and disappears, and still there is eternity. Silent, unopposed, brooding, forever . . .

But the soul survives. The soul lives on forever. It is the soul that must be saved, because the soul endures. And so when the burden of being nothing lifts from one's thoughts the idea of the immortality of the soul is like a light in a blinding storm. Dear God! the spirit cries out, my soul will live forever!

And so we hurried to catechism! The trying forty days of Lent lay ahead of us, then the shining goal, Easter Sunday and first holy communion! Very little else mattered in my life. School work was dull and uninspiring compared to the mysteries of religion. Each new question, each new catechism chapter, each new story seemed to open up a thousand facets concerning the salvation of my soul. I saw very little of Ultima, or even of my mother and father. I was concerned with myself. I knew that eternity lasted forever, and a soul because of one mistake could spend that eternity in hell.

The knowledge of this was frightful. I had many dreams in which I saw myself or different people burning in the fires of hell. One person especially continually haunted my nightmares. It was Florence. Inevitably it was he whom I saw burning in the roaring inferno of eternal damnation.

But why? I questioned the hissing fires, Florence knows all the answers!

But he does not accept, the flames lisped back.

"Florence," I begged him that afternoon, "try to answer."

He smiled. "And lie to myself," he answered.

"Don't lie! Just answer!" I shouted with impatience.

"You mean, when the priest asks where is God, I am to say God is everywhere: He is the worms that await the summer heat to eat Narciso, He shares the bed with Tenorio and his evil daughters—"

"Oh, God!" I cried in despair.

Samuel came up and touched me on the shoulder. "Perhaps things would not be so difficult if he believed in the golden carp," he said softly.

"Does Florence know?" I asked.

"This summer he shall know," Samuel answered wisely.

"What's that all about?" Ernie asked.

"Nothing," I said.

"Come on!" Abel shouted, "bell's ringing—"

It was Friday and we ran to attend the ritual of the Stations of the Cross. The weather was beginning to warm up but the winds still blew, and the whistling of the wind and the mournful cou-rouing of the pigeons and the burning incense made the agony of Christ's journey very sad. Father Byrnes stood at the first station and prayed to the bulto on the wall that showed Christ being sentenced by Pilate. Two high-school altar boys accompanied the priest, one to hold the lighted candle and the other to hold the incense burner. The hushed journeyers with Christ answered the priest's prayer. Then there was an interlude of silence while the priest and his attendants moved to the second station, Christ receiving the cross.

Horse sat by me. He was carving his initials into the back of the seat in front of us. Horse never prayed all of the stations, he waited until the priest came near, then he prayed the one he happened to be sitting by. I looked at the wall and saw that today he had picked to sit by the third fall of Christ.

The priest genuflected and prayed at the first fall of Christ. The incense was thick and sweet. Sometimes it made me sick inside and I felt faint. Next Friday would be Good Friday. Lent had gone by fast. There would be no stations on Good Friday, and maybe no catechism. By then we would be ready for confession Saturday and then the receiving of the sacrament on the most holy of days, Easter Sunday.

"What's Immmm-ack-que-let Con-sep-shion?" Abel asked. And Father Byrnes moved to the station where Christ meets his mother. I tried to concentrate. I felt sympathy for the Virgin.

"Immaculate Conception," Lloyd whispered.

"Yeah?"

"The Virgin Mary—"

"But what does it mean?"

"Having babies without—"

"What?"

I tried to shut my ears, I tried to hear the priest, but he was moving away, moving to where Simon helped Christ carry the cross. Dear Lord, I will help.

"I don't know—" Everybody giggled.

"Shhh!" Agnes scowled at us. The girls always prayed with bowed heads throughout the stations.

"A man and a woman, it takes a man and a woman," Florence nodded.

But the Virgin! I panicked, the Virgin Mary was the mother of God! The priest had said she was a mother through a miracle.

The priest finished the station where Veronica wiped the bloodied face of Christ, and he moved to Christ's second fall.

The face of Christ was imprinted on the cloth. Besides the Virgin's blue robe, it was the holiest cloth on earth. The cross was heavy, and when He fell the soldiers whipped Him and struck Him with clubs. The people laughed. His agony began to fill the church and the women moaned their prayers, but the kids would not listen.

"The test is Saturday morning—"

Horse left his carving and looked up. The word "test" made him nervous.

"I, I, I'll pass," he nodded. Bones growled.

"Everybody will pass," I said, trying to be reassuring.

"Florence doesn't believe!" Rita hissed behind us.

"Shhhh! The priest is turning." Father Byrnes was at the back of the church, the seventh station. Now he would come down this side of the aisle for the remaining seven. Christ was speaking to the women.

Maybe that's why they prayed so hard, Christ spoke to them.

In the bell tower the pigeons cou-rouing made a mournful sound.

The priest was by us now. I could smell the incense trapped in his frock, like the fragrance of Ultima's herbs was part of her clothes. I bowed my head. The burning incense was sweet and suffocating; the glowing candle was hypnotizing. Horse had looked at it too long. When the priest moved on Horse leaned on me. His face was white.

"A la chingada," he whispered, "voy a tirar tripas—"

The priest was at the station of the Crucifixion. The hammer blows were falling on the nails that ripped through the flesh. I could almost hear the murmuring of the crowd as they craned their necks to see. But today I could not feel the agony.

"Tony—" Horse was leaning on me and gagging.

I struggled under his weight. People turned to watch me carrying the limp Horse up the aisle. Florence left his seat to help me and together we dragged Horse outside. He threw up on the steps of the church.

"He watched the candle too long," Florence said.

"Yes," I answered.

Horse smiled weakly. He wiped the hot puke from his lips and said, "ah la veca, I'm going to try that again next Friday—"

We managed to get through the final week of catechism lessons. The depression that comes with fasting and strict

penance deepened as Lent drew to its completion. On Good
Friday there was no school. I went to church with my mother
and Ultima. All of the saints' statues in the church were covered
with purple sheaths. The church was packed with women in
black, each one stoically suffering the three hours of the Crucifixion with the tortured Christ. Outside the wind blew and cut
off the light of the sun with its dust, and the pigeons cried
mournfully in the tower. Inside the prayers were like muffled
cries against a storm which seemed to engulf the world. There
seemed to be no one to turn to for solace. And when the dying
Christ cried, "My God, my God, why hast Thou forsaken me?"
the piercing words seemed to drive through to my heart and
make me feel alone and lost in a dying universe.

Good Friday was forlorn, heavy and dreary with the death
of God's son and the accompanying sense of utter hopelessness.

But on Saturday morning our spirits lifted. We had been
through the agony and now the ecstasy of Easter was just
ahead. Then too we had our first confession to look forward to
in the afternoon. In the morning my mother took me to town
and bought me a white shirt and dark pants and jacket. It was
the first suit I ever owned, and I smiled when I saw myself in
the store mirror. I even got new shoes. Everything was new, as it
should be for the first communion.

My mother was excited. When we returned from town she
would not allow me to go anywhere or do anything. Every five
minutes she glanced at the clock. She did not want me to be
late for confession.

"It's time!" she finally called, and with a kiss she sent me
scampering down the goat path, to the bridge where I raced the
Vitamin Kid and lost, then waited to walk to church with
Samuel.

"You ready?" I asked. He only smiled. At the church all the
kids were gathered around the steps, waiting for the priest to
call us.

"Did you pass?" everyone asked. "What did the priest ask
you?" He had given each one of us a quiz, asking us to answer
questions on the catechism lessons or to recite prayers.

"He asked me how many persons in one God?" Bones
howled.

"Wha'daya say?"

"Four! Four! Four!" Bones cried. Then he shook his head
vigorously. "Or five! I don't know?"

"And you passed?" Lloyd said contemptuously.

"I got my suit, don't I?" Bones growled. He would fight anyone who said he didn't pass.

"Okay, okay, you passed," Lloyd said to avoid a fight.

"Whad' did he ask you, Tony?"

"I had to recite the Apostles' Creed and tell what each part meant, and I had to explain where we get original sin—"

" ¡Oh sí!" " ¡Ah la veca!" " ¡Chingada!"

"Bullshit!" Horse spit out the grass he had been chewing.

"Tony could do it," Florence defended me, "if he wanted to."

"Yeah, Tony knows more about religion and stuff like that than anyone—"

"Tony's gonna be a priest!"

"Hey, let's practice going to confession and make Tony the priest!" Ernie shouted.

"Yeahhhhh!" Horse reared up. Bones snarled and grabbed my pant leg in his teeth.

"Tony be the priest! Tony be the priest!" they began to chant.

"No, no," I begged, but they surrounded me. Ernie took off his sweater and draped it around me. "His priest's dress!" he shouted, and the others followed. They took off their jackets and sweaters and tied them around my waist and neck. I looked in vain for help but there was none.

"Tony is the priest, Tony is the priest, yah-yah-yah-ya-ya!" they sang and danced around me. I grew dizzy. The weight of the jackets on me was heavy and suffocating.

"All right!" I cried to appease them, "I shall be your priest!" I looked at Samuel. He had turned away.

"Yea-aaaaaaaye!" A great shout went up. Even the girls drew closer to watch.

"Hail to our priest!" Lloyd said judiciously.

"Do it right!" Agnes shouted.

"Yeah! Me first! Do it like for reals!" Horse shouted and threw himself at my feet.

"Everybody quiet!" Ernie held up his hands. They all drew around the kneeling Horse and myself, and the wall provided the enclosure but not the privacy of the confessional.

"Bless me, father—" Horse said, but as he concentrated to make the sign of the cross he forgot his lines. "Bless me, father—" he repeated desperately.

"You have sinned," I said. It was very quiet in the enclosure.

"Yes," he said. I remembered hearing the confession of the dying Narciso.

"It's not right to hear another person's confession," I said, glancing at the expectant faces around me.

"Go on!" Ernie hissed and hit me on the back. Blows fell on my head and shoulders. "Go on!" they cried. They really wanted to hear Horse's confession.

"It's only a game!" Rita whispered.

"How long has it been since your last confession?" I asked Horse.

"Always," he blurted out, "since I was born!"

"What are your sins?" I asked. I felt hot and uncomfortable under the weight of the jackets.

"Tell him only your worst one," Rita coaxed the Horse. "Yeah!" all the rest agreed.

The Horse was very quiet, thinking. He had grabbed one of my hands and he clutched it tightly, as if some holy power was going to pass through it and absolve him of his sins. His eyes rolled wildly, then he smiled and opened his mouth. His breath fouled the air.

"I know! I know!" he said excitedly, "one day when Miss Violet let me go to the bathroom I made a hole in the wall! With a nail! Then I could see into the girls' bathroom! I waited a long time! Then one of the girls came and sat down, and I could see everything! Her ass! Everything! I could even hear the pee!" he cried out.

"Horse, you're dirty!" June exclaimed. Then the girls looked shyly at each other and giggled.

"You have sinned," I said to Horse. Horse freed my hand and began rubbing at the front of his pants.

"There's more!" he cried, "I saw a teacher!"

"No!"

"Yes! Yes!" He rubbed harder.

"Who?" one of the girls asked.

"Mrs. Harrington!" Everyone laughed. Mrs. Harrington weighed about two hundred pounds. "It was biggggggggg—!" he exploded and fell trembling on the ground.

"Give him a penance!" the girls chanted and pointed accusing fingers at the pale Horse. "You are dirty, Horse," they cried, and he whimpered and accepted their accusations.

"For your penance say a rosary to the Virgin," I said weakly. I didn't feel good. The weight of the jackets was making me sweat, and the revelation of Horse's confession and the way the kids were acting was making me sick. I wondered how the priest could shoulder the burden of all the sins he heard.

. . . the weight of the sins will sink the town into the lake of the golden carp . . .

I looked for Samuel. He was not joining in the game. Florence was calmly accepting the sacriligious game we were playing, but then it didn't matter to him, he didn't believe.

"Me next! Me next!" Bones shouted. He let go of my leg and knelt in front of me. "I got a better sin than Horse! Bless me, father! Bless me, father! Bless me, father!" he repeated. He kept making the sign of the cross over and over. "I got a sin! I got to confess! I saw a high school boy and a girl fucking in the grass by the Blue Lake!" He smiled proudly and looked around.

"Ah, I see them every night under the railroad bridge," the Vitamin Kid scoffed.

"What do you mean?" I asked Bones.

"Naked! Jumping up and down!" he exclaimed.

"You lie, Bones!" Horse shouted. He didn't want his own sin bettered.

"No I don't!" Bones argued. "I don't lie, father, I don't lie!" he pleaded.

"Who was it?" Rita asked.

"It was Larry Saiz, and that dumb gabacha whose father owns the Texaco station—please father, it's my sin! I saw it! I confess!" He squeezed my hand very hard.

"Okay, Bones, okay," I nodded my head, "it's your sin."

"Give me a penance!" he growled.

"A rosary to the Virgin," I said to be rid of him.

"Like Horse?" he shouted.

"Yes."

"But my sin was bigger!" he snarled and leaped for my throat. "Whaggggghhh—" he threw me down and would have strangled me if the others hadn't pulled him away.

"Another rosary for daring to touch the priest!" I shouted in self-defense and pointed an accusing finger at him. That made him happy and he settled down.

"Florence next!" Abel cried.

"Nah, Florence ain't goin' make it anyway," Lloyd argued.

"That's enough practice," I said and started to take off the cumbersome costume, but they wouldn't let me.

"Abel's right," Ernie said emphatically, "Florence needs the practice! He didn't make it because he didn't practice!"

"He didn't make it because he doesn't believe!" Agnes taunted.

"Why doesn't he believe?" June asked.

"Let's find out!" "Make him tell!" "¡Chingada!"

They grabbed tall Florence before he could bolt away and made him kneel in front of me.

"No!" I protested.

"Confess him!" they chanted. They held him with his arms pinned behind his back. I looked down at him and tried to let him know we might as well go along with the game. It would be easier that way.

"What are your sins?" I asked.

"I don't have any," Florence said softly.

"You do, you bastard!" Ernie shouted and pulled Florence's head back.

"You have sins," Abel agreed.

"Everybody has sins!" Agnes shouted. She helped Ernie twist Florence's head back. Florence tried to struggle but he was pinned by Horse and Bones and Abel. I tried to pull their hands away from him to relieve the pain I saw in his face, but the trappings of the priest's costume entangled me and so I could do very little.

"Tell me one sin," I pleaded with Florence. His face was very close to mine now, and when he shook his head to tell me again that he didn't have sins I saw a frightening truth in his eyes. He was telling the truth! He did not believe that he had ever sinned against God! "Oh my God!" I heard myself gasp.

"Confess your sins or you'll go to hell!" Rita cried out. She grabbed his blonde hair and helped Ernie and Agnes twist his head.

"Confess! Confess!" they cried. Then with one powerful heave and a groan Florence shook off his tormentors. He was long and sinewy, but because of his mild manner we had always underestimated his strength. Now the girls and Ernie and even Horse fell off him like flies.

"I have not sinned!" he shouted, looking me square in the eyes, challenging me, the priest. His voice was like Ultima's

when she had challenged Tenorio, or Narciso's when he had
tried to save Lupito.

"It is God who has sinned against me!" his voice thundered,
and we fell back in horror at the blasphemy he uttered.

"Florence," I heard June whimper, "don't say that—"

Florence grinned. "Why? Because it is the truth?" he questioned. "Because you refuse to see the truth, or to accept me
because I do not believe in your lies! I say God has sinned
against me because he took my father and mother from me
when I most needed them, and he made my sisters whores— He
has punished all of us without just cause, Tony," his look
pierced me, "He took Narciso! And why? What harm did Narciso ever do—"

"We shouldn't listen to him," Agnes had the courage to
interrupt Florence, "we'll have to confess what we heard and
the priest will be mad."

"The priest was right in not passing Florence, because he
doesn't believe!" Rita added.

"He shouldn't even be here if he is not going to believe in
the laws we learn," Lloyd said.

"Give him a penance! Make him ask for forgiveness for those
terrible things he said about God!" Agnes insisted. They were
gathering behind me now, I could feel their presence and their
hot, bitter breath. They wanted me to be their leader; they
wanted me to punish Florence.

"Make his penance hard," Rita leered.

"Make him kneel and we'll all beat him," Ernie suggested.

"Yeah, beat him!" Bones said wildly.

"Stone him!"

"Beat him!"

"Kill him!"

They circled around me and advanced on Florence, their
eyes flashing with the thought of the punishment they would
impose on the non-believer. It was then that the fear left me,
and I knew what I had to do. I spun around and held out my
hands to stop them.

"No!" I shouted, "there will be no punishment, there will be
no penance! His sins are forgiven!" I turned and made the sign
of the cross. "Go in peace, my son," I said to Florence.

"No!" they shouted, "don't let him go free!"

"Make him do penance! That's the law!"

"Punish him for not believing in God!"

"I am the priest!" I shouted back, "and I have absolved him of his sins!" I was facing the angry kids and I could see that their hunger for vengeance was directed at me, but I didn't care, I felt relieved. I had stood my ground for what I felt to be right and I was not afraid. I thought that perhaps it was this kind of strength that allowed Florence to say he did not believe in God.

"You are a bad priest, Tony!" Agnes lashed out at me.

"We do not want you for our priest!" Rita followed.

"Punish the priest!" they shouted and they engulfed me like a wave. They were upon me, clawing, kicking, tearing off the jackets, defrocking me. I fought back but it was useless. They were too many. They spread me out and held me pinned down to the hard ground. They had torn my shirt off so the sharp pebbles and stickers cut into my back.

"Give him the Indian torture!" someone shouted.

"Yeah, the Indian torture!" they chanted.

They held my arms while Horse jumped on my stomach and methodically began to pound with his fist on my chest. He used his sharp knuckles and aimed each blow directly at my breastbone. I kicked and wiggled and struggled to get free from the incessant beating, but they held me tight and I could not throw them off.

"No! No!" I shouted, but the raining blows continued. The blows of the knuckles coming down again and again on my breastbone were unbearable, but Horse knew no pity, and there was no pity on the faces of the others.

"God!" I cried, "God!" But the jarring blows continued to fall. I jerked my head from side to side and tried to kick or bite, but I could not get loose. Finally I bit my lips so I wouldn't cry, but my eyes filled with tears anyway. They were laughing and pointing down at the red welt that raised on my chest where the Horse was pounding.

"Serves him right," I heard, "he let the sinner go—"

Then, after what seemed an eternity of torture, they let me go. The priest was calling from the church steps, so they ran off to confession. I slowly picked myself up and rubbed the bruises on my chest. Florence handed me my shirt and jacket.

"You should have given me a penance," he said.

"You don't have to do any penance," I answered. I wiped my eyes and shook my head. Everything in me seemed loose and disconnected.

"Are you going to confession?" he asked.

"Yes," I answered and finished buttoning my shirt.

"You could never be their priest," he said.

I looked at the open door of the church. There was a calm in the wind and the bright sunlight made everything stark and harsh. The last of the kids went into the church and the doors closed.

"No," I nodded. "Are you going to confession?" I asked him.

"No," he muttered. "Like I said, I only wanted to be with you guys— I cannot eat God," he added.

"I have to," I whispered. I ran up the steps and entered the dark, musky church. I genuflected at the font of holy water, wet my fingertips, and made the sign of the cross. The lines were already formed on either side of the confessional, and the kids were behaving and quiet. Each one stood with bowed head, preparing himself to confess all of his sins to Father Byrnes. I walked quietly around the back pew and went to the end of one line. I made the sign of the cross again and began to say my prayers. As each kid finished his confession the line shuffled forward. I closed my eyes and tried not to be distracted by anything around me. I thought hard of all the sins I had ever committed, and I said as many prayers as I could remember. I begged God forgiveness for my sins over and over. After a long wait, Agnes, who had been in front of me came out of the confessional. She held the curtain as I stepped in, then she let it drop and all was dark. I knelt on the rough board and leaned against the small window. I prayed. I could hear whisperings from the confessional on the other side. My eyes grew accustomed to the gloom and I saw a small crucifix nailed to the side of the window. I kissed the feet of the hanging Jesus. The confessional smelled of old wood. I thought of the million sins that had been revealed in this small, dark space.

Then abruptly my thoughts were scattered. The small wooden door of the window slid open in front of me, and in the dark I could make out the head of Father Byrnes. His eyes were closed, his head bowed forward. He mumbled something in Latin then put his hand on his forehead and waited.

I made the sign of the cross and said, "Forgive me, Father, for I have sinned," and I made my first confession to him.

Diecinueve

Easter Sunday. The air was clear and smelled like the new white linen of the Resurrection. Christ was risen! He had walked in hell for three days and on the third day he had risen and was sitting at the right hand of God, the Father Almighty, Creator of Heaven and Earth—

The two lines stretched from the steps of the church out to the street. The girls' line was neat; they looked like angels in their starched white dresses, each pair of hands holding a white prayer book and a rosary. The boys' line was uneven, fidgeting nervously. We pulled at our ties and tugged at the tight fitting jackets. We did not hold our prayer books or rosaries in palmed hands. Around us proud parents smiled at each other, waiting for the priest to open the doors. From time to time a mother would move to the line and straighten this or that on a nervous kid.

Behind me Horse whinnied into the clear Christian air.

Bones snapped at him, and one of the high school sodality girls whose job it was to keep us in line whacked him on the head.

—Christ will come to judge the living and the dead—

I knew.

"What was your penance?" Horse asked Lloyd.

"Ain't supposed to tell," Lloyd sneered.

"Bones got a whole rosary!"

Everybody laughed. "Shhhhh!" the high school girl said.

"Hey! There's Florence!" Florence was standing against the wall, sunning himself in the morning sun that was just now beginning to warm the cool morning air.

"He's going to hell," Rita whispered next to me and Agnes agreed.

"Augh, augh, augh, hummmmph," the Horse neighed nervously at the mention of hell. His large teeth chomped hard and a white spittle formed around the edges of his mouth. The air smelled of fresh-cut hay.

Up in the bell tower the pigeons ducked and bobbed at each other and sang their soft couing song. Christ was risen. He was in the holy chalice awaiting us.

"I heard Rita's confession," Abel bragged.

"You damn liar!" Rita hissed back.

"Ah, ah, black spot on your soul," Lloyd said and shook his finger at her.

"Shhhhhh!" the high school girl warned us. She hit Bones again. She hit him hard because I could hear her knuckles striking the bone of his skull and her exclamation when it hurt her.

"The door's opening!" someone whispered. Father Byrnes stood at the entry way, smiling, surveying his flock. The parents returned his smile. They were pleased that he had done so well with us. I turned and looked at my father and mother and Ultima. Then the lines started moving forward.

"Remember your instructions!" the high school girl threatened us.

"Don't go drop God on the floor!" Bones volunteered as he went by, and she whacked him again.

We had been told to take the Host carefully in our tongue and swallow it immediately. No part of the Host must be lost from the time it left the chalice to the time it entered our mouths.

"Don't go bite on God," Horse whispered.

Swallow Him carefully, don't chew on Him. I wondered how God must feel to go into Horse's stinking mouth.

Above us the choir sang. The two lines moved without incident down the aisle then filed into the front row of seats. Father Byrnes went up to the altar, the altar bell rang and mass

began. All during the mass I prayed. I thought back to yesterday's confession and about the mixed feelings that the revealing
of my thoughts had left in me. But I had told everything, everything I thought was a sin. I had cleansed myself completely and
prepared to take God into my body. Since the confession I had
talked only to Ultima and my mother. I had kept myself pure.

On the altar the priest began the ceremony of changing the
bread into flesh and the wine into blood. The body and blood
of the risen Christ. Soon He would be with me, in me, and He
would answer all the questions I had to ask.

The altar bell tinkled and we knelt; we bowed our heads and
with our right fist softly beat our hearts, saying we believed in
the mystery taking place before our eyes.

"It's blood now," Abel whispered when the priest raised the
chalice with the wine, and his thin voice mixed mysteriously
into the ringing altar bell. I peeped and saw the chalice raised
high, into the couing of the pigeons, into the mystery of the
sky.

"Aggggh—" Horse spit on the floor, "blood—"

*The blood of Lupito, the blood of Narciso, winding its way
along the river, crying on the hills of the llano . . .*

"Florence said it's wine, and the priest drinks it because he's
a wino," Lloyd said.

"Florence said he wouldn't eat God," Bones added.

I looked again and saw the flat round piece of bread the
priest held up. That thin wafer was becoming God, it was becoming flesh.

". . . Bread made flesh . . ."

"Meat," Bones growled.

"No Bones, not like that!" I nodded my head. Somehow I
couldn't understand, the mystery was beginning to escape me! I
shut my eyes tightly and prayed for forgiveness.

"It's time—"

"What?"

"It's time, the priest is waiting!"

"¡Chingada!"

I opened my eyes and stood. My heart was pounding. Was I
ready? The line filed towards the altar railing. We knelt clumsily
at the railing and tucked our hands beneath the white cloth that
stretched over the top. The priest was at the far end of the
railing; the girls were getting the communion first. There was
still time to pray.

Oh my God I am sorry for all my sins, "Because they displease Thee, Lord, Who art all good and deserving . . ."

"Shhhhh!" the high school girl said.

We waited quietly. Then the priest came to our side. The girls were already filing back to their seats. The altar boy held the gold platter under each chin, the priest mumbled something in Latin and placed the host on the tongue. He moved fast.

"Aghhhhhhh—" Out of the corner of my eyes I saw Bones jump up and push his finger into his mouth. The host had stuck to the roof of his mouth. He was jabbing God with his finger, trying to free Him, choking on Him.

Then suddenly the priest was in front of me. I caught a glimpse of the small, white wafer, the risen Christ, and then I closed my eyes and felt the host placed on my tongue. I received Him gladly, and swallowed Him. At last! I flooded the sticky piece of bread with hot saliva and swallowed it. God. Now I would know the answers! I bowed my head and waited for Him to speak to me.

"Tony! Tony!"

"Yes!" I cried.

"Go on! Go on!" It was the Kid poking me. "The line's moving!"

Bones passed by me, still fingering his mouth. I was holding up the line, confusing them. I moved quickly to get back in step. We filed back into the pew and knelt.

"Lord—" I whispered, still seeking God's voice.

"Dumb ass!" Ernie poked me, "you got everybody mixed up!"

"Damn! I nearly choked!" Bones whimpered through watery eyes.

I closed my eyes and concentrated. I had just swallowed Him, He must be in there! For a moment, on the altar railing, I thought I had felt His warmth, but then everything moved so fast. There wasn't time just to sit and discover Him, like I could do when I sat on the creek bank and watched the golden carp swim in the sun-filtered waters.

God! Why did Lupito die?

Why do you allow the evil of the Trementinas?

Why did you allow Narciso to be murdered when he was doing good?

Why do you punish Florence? Why doesn't he believe?

Will the golden carp rule—?

A thousand questions pushed through my mind, but the Voice within me did not answer. There was only silence. Perhaps I had not prepared right. I opened my eyes. On the altar the priest was cleaning the chalice and the platters. The mass was ending, the fleeting mystery was already vanishing.

"Did you feel anything?" I urgently asked Lloyd and clutched his arm.

"I feel hungry," Lloyd answered.

My own stomach rumbled from the morning fast and I simply nodded. I glanced around, trying to find in someone's face or eyes the answer that had escaped me. There was nothing, only the restlessness to get home to breakfast.

We were standing now, the priest was talking to us. He said something about being Christians now, and how it was our duty to remind our parents to contribute to the collection box every Sunday so that the new school building could be built and sisters could come to teach us.

I called again to the God that was within me, but there was no answer. Only emptiness. I turned and looked at the statue of the Virgin. She was smiling, her outstretched arms offering forgiveness to all.

"Ite, missa est," the priest said.

"Deo gratis," the choir sang back and the people stood to leave.

It was over.

Veinte

After Easter I went to confession every Saturday and on Sunday morning I took communion, but I was not satisfied. The God I so eagerly sought was not there, and the understanding I thought to gain was not there. The bad blood of spring filled us with strange yearnings and tumult, and the boys from Los Jaros split off from the boys from town and there were gang fights. Since I was not from across the tracks or from town, I was caught in the middle.

"It's all part of growing up, Anthony," Miss Violet told me one afternoon after school when I stayed to help her.

"Growing up is not easy sometimes," I said. She smiled. "I will come to see you next year when school begins," I told her.

"That would be nice," she said and touched my head. "What will you do this summer—"

I wanted to tell her that I was searching for something, but sometimes I didn't even know what it was I sought. I would see the golden carp, but I couldn't tell her about that. "Play," I answered, "fish, take care of my animals, and go to El Puerto to learn about farming from my uncles—"

"Do you want to become a farmer?" She asked. It was difficult to leave her, but outside I would hear the clamor of the departing kids. I had to get home.

"I don't know," I said, "it's part of the thing I must learn about myself. There are so many dreams to be fulfilled, but Ultima says a man's destiny must unfold itself like a flower, with only the sun and the earth and water making it blossom, and no one else meddling in it—"

"She must be a wise woman—" Miss Violet said. I looked at her and saw that she was tired, and somehow she seemed older. Perhaps we were all older.

"Yes," I said. "Goodbye."

"Goodbye," she smiled and waved after me.

I ran very hard, so that by the time I was at the bridge I was exhausted. My lungs were bursting with clean air and my heart was pounding, still I had the nerve to call out a challenge to the Kid.

"Raaaaaaaaaaaaa-ssssss . . ." I shouted. He was walking with Ida. I had never seen the Vitamin Kid walking before, but there he was, just starting across the bridge, side by side with Ida. I raced by him and called the challenge again. I put all I had into that race, I ran as hard as I could, but the Kid never passed me. I reached the end of the bridge and turned to look back. Through watering eyes I saw the Kid and Ida, still walking side by side across the bridge. I couldn't believe it. I had beaten the Kid across the bridge! Andrew said that someday I would beat the Kid across, I remembered. But there was no sweetness to the victory, instead I felt that something good had ended.

In a way I felt relieved school was over. I had more time to spend with Ultima, and in her company I found a great deal of solace and peace. This was more than I had been able to find at church or with the kids at school. The llano had come alive with spring, and it was comforting to walk in the hills and see the new birth take root and come-alive-green. But even in the new season and in the hills there were ominous signs. We found tracks near the junipers that surrounded the house. I asked Ultima about them and she laughed and said it was someone out hunting rabbits, but I saw how she studied the footprints carefully and then took a dry juniper branch and erased the prints in the sand. And at night I heard the owl cry in warning, not the soft rhythmic song we were so used to, but cries of alarm.

"It is Tenorio," I said.

"Bah, do not bother your mind about that wolf," she laughed.

But I had heard the grown-ups rumor that Tenorio's second daughter was dying and that she would not last the summer, and I remembered his threat. And then there were the rumors about the evil things happening on the Agua Negra ranch. A curse had been placed on one of the families of the Agua Negra, and because the man knew my father and about Ultima's powers he came seeking help.

"¿Cómo estás Téllez?" my father greeted the thin, weather-beaten man with an abrazo.

"Aye, Gabriel Márez," the gray, emaciated face smiled weakly, "it does my heart good to see an old compadre, an old vaquero—"

They came arm in arm into the house where the man called Téllez greeted my mother and Ultima. The formalities did not last long, we all knew the man had come to seek Ultima's help. My father would gladly give his help to anyone of his old compadres, it only remained to be seen if my mother would allow Ultima to go help. My mother had been very afraid for Ultima since the night Tenorio and his mob came, and she had not allowed Ultima to help anyone since.

"People are ungrateful," she said, "they seek her help and after la Grande has risked her life to help them then they brand her a witch. Nonsense! We have no use for that kind of people!"

But now we listened intently while the man told of the horror that had enveloped his life.

"I swear before God Almighty," Téllez' voice cracked with the tremble of fear in it, "that there are things that have happened to my family that are directed by the devil himself!"

"¡Ave María Purísima!" my mother exclaimed and crossed her forehead.

"The pots and pans, the dishes lift into the air and crash against the walls! We cannot eat! The skillet full of hot grease badly burned one of my children. Just yesterday morning I reached for the coffee pot and it jumped up and spilled the scalding coffee on me." He rolled up his sleeve and showed us the blistered pink flesh of the burn on his forearm.

"Téllez," my father said calmly, "the imagination—"

"The imagination!" Téllez laughed sardonically, "this is not imagined!" He pointed again to the arm. "It was not an accident!" he insisted, "and I had not been drinking!"

"Perhaps it is a bad joke, someone who has a grudge against you," my father the skeptic questioned.

"Gabriel, the people of the Agua Negra are good people.

You know that! Who would carry out a joke this far. And who could make stones rain from the skies!"

"Stones from the skies!" my mother gasped.

"¡Sí! Day and night, without reason, the stones fall and pelt the house! Why? And how is this done? I am at my wit's end! It is the devil's work—" Téllez moaned.

"Courage," my father said and reached across and placed his hand on Téllez' shoulder.

"There was a curse like that at El Puerto when I was a little girl," my mother nodded, "the dishes would move, the statues of the saints themselves were found in the pigpens and the outhouse, and stones would fall like rain on the house—"

"Sí, sí," Téllez nodded in agreement. He knew if my mother believed then he could get Ultima's help.

"The curse was lifted when the priest blessed the house with holy water—" she did not finish.

"Ay, mujer," Téllez groaned, "do you think my good wife did not think of that! The priest from Vaughn came and blessed the entire house. It did not help. Now he will not come anymore. He says no evil can withstand the blessing by holy water, and so we must be making up stories. Stories—" He nodded his head and laughed bitterly. "Such stories! We cannot eat, we cannot sleep. My children are like walking zombies, the evil presence moves them like ghosts and the priest says we make up stories! It is too much—" He cupped his head in his hands and cried.

So again the power of the priest has failed, I thought. Why can't the power of God work against the evils that beset the family of Téllez? Why is it allowed to continue?

"What can I do?" my father asked, trying to console the poor man.

"Come with me and see with your very eyes the things I speak about. Someone must believe!" Téllez exclaimed, taking some faith in my father's offer.

"I will go," my father nodded.

"¡Ay, gracias a Dios!" Téllez stood and embraced my father.

They left immediately, and my father did not return until late that night. The lights of the truck came bouncing up the goat path and I ran to meet him, but he did not greet me when he stepped down from the truck, in fact he did not seem to see me. He walked mechanically into the house, his eyes wide and staring straight ahead. He looked very tired.

"Gabriel," my mother said, but he did not answer. He sat in his chair and looked ahead, as if peering into a dream; and it was not until he took a long drink of the hot coffee Ultima put in his hand that he spoke.

"At first I did not believe Téllez," he whispered. "I am not a believer in spirits, good or bad, but—" and he turned and looked at us as if he were coming back to reality, his eyes bright and watery, "but I saw the things Téllez spoke about. I still cannot believe it—" his chin sank to his chest.

"¡Ave María Purísima!" my mother cried, then she turned and went to the sala to pray. Meantime, we waited in the kitchen.

"What is it that is happening out there at that ranch?" my father asked. He did not look at Ultima, but it was obvious he was seeking some understanding from her.

"A curse has been laid," she said simply.

"Like on my uncle Lucas?" I asked. I was already wondering if she would take me to help this time.

"No," she said, addressing my father, "this curse was not laid on a person, the curse was put on a bulto, a ghost. It is the bulto that haunts the house—"

"I don't understand," my father said. He looked up at her searchingly.

"A long time ago," she began, "the llano of the Agua Negra was the land of the Comanche Indians. Then the comancheros came, then the Mexican with his flocks—many years ago three Comanche Indians raided the flocks of one man, and this man was the grandfather of Téllez. Téllez gathered the other Mexicans around him and they hanged the three Indians. They left the bodies strung on a tree; they did not bury them according to their custom. Consequently, the three souls were left to wander on that ranch. The brujas who laid the curse knew this, so instead of placing the curse on a member of the family and taking the chance of getting caught, they simply awakened the ghosts of the three Indians and forced them to do the wrong. The three tortured spirits are not to blame, they are manipulated by brujas—"

"It is unbelievable," my father said.

"Yes," Ultima agreed.

"Can they be stopped?" my father asked.

"Of course," Ultima smiled, "all evil can be stopped."

At that moment my mother returned from praying to the Virgin. "Téllez is your friend," she said to my father.

"Of course," my father answered, "we grew up on the llano together. We all count each other as brothers—"

"And he needs help," she said, tracing the very simple steps for us to hear.

"There is no one more deserving of help at this moment," my father said.

"Well then, we must help in any way we can," she said with finality. She started to turn to Ultima, but my father motioned her to be still. He got up and went to Ultima.

"Will you help this poor family, will you help my friends?" he asked.

"You know the rules that guide the interference with any man's destiny," Ultima said.

"I know," my father said. "I have tried to lead my own life, and I have given other men room and respect to live theirs. But I feel I must do this for my friends, so let the bad consequences in your chain of destiny fall on my head."

"We will leave tomorrow at sunup," Ultima said.

I was allowed to go, and so early next morning we got in my father's truck and headed westward. We traveled halfway to Las Pasturas and then left the paved road and turned southward on a dirt road of the llano. The llano was beautiful in the early morning, beautiful before the summer sun of August burned it dry. The mesquite bushes were green, and even the dagger yucca was stately as it pushed up the green stem that blossomed with white bell flowers. Jackrabbits bolted from shady thickets at the approach of the truck and bounded away into the rolling hills spotted with dark juniper trees. The sun grew very white and warm in the clear, azure sky. It was hard to believe that in this wide beauty there roamed three souls trapped to do evil.

We had left home in the gray of dawn, and we had all been quiet. But now the lovely expanse of the llano filled our hearts and we forgot for awhile the strange, forboding job ahead of us.

"Ah, there is no freedom like the freedom of the llano!" my father said and breathed in the fresh, clean air.

"And there is no beauty like this earth," Ultima said. They looked at each other and smiled, and I realized that from these two people I had learned to love the magical beauty of the wide, free earth. From my mother I had learned that man is of the earth, that his clay feet are part of the ground that nourishes him, and that it is this inextricable mixture that gives man his measure of safety and security. Because man plants in the earth he believes in the miracle of birth, and he provides a home

. . . home of Téllez. It was a simple adobe ranch house, squatting

low to the good earth, its tin roof shielding it from the hot sun.

for his family, and he builds a church to preserve his faith and the soul that is bound to his flesh, his clay. But from my father and Ultima I had learned that the greater immortality is in the freedom of man, and that freedom is best nourished by the noble expanse of land and air and pure, white sky. I dreaded to think of a time when I could not walk upon the llano and feel like the eagle that floats on its skies: free, immortal, limitless.

"There is power here, a power that can fill a man with satisfaction," my father said.

"And there is faith here," Ultima added, "a faith in the reason for nature being, evolving, growing—"

And there is also the dark, mystical past, I thought, the past of the people who lived here and left their traces in the magic that crops out today.

Enveloped in our thoughts, we bounced down the sandy road that at times was no more than a cow path. I was lost in the immensity of land and sky, but my father knew where to go. At the foot of a hill ahead of us crouched the troubled home of Téllez. It was a simple adobe ranch house, squatting low to the good earth, its rusted tin roof shielding it from the hot sun. To the side of the house were the corrals.

"That is his place," my father announced. He drove the truck near the corral and stopped. Téllez came running.

"¡Gracias a Dios que venites!" he cried. He believed in Ultima's power, and he knew it was his last source of help. He took Ultima's hand and kissed it, then led us excitedly into the house. A frail, thin woman and the children cringed against the wall when we entered. "It is all right, it is all right," Téllez said soothingly, "la Grande has come to help us."

Only then did the woman, whose eyes were burning with fever, come forth and greet Ultima. "Grande," she said simply and kissed her hand.

"Dorotea Téllez," Ultima greeted the woman.

"These are bad times," Téllez' wife whimpered, "I am sorry but I can offer you nothing to eat or drink—" Her voice broke and she went to the table, sat, bowed her head on the rough wooden planks and cried.

"It has been like this!" Téllez threw up his arms in exasperation, "since the evil thing came—"

As he spoke a strange thing happened. A cloud passed overhead and darkened the house. Téllez looked up and cried, "It's here! It's here!"

"Benditos sean los dulces nombres," his wife moaned. She crossed herself and fell to her knees.

A few moments ago the sky had been clear, and now in the gloom we saw each other as dark bultos. My father started for the door but Téllez leaped in his way and shouted, "No! Do not go! The evil is out there!"

Then the pounding began. The darkness had already terrified me, but now the strange pounding noise on the roof made me seek Ultima's hand. She stood quietly, listening to the devil's bombardment that held us with such terror that we could not move. The fear of the deafening, evil noise held us prisoners. The children cringed around their mother, but they did not cry. They seemed accustomed to the devil's beating on the roof.

"¡Jesús, María y José! my father cried out, and he crossed his forehead.

"Aiiiiiiiie!" Téllez groaned, "it is the devil dancing on my roof—" His body twisted to the crescendo of the fearful drum beat. But almost as quickly as it had begun the noise stopped and the dark cloud moved away. My father ran to the door and we followed.

It was incredible, but we stepped out into the perfectly quiet day we had known earlier. The llano was so quiet I could hear the drone of the grasshoppers and crickets in the grass.

"The rocks!" my father muttered, "they weren't here when we came—" He pointed at the melon-sized stones that lay around the house. That is what had pounded on the roof! But where had they come from? We looked up. There was not a cloud in the sky.

"Incredible," my father said and shook his head. "The cloud darkened only the house, and the stones fell only on the roof—" As he spoke the two boys who had been inside with their mother came outside. Without a word they began picking up the rocks and carrying them to the nearby corral where there was already a pile of rocks.

"We stack the devil's work in the corral," Téllez said. "This is the third time the rocks have fallen—"

"But from where?" my father cried, "and how?" Téllez only shrugged. "You have searched around the house, into the hills?" Téllez nodded. "My God!" my father shivered.

"It is the work of the devil, I tell you," Téllez murmured.

Ultima, who had stood quietly by us, answered. "It is the work of man," she said. "But let us not waste time while the spirits grow stronger. Gabriel, I want you to erect a platform here." She pointed to the ground and marked four spots. "Make the holes there. Use some of those cedar posts in the corral, make it this high." She held her hand above her head. "Place many juniper branches on the platform. Cut many branches because we may have to burn a long time. Have Antonio cut them, he understands the power in the tree—" Then she turned and herded the family back into the house. After that we did not see her for a long time.

My father found an axe in the tool shed and gave it to me. I went into the hills and began cutting juniper branches. Where possible I took dead dry branches because Ultima had said we would be burning them, but when I had to cut into a live tree I first talked to the tree and asked it for its medicine, as Ultima had instructed me to do with every living plant. I dragged the branches to where my father worked on the platform. He dug four holes and placed the cedar posts in them. "Notice," he said, "it is not square but long, as if it could hold a coffin." With wire he securely tied some rafters across the top of the posts then we put the juniper branch roof on the platform. When we were done we rested, and looked at the altar that we had erected.

The day was very long. We had not brought food and so the only thing we had was water from the well, which tasted brackish. "That is why they call these the ranches of the Agua Negra," my father explained. I wondered if the water which flowed beneath this earth connected to the waters beneath our town, the waters of the golden carp.

"Strange that there are no animals around the ranch," my father said. "The animals sense this bad business and stay clear of it—just as we have stayed clear of those evil rocks." He pointed to the pile of rocks in the corral. "What we have seen today is incredible," he finished.

"It is good that we have Ultima to explain it," I told him, and he only shrugged. We waited. A strange singing, a low chanting song emanated from the house all day long. Finally, at dusk when the nightjars and bats began to fly and the setting sun had passed from orange to gray, Ultima came through the front door of the house. She carried what appeared to be three bundles, and she stepped to the platform quickly.

"You have done well," she said and placed the three bundles at the foot of the platform. "Place the bundles on the platform and set fire to it," she commanded and stepped back. My father was surprised when he picked up the first bundle and found it heavy. Ultima had carried the three lightly but he had to strain to lift them up on the platform. There was another strange thing about Ultima as she stood with her arms crossed, quietly watching my father work. The way she stood, the bright sash around her waist, and the two glossy braids falling over her shoulders made me feel that she had performed this ceremony in some distant past.

My father picked up a dry brush of yerba de la vívora and striking a match to it he used it as a torch to set fire to the platform. The fire sputtered at first, but as it found the drier branches it hissed and crackled then whooshed up in a ball of yellow fire. The fragrance of the dry bush had been sharp and tangy, but as the green branches caught fire the sweet, spermy smell of the evergreen filled the air.

"Continue feeding the fire until I return," Ultima commanded, and she turned and walked back to the house. We piled branches beneath the platform and kept it burning. Soon even the cedar posts were burning. Their popping sound and their sweet scent filled the night air. Somehow the fire seemed to dispel the brooding mystery we had felt since the shower of rocks.

"What is it we burn?" I asked my father as we watched the inferno envelop the bundles.

"I don't know," my father answered, "it is all so strange. My father once told me a story about the early comancheros on this llano, and what they learned from the Indians about their burial ceremony. They did not bury their dead the way we do, but they made a platform like this one and cremated the body. It was part of their way of life—"

He paused and I asked, "Are these the—" but before I could finish he said, "I don't know, but if it will help Téllez be rid of these ungodly things who are we to question old ways—"

In the dark night we heard an owl sing. It was Ultima's owl. It seemed the first sign of life we had heard around the ranch all day, and it lifted our spirits. Somehow the memory of the falling rocks faded with the owl's cry, and what had been frightening and unexplainable grew distant. I looked for the rock pile in the corral, but I could not see it. Perhaps it was because the bright fire made the shadows around us very dark.

"¡Cuidado!" my father shouted. I turned and jumped back

as the top of the platform toppled into the ashes beneath. A flower of sparks blossomed into the night air. The four posts which had held the platform continued to burn like torches, one for each of the directions of the wind. We threw the rest of the juniper branches in the fire. Already the platform and the three bundles were only white ashes.

"You two are good workers," Ultima said. We had not heard her and were startled at her approach. I went to her and took her hand. She smelled sweet with incense. "It is done," she said.

"Good," my father answered and wiped his hands.

"You know, Gabriel," she said to my father, "I am getting old. Perhaps this would be the best burial you could provide me—" She peered into the dying fire and smiled. I could see that she was very tired.

"It is a good way to return to the earth," my father agreed. "I think the confines of a damp casket will bother me too. This way the spirit soars immediately into the wind of the llano, and the ashes blend quickly into the earth—"

Téllez came and stood by us. He too peered into the embers of the strange fire. "She says the curse is lifted," he said dumbly. He too looked very tired.

"Then it is," my father answered.

"How can I pay you?" Téllez asked Ultima.

"Instead of my silver," she said, "you can bring us a nice lamb the next time you come to Guadalupe—"

"I will bring a dozen," he smiled weakly.

"And stay away from the one-eyed Tenorio," she finished.

"¡Ay! That devil was in this too!" my father exclaimed.

"I was at El Puerto about a month ago," Téllez said, "I went to the saloon for a drink, and to play some cards. I tell you, Gabriel, that man has nothing but revenge in his heart for la Grande. He said something insulting, and I answered him. I thought nothing of it, I was only upholding my honor, our honor, the pride of those from Las Pasturas. Well, a week later the bad things started here—"

"You picked a bad one to tangle with," my father shook his head thoughtfully as he stared into the dying fire, "Tenorio has already murdered one of our friends—"

"I know now of his true evil," Téllez muttered.

"Well, what's done is done," my father nodded. "Now we must be on our way."

"I can never thank you enough, old friend," Téllez said and embraced my father warmly, then he embraced and kissed Ultima.

"Adiós."

"Adiós." We climbed into the truck and drove away, leaving Téllez standing by the dying embers of the fire. The bouncing lights of the truck cut a jerky path through the night as we traveled out of the dark llano back to Guadalupe. My father rolled a Bull Durham cigarette and smoked. The fatigue of the day and the humming sound of the tires on the highway made me sleep. I do not remember my father carrying me in when we arrived home.

In my dreams that night I did not recall the strange events that happened on the Agua Negra, instead I saw my three brothers. They were three dark figures driven to wander by the wild sea-blood in their veins. Shrouded in a sea-mist they walked the streets of a foreign city.

Toni-eeeeee, they called in the night fantasy, Tony-reelooooo! Where are you?

Here, I answered, here by the river!

The brown swirling waters lapped at my feet, and the monotonous chirping of the grillos as they sang in the trees mixed into a music which I felt in the roots of my soul.

Oooooo Tony . . . they cried with such a mournful sound that I felt a chill in my heart . . . Help us, Toni-eeeeee. Give us, grant us rest from this sea-blood!

I have no magic power to help you, I cried back.

I carefully marked where the churning waters eddied into a pool. There the catfish would lurk, greedy for meat. From my disemboweled brothers I took three warm livers and baited my hook.

But you have the power of the church, you are the boy-priest! they cried. Or choose from the power of the golden carp or the magic of your Ultima. Grant us rest!

They cried in such pain for release that I took their livers from the hook and cast them into the raging, muddy waters of the River of the Carp.

Then they rested, and I rested.

Veintiuno

The days grew warmer and the Blue Lake opened for swimming, but Cico and I avoided the glistening, naked boys who dared the deep-blue power of the lake. Instead we worked our way around the teeming lake and towards the creek. It was time for the arrival of the golden carp!

"He will come today," Cico whispered, "the white sun is just right." He pointed up at the dazzling sky. Around us the earth seemed to groan as it grew green. We had waited many days, but today we were sure he would come. We crawled through the green thicket and sat by the edge of the pond. Around us sang the chorus of insects which had just worked their way out of winter nests and cocoons.

While we waited time flowed through me and filled me with many thoughts. I was still concerned with the silence of God at communion. Every Saturday since Easter I had gone to confession, and every Sunday morning I went to the railing and took communion. I prepared my body and my thoughts for receiving God, but there was no communication from Him. Sometimes, in moments of great anxiety and disappointment, I wondered if God was alive anymore, or if He ever had been. He had not been able to cure my uncle Lucas or free the Téllez family from their curse, and He had not been able to save Lupito or Narciso. And yet, He had the right to send you to hell or heaven when you died.

"It doesn't seem right—" I said aloud.

"What?" Cico asked.

"God."

"Yeah," he agreed.

"Then why do you go to church?" I asked.

"My mother believes—" he answered, "I go to please her—"

"I used to think everyone believed in God," I said.

"There are many gods," Cico whispered, "gods of beauty and magic, gods of the garden, gods in our own backyards—but we go off to foreign countries to find new ones, we reach to the stars to find new ones—"

"Why don't we tell others of the golden carp?" I asked.

"They would kill him," Cico whispered. "The god of the church is a jealous god, he cannot live in peace with other gods. He would instruct his priests to kill the golden carp—"

"What if I become a priest, like my mother wants me to—"

"You have to choose, Tony," Cico said, "you have to choose between the god of the church, or the beauty that is here and now—" He pointed and I looked into the dark, clear water of the creek. Two brown carp swam from under the thicket into the open.

"He comes—" We held our breath and peered into the water beneath the overhanging thicket. The two brown carp had seen us, and now they circled and waited for their master. The sun glittered off his golden scales.

"It's him!"

The golden fish swam by gracefully, cautiously, as if testing the water after a long sleep in his subterranean waters. His powerful tail moved in slow strokes as he slid through the water towards us. He was beautiful; he was truly a god. The white sun reflected off his bright orange scales and the glistening glorious light blinded us and filled us with the rapture true beauty brings. Seeing him made questions and worries evaporate, and I remained transfixed, caught and caressed by the essential elements of sky and earth and water. The sun warmed us with its life-giving power, and up in the sky a white moon smiled on us.

"Damn, he's beautiful—" Cico whistled as the golden carp glided by.

"Yes," I agreed, and for a long time we did not speak. The

arrival of the golden carp rendered us silent. We let the sun beat down on us, and like pagans we listened to the lapping water and the song of life in the grass around us.

Whose priest will I be, I thought. The idea that there could be other gods besides the God of heaven ran through my mind. Was the golden carp a god of beauty, a god of here and now like Cico said. He made the world peaceful—

"Cico," I said, "let's tell Florence!" It was not right, I thought, that Florence did not know. Florence needed at least one god, and I was sure he would believe in the golden carp. I could almost hear him say as he peered into the waters, "at last, a god who does not punish, a god who can bring beauty into my life—"

"Yes," Cico said after a long pause, "I think Florence is ready. He has been ready for a long time; he doesn't have gods to choose between."

"Does one have to choose?" I asked. "Is it possible to have both?"

"Perhaps," he answered. "The golden carp accepts all magic that is good, but your God, Tony, is a jealous God. He does not accept competition—" Cico laughed cynically.

I had to laugh with him because I was excited and happy that we were going to let Florence in on our secret. Perhaps later Jasón would know, and then maybe others. It seemed like the beginning of adoration of something simple and pure.

We made our way up the creek until we were just below the Blue Lake. On this side of the lake there was a concrete wall with a spillway. As the lake filled it emptied in a slow trickle into el Rito. No one was allowed to swim along the wall because the water was very deep and full of thick weeds, and because the lifeguard was on the other side. But as we came up the gentle slope we heard the shouts of swimmers. I recognized Horse and the others shouting and waving at us.

"They're not supposed to be here," Cico said.

"Something's wrong," I answered. I heard the pitch of fear in their voices as they called and gestured frantically.

"Remember, we tell only Florence," Cico cautioned.

"I know," I replied.

"Hurry! Hurry!" Abel cried.

"It's a joke," Cico said as we neared the gang.

"No, something's happened—" We sprinted the last few yards and came to the edge of the culvert. "What?" I asked.

"Florence is down there!" Bones cried.

"Florence hasn't come up! He hasn't come up!" Abel sobbed and tugged at my arm.

"How long?" I shouted and worked myself loose from Abel. It was not a joke. Something was wrong!

"A long time!" Horse nodded through the spittle in his mouth. "He dived!" he pointed into the deep water, "and he didn't come up! Too long!"

"Florence," I groaned. We had come seeking Florence to share our secret with him, a secret of the dark, deep-blue water in which he swam.

"He drowned, he drowned," Bones whimpered.

"How long?" I wanted to know, "how long has he been in the water?" But their fright would not let them answer. I felt Cico's hand on my shoulder.

"Florence is a good swimmer," Cico said.

"But he's been down too long," Abel whimpered.

"What do we do?" Horse asked nervously. He was frightened.

I grabbed Abel. "Go get the lifeguard!" I pointed across the lake where the high school boys loitered on the pier and dove off the high board to show off for the girls. "Tell anyone you can find there's been an accident here!" I shouted into his fear-frozen face. "Tell them there's a drowning!" Abel nodded and scampered up the path that cut around the side of the lake. He was instantly lost in the tall green reeds of the cattails.

It was a warm day. I felt the sweat cold on my face and arms. The sun glistened on the wide waters of the lake.

"Wha—?"

"Dive after him!"

"No! No!" Horse shook his head violently and bolted back.

"I'll dive," Cico said. He began to strip.

"Too late!"

We looked and saw the body come up through the water, rolling over and over in a slow motion, reflecting the sunlight. The long blonde hair swirled softly, like golden seaweed, as the lake released its grip and the body tumbled up. He surfaced near where we stood on the edge of the culvert. His open eyes stared up at us. There was a white film over them.

"Oh my God—"

"Help me!" Cico said and grabbed an arm. We pulled and tried to tear the dead weight of his body from the waters of the lake.

There was a red spot on Florence's forehead where he must have hit bottom or the edge of the culvert. And there was some rusty-black barbed wire around one arm. That must have held him down.

"Horse!" I shouted, "help us!" The weight was too much for Cico and me. Horse hesitated, closed his eyes and grabbed a leg. Then he pulled like a frightened animal. At first he almost tipped us all back into the water, but he lunged and his frantic strength pulled Florence over the side of the culvert.

Bones would not come near. He stood away, a dry, rattling sound echoing from his throat. He was vomiting and the vomit ran down his chest and stomach and dirtied his swimming trunks. He didn't know he was vomiting. His wild eyes just stared at us as we pulled Florence on the sand.

I looked across the lake and saw the high school boys pointing excitedly toward us. Some were already convinced something was wrong and were sprinting up the path. They would be here in seconds.

"Damn!" Cico cursed, "he's dead for sure. He's cold and heavy, like death—"

"¡Chingada!" Horse muttered and turned away.

I dropped to my knees beside the bronzed, wet body. I touched his forehead. It was cold. His hair was matted with moss and water. Sand clung to his skin, and as he dried little black sand ants began to crawl over him. I crossed my forehead and prayed an Act of Contrition like I had for Narciso, but it was no good. Florence had never believed.

The lifeguard was the first one there. He pushed me aside and he and another high school boy turned Florence on his stomach. He began pushing down on Florence's back and a sickening white foam flowed from Florence's mouth.

"Damn! How long was he under?" he asked.

"About five or ten minutes!" Bones growled through his vomit.

"You fucking little bastards!" the lifeguard cursed back, "I've told you guys a hundred times not to swim here! Two years I've had a perfect record here—now this!" He continued pushing down on Florence's back and the white froth continued to flow from his mouth.

"Think we should get a priest?" the other high school boy asked worriedly. Quite a few people were already gathered around the body, watching the lifeguard work, asking, "Who is it?"

I wasn't looking at Florence anymore, I wasn't looking at anybody. My attention was centered on the northern blue skies. There two hawks circled as they rode the warm air currents of the afternoon. They glided earthward in wide, concentric circles. I knew there was something dead on the road to Tucumcari. I guess it was the sound of the siren or the people pushing around me that shattered my hypnotic gaze. I didn't know how long I had been concerned with the hawks free flight. But now there were many people pushing around me and the sound of the siren grew louder, more urgent. I looked around for Cico, but he was gone. Bones and Horse were eagerly answering questions for the crowd.

"Who is he?"

"Florence." "He's our friend."

"How did he drown? What happened?"

"He dove in and got caught in the wire. We told him not to go swimming here, but he did. We dove in and pulled him out—"

I didn't want to hear anymore. My stomach turned and made me sick. I pushed my way through the crowd and began to run. I don't know why I ran, I just knew I had to be free of the crowd. I ran up the hill and through the town's quiet streets. Tears blinded my eyes, but the running got rid of the sick feeling inside. I made my way down to the river and waded across. The doves that had come to drink at the river cried sadly. The shadows of the brush and the towering cottonwoods were thick and dark.

The lonely river was a sad place to be when one is a small boy who has just seen a friend die. And it grew sadder when the bells of the church began to toll, and the afternoon shadows lengthened.

Veintidós

In my dreams that night I saw three figures. At first I thought the three men were my brothers. I called to them. They answered in unison.

This is the boy who heard our last confession on earth, they chanted as if in prayer. In his innocence he prayed the Act of Final Contrition for us who were the outcasts of the town.

Who is it? I called, and the three figures drew closer.

First I saw Narciso. He held his hands to the gaping, bloody wound at his chest. Behind him came the mangled body of Lupito, jerking crazily to the laughter of the townspeople. And finally I saw the body of Florence, floating motionlessly in the dark water.

These are the men I have seen die! I cried. Who else will my prayers accompany to the land of death?

The mournful wind moved like a shadow down the street, swirling in its path chalky dust and tumbleweeds. Out of the dust I saw the gang arise. They fell upon each other with knives and sticks and fought like animals.

Why must I be witness to so much violence! I cried in fear and protest.

The germ of creation lies in violence, a voice answered.

Florence! I shouted as he appeared before me, is there no God in heaven to bear my burden?

Look! He pointed to the church where the priest desecrated the altar by pouring the blood of dead pigeons into the holy chalice. The old gods are dying, he laughed.

Look! He pointed to the creek where Cico lay in wait for the golden carp. When the golden carp appeared Cico struck with his spear and the water ran blood red.

What is left? I asked in horror.

Nothing, the reply rolled like silent thunder through the mist of my dream.

Is there no heaven or hell?

Nothing.

The magic of Ultima! I insisted.

Look! He pointed to the hills where Tenorio captured the night-spirit of Ultima and murdered it, and Ultima died in agony.

Everything I believed in was destroyed. A painful wrenching in my heart made me cry aloud, "My God, my God, why have you forsaken me!"

And as the three figures departed my pesadilla they cried out longingly. We live when you dream, Tony, we live only in your dreams—

"What is it?" Ultima asked. She was at my bedside, holding me in her arms. My body was shaking with choking sobs that filled my throat.

"A nightmare," I mumbled, "pesadilla—"

"I know, I know," she crooned and held me until the convulsions left me. Then she went to her room, heated water, and brought me medicine to drink. "This will help you sleep," she said. "It is the death of your young friend," she talked as I drank the bitter potion, "perhaps it is all the things in your mind of late that cause the pesadilla—anyway, it is not good. The strengthening of a soul, the growing up of a boy is part of his destiny, but you have seen too much death. It is time for you to rest, to see growing life. Perhaps your uncles could best teach you about growth—"

She laid me back on my pillow and pulled the blanket up to my neck. "I want you to promise that you will go with them. It will be good for you." I nodded my head in agreement. The medicine put me to sleep, a sleep without dreams.

When Florence was buried I did not go to the funeral. The

bells of the church kept ringing and calling, but I did not go. The church had not given him communion with God and so he was doomed to his dream-wanderings, like Narciso and Lupito. I felt that there was nothing the church or I could give him now.

I overheard Ultima talking to my father and mother. She told them I was sick and that I needed rest. She talked about how beneficial a stay at El Puerto would be. My parents agreed. They understood that I had to be away from the places that held the memories of my friend. They hoped that the solitude of the small village and the strength of my uncles would lend me the rest I needed.

"I will be saddened at leaving you," I told Ultima when we were alone.

"Ay," she tried to smile, "life is filled with sadness when a boy grows to be a man. But as you grow into manhood you must not despair of life, but gather strength to sustain you—can you understand that."

"Yes," I said, and she smiled.

"I would not send you if I thought the visit would not be good for you, Antonio, but it will be. Your uncles are strong men, you can learn much from them, and it will be good for you to be away from here, where so much has happened. One thing—" she cautioned.

"Yes?" I asked.

"Be prepared to see things changed when you return—"

I thought awhile. "Andrew said things had changed when he returned from the army—do you mean in that way?"

She nodded. "You are growing, and growth is change. Accept the change, make it a part of your strength—"

Then my mother came to give me her blessings. I knelt and she said, "te doy esta bendición en el nombre del Padre, del Hijo, y el Espíritu Santo," and she wished that I would prosper from the instruction of her brothers. Then she knelt by my side and Ultima blessed us both. She blessed without using the name of the Trinity like my mother, and yet her blessing was as holy. She only wished for strength and health within the person she blessed.

"Your father is waiting," my mother said as we rose. Then I did something I had never done before. I reached up and kissed Ultima. She smiled and said, "Adiós, Antonio—"

"Adiós," I called back. I grabbed the suitcase with my clothes and ran out to the truck where my father waited.

"¡Adiós!" they called, trailing after me, "send my love to papá!"

"I will," I said, and the truck jerked away.

"Ay," my father smiled, "women take an hour saying good-byes if you let them—"

I nodded, but I had to turn and wave for the last time. Deborah and Theresa had run after the truck; my mother and Ultima stood waving by the door. I think I understood then what Ultima said about things changing, I knew that I would never see them in that beauty of early-morning, bright-sunlight again.

"It will be good for you to be on your own this summer, to be away from your mother," my father said after we left the town and the truck settled down to chugging along the dusty road to El Puerto.

"Why?" I asked him.

"Oh, I don't know," he shrugged, and I could tell he was in a good mood, "I can't tell you why, but it is so. I left my own mother, may God rest her soul, when I was seven or eight. My father contracted me to a sheep camp on the llano. I spent a whole year on my own, learning from the men in the camp. Ah, those were days of freedom I wouldn't trade for anything— I became a man. After that I did not depend on my mother to tell me what was right or wrong, I decided on my own—"

"And that is what I must do," I said.

"Eventually—"

I understood what he said and it made sense. I did not understand his willingness to send me to my mother's brothers. So I asked him.

"It does not matter," he answered regretfully, "you will still be with the men, in the fields, and that is what matters. Oh, I would have liked to have sent you to the llano, that is the way of life I knew, but I think that way of life is just about gone, it is a dream. Perhaps it is time we gave up a few of our dreams—"

"Even my mother's dreams?" I asked.

"Ay," he murmured, "we lived two different lives, your mother and I. I came from a people who held the wind as brother, because he is free, and the horse as companion, because he is the living, fleeting wind—and your mother, well, she came from men who hold the earth as brother, they are a steady, settled people. We have been at odds all of our lives, the wind and the earth. Perhaps it is time we gave up the old differences—"

["Then maybe I do not have to be just Márez, or Luna, perhaps I can be both—" I said.]

"Yes," he said, but I knew he was as proud as ever of being Márez.

"It seems I am so much a part of the past—" I said.

"Ay, every generation, every man is a part of his past. He cannot escape it, but he may reform the old materials, make something new—"

"Take the llano and the river valley, the moon and the sea, God and the golden carp—and make something new," I said to myself. That is what Ultima meant by building strength from life.["Papá," I asked, "can a new religion be made?"]

"Why, I suppose so," he answered.

"A religion different from the religion of the Lunas," I was again talking to myself, intrigued by the easy flow of thoughts and the openness with which I divulged them to my father. "The first priest here," I nodded towards El Puerto, "he was the father of the Lunas wasn't he—"

My father looked at me and grinned. "They do not talk about that, they are very sensitive about that," he said.

But it was true, the priest that came with the first colonizers to the valley of El Puerto had raised a family, and it was the branches of this family that now ruled the valley. Somehow everything changed. The priest had changed, so perhaps his religion could be made to change. If the old religion could no longer answer the questions of the children then perhaps it was time to change it.

"Papá," I asked after awhile, "why is there evil in the world?"

"Ay, Antonio, you ask so many questions. Didn't the priest at the church explain, didn't you read in your catechism?"

"But I would like to know your answer," I insisted.

"Oh well, in that case—well, I will tell you as I see it.[I think most of the things we call evil are not evil at all; it is just that we don't understand those things and so we call them evil.] And we fear evil only because we do not understand it. When we went to the Téllez ranch I was afraid because I did not understand what was happening, but Ultima was not afraid because she understood—"

"But I took the holy communion! I sought understanding!" I cut in.

My father looked at me and the way he nodded his head

made me feel he was sorry for me. "Understanding does not
come that easy, Tony—"

"You mean God doesn't give understanding?"

"Understanding comes with life," he answered, "as a man
grows he sees life and death, he is happy and sad, he works,
plays, meets people—sometimes it takes a lifetime to acquire
understanding, because in the end understanding simply means
having a sympathy for people," he said. "Ultima has sympathy
for people, and it is so complete that with it she can touch their
souls and cure them—"

"That is her magic—"

"Ay, and no greater magic can exist," my father nodded.
"But in the end, magic is magic, and one does not explain it so
easily. That is why it is magic. To the child it is natural, but for
the grown man it loses its naturalness—so as old men we see a
different reality. And when we dream it is usually for a lost
childhood, or trying to change someone, and that is not good.
So, in the end, I accept reality—"

"I see," I nodded. Perhaps I did not understand completely,
but what he had said was good. I have never forgotten that
conversation with my father.

The rest of the summer was good for me, good in the sense
that I was filled with its richness and I made strength from
everything that had happened to me, so that in the end even the
final tragedy could not defeat me. And that is what Ultima tried
to teach me, that the tragic consequences of life can be overcome by the magical strength that resides in the human heart.

All of August I worked in the fields and orchards. I worked
alongside my uncles and cousins and their companionship was
good. Of course I missed my mother and Ultima, and sometimes
the long, gray evenings were sad, but I learned to be at ease in
the silence of my uncles, a silence steeped as deep as a child's. I
watched closely how they worked the earth, the respect they
showed it, and the way they cared for living plants. Only Ultima
equaled them in respect for the life in the plant. Never once did
I witness any disharmony between one of my uncles and the
earth and work of the valley. Their silence was the language of
the earth.

After a hard day's work and supper we sat out in the open
night air and listened to stories. A fire would be lit and dried
cow dung put in to burn. Its smoke kept the mosquitoes away.
They told stories and talked about their work, and they looked

into the spermy-starred sky and talked about the heavens, and
the rule of the moon. I learned that the phases of the moon
ruled not only the planting but almost every part of their lives.
That is why they were the Lunas! They would not castrate or
shear animals unless the moon was right, and they would not
gather crops or save next year's seeds unless the moon dictated.
And the moon was kind to them. Each night it filled the valley
with her soft light and lighted a way for the solitary man standing in his field, listening to the plants sleep, listening to the
resting earth.

The bad dreams which had plagued me did not come, and I
grew strong with the work and good food. I learned much from
those men who were as dark and quiet as the earth of the valley,
and what I learned made me stronger inside. I knew that the
future was uncertain and I did not yet know if I could follow in
their footsteps and till the earth forever, but I did know that if I
chose that life that it would be good. Sometimes when I look
back on that summer I think that it was the last summer I was
truly a child.

My uncles were pleased with my progress. They were not
men who were free with their compliments, but because I was
the first of their sister's sons who had come to learn their ways
they were happy. It was the last week of my stay, school was
almost upon me again, when my uncle Pedro came to speak to
me.

"A letter from your mother," he said waving the open letter.
He came to where I stood directing the waters of the acequia
down the rows of corn. He handed me the letter and as I read
he told me what it said. "They will come in a few days—"

"Yes," I nodded. It was strange, always I made the trip with
them and now I would be here to greet them as they arrived. I
would be glad to see them.

"School starts early this year," he said and leaned against the
apple tree by the water ditch.

"It always comes early," I said and put the folded letter in
my pocket.

"Your mother says you do well in school. You like school—"

"Yes," I answered, "I like it."

"That is good," he said, "a man of learning can go far in this
world, he can be anything— It makes your mother very proud,
and," he looked down at the earth beneath his feet and as was
their custom caressed it with his boot, "it makes us proud. It

has been a long time since there was an educated Luna, a man of the people," he nodded and pondered.

"I am Márez," I answered. I did not know why I said it, but it surprised him a little.

"Wha—" Then he smiled. "That is right, you are Márez first, then Luna. Well, you will be leaving us in a few days, going back to your studies, as it should be. We are pleased with your work, Antonio, all of your uncles are pleased. It has been good for us to have one of María's sons work with us. We want you to know that there will always be a place here for you. You must choose what you will do as a grown man, but if you ever decide to become a farmer you will be welcomed here, this earth that was your mother's will be yours—"

I wanted to thank him, but as I started to respond my uncle Juan came hurrying towards us. My uncle Juan never hurried anywhere and so we turned our attention to him, knowing something important must have happened. When he saw me with my uncle he stopped and motioned.

"Pedro, may I see you a minute!" he called excitedly.

"What is it, brother Juan?" my uncle Pedro asked.

"Trouble!" my uncle Juan whispered hoarsely, but his voice carried and I could hear, "trouble in town! Tenorio's daughter, the one who has been sick and wasting away, death has come for her!"

"But when?" my uncle asked, and he turned and looked at me.

"I guess it happened just after we came to the fields, I heard it just now from Esquivel. I met him on the bridge. He says the town is in an uproar—"

"How? Why?" my uncle Pedro asked.

"Tenorio has taken the body into town, and like the mad-man that he is, he has stretched out the corpse on the bar of his saloon!"

"No!" my uncle gasped, "the man is insane!"

"Well, that is a truth that does not concern us," my uncle Juan agreed, "but what does concern me is that the man has been drinking all day and howling out his vengeance on la cur-andera, Ultima."

When I heard that the hair on my back bristled. I had seen the devil Tenorio murder Narciso, and now there was no telling what he might do to avenge his daughter's death. I had not thought of Tenorio all summer even though the man lived on the black mesa down the river and had his saloon in town, but now he was here again, plotting to bring another tragedy into my life. I felt my heart pounding even though I had not moved from where I stood.

My uncle Pedro stood looking down at the ground for a long time. Finally he said, "Ultima helped restore our brother's life —once before she needed help and we stood by idly. This time I must act—"

"But papá will not like—"

"—The interference," my uncle Pedro finished. Again he turned and looked at me. "We indebted ourselves to her when she saved our brother, a debt I will gladly pay."

"What will you do?" my uncle Juan asked. His voice was tense. He was not committed to act, but he would not interfere.

"I will take the boy, we will drive back to Guadalupe tonight—hey, Antonio!" he called and I went to them. He smiled down at me. "Listen, something has come up. Not a big emergency, but we must act to help a friend. We will drive to Guadalupe immediately after supper. In the meantime, there are only a few hours of work left in this day, so go to your grandfather's house and pack your clothes. If anyone asks why you are back early, tell them you got time off for being such a good worker, eh?" He smiled.

I nodded. The fact that my uncle would go to Guadalupe tonight to tell of what had happened with Tenorio lessened my anxiety. I knew that my uncle treated the matter lightly so as not to alarm me, and besides, if Tenorio was drinking it would take a long time before he gathered enough courage to act. By that time my uncle and I would be in Guadalupe, and Ultima would be safe with my uncle and my father there. Also, I doubted that Tenorio would go to our house in Guadalupe. He knew if he trespassed once again on our land my father would kill him.

"Very well, tío," I said. I handed him the hoe I had been using on the weeds.

"Hey! You know the way?" he called as I jumped over the acequia.

"Sure," I replied. He was still making light of the matter so as not to arouse my suspicions.

"Go straight to your grandfather's house—take a rest. We will be in as soon as this field is done and the tools collected!"

"¡Adiós!" I called and turned up the road. Once the road

left the flat river bottom it got very sandy. Lush, green mesquite bordered the road and shut off most of the horizon. But
in the west I could see the summer sun was already low, hover-
ing in its own blinding light before it wedded night. I walked
carelessly up the road, unaware of what the coming darkness
would reveal to me. The fact that I would be back home in a
few hours excited me, and it put me so much at ease that I did
not think about what Tenorio might do. As I walked I gathered
ripe mesquite pods and chewed them for the sweet juice.

Half a mile from my uncles' fields the narrow wagon road
turned into the road that crossed the bridge and led into town.
Already I could see in the setting sun the peaceful adobe houses
on the other side of the river. The river was at its flood stage
and swollen with muddy waters and debris, and so as I crossed
the narrow, wooden bridge my attention was drawn to the raging waters. And so it was not until the horseman was almost
upon me that I was aware of him. The sharp, reverberating
hoofbeats that moments ago had mixed into the surging sound
of the river were now a crescendo upon me.

"¡Cabroncito! ¡Hijo de la bruja!" the dark horseman cried
and spurred his black horse upon me. It was Tenorio, drunk
with whiskey and hate, and he meant to run me down! Fear
glued me to the spot for long, agonizing seconds, then instinct
made me jump aside at the last moment. The huge, killer horse
swept by me, but Tenorio's foot hit me and sent me spinning to
the floor of the bridge.

"Hie! Hie! Hie!" the madman shrieked and spurred his horse
around for a second pass. "I have you where I want you hijo de
la chingada bruja!" he shouted with anger. He spurred the black
horse so savagely that blood spurted from the cuts in the flanks.
The terrified animal cried in pain and reared up, its sharp
hooves pawing the air. I rolled and the hooves came down beside me. He would have forced me over the side of the bridge if
I had not reached up and grabbed the reins. The horse's jerk
pulled me to my feet. I hit his nose as hard as I could and when
he turned I hit the sensitive flank the spurs had cut open. He
cried and bolted.

"¡Ay diablo! ¡Diablo!" Tenorio shouted and tried to bring
the horse under control.

The bucking horse trying to throw its tormentor blocked the
way towards the village, and so I turned and ran in the opposite
direction. As I neared the end of the bridge I heard the clatter

of hooves and the wild curses of Tenorio. I knew that if I stayed on the road back to my uncles' fields that I would be trapped and Tenorio would run me down, so as I felt the hot breath of the horse on my neck I jumped to the side and rolled down the embankment. I fell headlong into the brush at the bottom of the sandy bank and lay still.

Tenorio turned his killer horse and came to the edge of the bank and looked down. I could see him through the thick branches but he could not see me. I knew he would not follow me with his horse into the brush, but I did not know if he would dismount and come after me on foot. His sweating horse pranced nervously at the edge of the bank while Tenorio's evil eye searched the brush for me.

"I hope you have broken your neck, you little bastard!" He leaned over the saddle and spit down.

"You hear me, cabroncito!" he shouted, "I hope you rot in that hole as your bruja will rot in hell!" He laughed fiendishly, and the laughter carried down the empty road. There was no one to help me. I was trapped on this side of the road, away from my uncles, and the river was too flooded to swim across to the village and the safety of my grandfather's home.

"You two have been a thorn at my side!" he cursed, "but I will avenge my daughter's death. This very night I will avenge the death of my two daughters! It is the owl! Do you hear, little bastard! It is the owl that is the spirit of the old witch, and tonight I will send that miserable bird to hell, as I hope I have sent you—!" And he laughed like a madman, while the crazy horse snorted blood and froth.

It was when he said that the owl was the spirit of Ultima that everything I had ever known about Ultima and her bird seemed to make sense. The owl was the protective spirit of Ultima, the spirit of the night and the moon, the spirit of the llano! The owl was her soul!

Once that thought fitted into the thousand fragments of memory flitting through my mind, the pain of the scratches and the scraped skin left me. The fear left me, or rather the fear for myself left me and I was afraid for Ultima. I realized the evil Tenorio had found a way to hurt Ultima, and that he would do anything to hurt her. Hadn't he, almost within sight of the village, tried to trample me with his horse! I turned into the brush and fled.

"¡Ay cabroncito!" he cried at the noise, "so you yet crawl

about! That is good, the coyotes will have sport when they
devour you tonight—!'"

I ran through the brush with only one thought in mind, to
get to Ultima and warn her of Tenorio's intents. The thick
brush scratched at my face and arms, but I ran as hard as I
could. A long time afterwards I thought that if I had waited and
gone to my uncles, or somehow sneaked across the bridge and
warned my grandfather that things would have turned out dif-
ferently. But I was frightened and the only thing I was sure of
was that I could run the ten miles to Guadalupe, and I knew
that being on this side of the river I would come almost directly
on the hills in which our home huddled. The only other thing
that I thought about was Narciso's mad rush through the snowstorm to warn Ultima, and not until now had I ever understood
the sacrifice of his commitment. For us Ultima personified
goodness, and any risk in defense of goodness was right. She
was the only person I had ever seen defeat evil where all else
had failed. That sympathy for people my father said she possessed had overcome all obstacles.

I ran miles before I could run no more and then fell to the
ground. My heart was pounding, my lungs burned, and in my
side there was a continuous stabbing pain. For a long time I lay
on the ground, gasping for breath and praying that I would not
die from the pain that racked my body before I could warn
Ultima. When I had rested and was able to run again I paced
myself so as not to tire myself as I had in the wild, first dash.
The second time I stopped to rest I saw the flaming sun go
down over the tops of the cottonwood trees, and the thick,
heavy shadows brought dusk. The melancholy mood of evening
spread along the river, and after the strange cries of birds set-
tling to roost were gone, a strange silence fell upon the river.

With darkness upon me I had to leave the brush and run up
in the hills, just along the tree line. I knew that if I left the
contour of the river that I could save a mile or two, but I was
afraid to get lost in the hills. Over my shoulder the moon rose
from the east and lighted my way. Once I ran into a flat piece
of bottom land, and what seemed solid earth by the light of the
moon was a marshy quagmire. The wet quicksand sucked me
down and I was almost to my waist before I squirmed loose.
Exhausted and trembling I crawled onto solid ground. As I
rested I felt the gloom of night settle on the river. The dark
presence of the river was like a shroud, enveloping me, calling to

me. The drone of the grillos and the sigh of the wind in the trees whispered the call of the soul of the river.

Then I heard an owl cry its welcome to the night, and I was reminded again of my purpose. The owl's cry reawakened Tenorio's threat:

"This very night I will avenge the death of my two daughters! It is the owl that is the spirit of the old witch—"

It was true that the owl was Ultima's spirit. It had come with Ultima, and as men brought evil to our hills the owl had hovered over us, protecting us. It had guided me home from Lupito's death, it had blinded Tenorio the night he came to hurt Ultima, the owl had driven away the howling animals the night we cured my uncle, and it had been there when the misery of the Téllez family was removed.

The owl had always been there. It sang to me the night my brothers came home from the war, and in my dreams I sometimes saw it guiding their footsteps as they stumbled through the dark streets of their distant cities. My brothers, I thought, would I ever see my brothers again. If my sea-blood called me to wander and sailed me away from my river and my llano, perhaps I would meet them in one of the dazzling streets of their enchanting cities—and would I reach out and whisper my love for them?

I ran with new resolution. I ran to save Ultima and I ran to preserve those moments when beauty mingled with sadness and flowed through my soul like the stream of time. I left the river and ran across the llano; I felt light, like the wind, as my even strides carried me homeward. The pain in my side was gone, and I did not feel the thorns of the cactus or the needles of yucca that pierced my legs and feet.

The full moon of the harvest rose in the east and bathed the llano in its light. It had knocked softly on the door of my uncles' valley, and they had smiled and admitted her. Would they smile when they learned I doubted the God of my forefathers, the God of the Lunas, and knew I praised the beauty of the golden carp?

Would I ever race like a kid again, a wild cabrito rattling the pebbles on the goat path; and would I ever wrestle the crazy Horse and wild Bones again? And what dream would form to guide my life as a man? These thoughts tumbled through my mind until I saw the lights of the town across the river. I had arrived. Just ahead were the juniper-spotted hills I knew so well.

My pounding heart revived at their sight, and with a burst of speed I urged myself forward and reached the top of the gentle hill. From here I could see our huddled home. There was a light shining through the kitchen door, and from where I stood I could make out the silhouette of my father. All was peaceful. I paused to catch my breath and for the first time since I began my race I slowed down to a walk. I was thankful that I had arrived in time.

But the tranquility of the night was false. It was a moment of serenity, lasting only as long as my sigh of relief. A truck came bouncing over the goat path and pulled to a screeching stop in front of the kitchen door.

"Antonio! Has Antonio come?" I heard my uncle Pedro shout.

"¿Qué? ¿Qué pasa?" My father appeared at the door. Ultima and my mother were behind him.

I was about to shout and answer that I was here and well when I saw the lurking shadow under the juniper tree.

"¡Aquí!" I screamed, "Tenorio is here!" I froze as Tenorio turned and pointed his rifle at me.

"—¡Espíritu de mi alma!" I heard Ultima's command ring in the still night air, and a swirling of wings engulfed Tenorio.

He cursed and fired. The thundering report of the rifle followed the flash of fire. That shot destroyed the quiet, moonlit peace of the hill, and it shattered my childhood into a thousand fragments that long ago stopped falling and are now dusty relics gathered in distant memories.

"Ultima!" I cried.

My father came running up the hill, but my uncle Pedro who had remained in his truck raced past him. The bouncing headlights of the truck revealed Tenorio on his hands and knees, searching the ground at the foot of the tree.

"Aiiiiiii-eeeee!" he cried like a fiend when he found the object of his search. He jumped up and waved the dead body of Ultima's owl over his head.

"No," I groaned when I saw the ruffled, bloodied feathers, "Oh God, no—"

"I win! I win!" he howled and danced. "I have killed the owl with a bullet molded by the Prince of Death!" he shouted at me. "The witch is dead, my daughters are avenged! And you, cabroncito, who escaped me on the bridge will follow her to hell!" With his evil eye blazing down the rifle's barrel he aimed at my forehead and I heard the shot ring out.

There was a loud ringing in my ears, and I expected the wings of death to gather me up and take me with the owl. Instead I saw Tenorio's head jerk in surprise, then he dropped the owl and his rifle and clutched at his stomach. He turned slowly and looked at my uncle Pedro who stood on the running board of the truck. He held the smoking pistol still aimed at Tenorio, but a second shot was not needed. Tenorio's face twisted with the pain of death.

"Aieee . . ." He moaned and tumbled into the dust.

"May your evil deeds speed your soul to hell," I heard my uncle whisper as he tossed the pistol on the ground, "and may God forgive me—"

"¡Antonio!" my father came running through the dust and smoke. He gathered me in his arms and turned me away. "Come away, Antonio," he said to me.

"Si, papá," I nodded, "but I cannot leave the owl." I went to Tenorio's side and carefully picked up Ultima's owl. I had prayed that it would be alive, but the blood had almost stopped flowing. Death was carrying it away in its cart. My uncle handed me a blanket from the truck and I wrapped the owl in it.

"¡Antonito! Antonito, mi hijito!" I heard my mother's frantic cries and I felt her arms around me and her hot tears on my neck. "¡Ave María Purísima!"

"Ultima?" I asked, "Where is Ultima?"

"But I thought she was with me." My mother turned and looked into the darkness.

"We must go to her—"

"Take him," my father said. "It is safe now. Pedro and I will go for the sheriff—"

My mother and I stumbled down the hill. I did not think she or my father understood what the owl's death meant, and I who shared the mystery with Ultima shuddered at what I would find. We rushed into the still house.

"¡Mamá!" Deborah cried. She held trembling Theresa.

"It is all right," she reassured them, "it is over."

"Take them to their room," I said to my mother. It was the first time I had ever spoken to my mother as a man; she nodded and obeyed.

I entered Ultima's room softly. Only a candle burned in the room, and by its light I saw Ultima lying on the bed. I placed the owl by her side and knelt at the side of the bed.

"The owl is dead—" was all I could say. I wanted to tell her that I had tried to come in time, but I could not speak.

"Not dead," she smiled weakly, "but winging its way to a new place, a new time—just as I am ready to fly—"

"You cannot die," I cried. But in the dim, flickering light I saw the ashen pallor of death on her face.

"When I was a child," she whispered, "I was taught my life's work by a wise old man, a good man. He gave me the owl and he said that the owl was my spirit, my bond to the time and harmony of the universe—"

Her voice was very weak, her eyes already glazed with death.

"My work was to do good," she continued, "I was to heal the sick and show them the path of goodness. But I was not to interfere with the destiny of any man. Those who wallow in evil and brujería cannot understand this. They create a disharmony that in the end reaches out and destroys life— With the passing away of Tenorio and myself the meddling will be done with, harmony will be reconstituted. That is good. Bear him no ill will— I accept my death because I accepted to work for life—"

"Ultima—" I wanted to cry out, don't die, Ultima. I wanted to rip death away from her and the owl.

"Shhh," she whispered, and her touch calmed me. "We have been good friends, Antonio, do not let my passing diminish that. Now I must ask you to do me a favor. Tomorrow you must clean out my room. At sunrise you must gather my medicines and my herbs and you must take them somewhere along the river and burn everything—"

"Sí," I promised.

"Now, take the owl, go west into the hills until you find a forked juniper tree, there bury the owl. Go quickly—"

"Grande," my mother called outside.

I dropped to my knees.

"Bless me, Ultima—"

Her hand touched my forehead and her last words were, "I bless you in the name of all that is good and strong and beautiful, Antonio. Always have the strength to live. Love life, and if despair enters your heart, look for me in the evenings when the wind is gentle and the owls sing in the hills, I shall be with you—"

I gathered up the owl and slipped out of the room without looking back. I rushed past my worried mother who cried after me then ran to tend Ultima. I ran into the darkness of the quiet hills. I walked for a long time in the moonlight, and when I found a forked juniper tree I dropped to my knees and with my hands I carved out a hole big enough to hold the owl. I placed the owl in the grave and I put a large stone over it so the coyotes would not dig it out, then I covered the hole with the earth of the llano. When I stood up I felt warm tears on my cheeks.

Around me the moonlight glittered on the pebbles of the llano, and in the night sky a million stars sparkled. Across the river I could see the twinkling lights of the town. In a week I would be returning to school, and as always I would be running up the goat path and crossing the bridge to go to church. Sometime in the future I would have to build my own dream out of those things that were so much a part of my childhood.

I heard the sound of a siren somewhere near the bridge and I knew my father and my uncle were returning with the sheriff. The dead Tenorio who had meddled with the fate of Narciso and Ultima would be carted away from our hills. I did not think that my uncle Pedro would be punished for killing such a man. He had saved my life, and perhaps if we had come earlier we would have saved Ultima. But it was better not to think that way. Ultima said to take life's experiences and build strength from them, not weakness.

Tomorrow the women who came to mourn Ultima's death would help my mother dress her in black, and my father would make her a fine pine coffin. The mourners would bring food and drink, and at night there would be a long velorio, the time of her wake. In two days we would celebrate the mass of the dead, and after mass we would take her body to the cemetery in Las Pasturas for burial. But all that would only be the ceremony that was prescribed by custom. Ultima was really buried here. Tonight.

3-86-041

F   Anaya, Rudolfo A.
           Bless me, Ultima.

GAYLORD FG